W9-DJF-392

DEADLINE
IN
ROME

DEADLINE
IN
ROME

MAX CALL

Published by

√chosen books

Lincoln, Virginia 22078

Distributed by Word Books • Waco, Texas 76703

Scripture quotations at the beginning of each chapter are from the King
James Version of the Bible.

Library of Congress Cataloging in Publication Data

Call, Max.
 Deadline in Rome.

 I. Title.
PZ4.C15583De   [PS3553.A4214]   813'.54   80–66693

ISBN 0–912376–54–6

Copyright © 1980 by Max Call
Published by Chosen Books Publishing Co., Ltd.
Distributed by Word Books
All Rights Reserved
Printed in the United States of America

*Every man needs a Phoebe
and mine is named Murney.*

PROLOGUE

Rejoice with them that do rejoice, and weep with them that weep.

ROMANS 12:15

WHEN the apostle Paul wrote his letter to the Romans, Christianity in the west was being severely threatened by false teachings and traditions that circumvented Christ's message of salvation. Rome was a city of more than 2 million souls and Christ was in the hearts of less than a thousand.

The Messianic Jews in the imperial capital still maintained that a Gentile had to become a Jew in order to follow Jesus. Nero sat on the throne of the Caesars with his 19-year-old mind obsessed by dreams of immortality, and Paul sent a woman to Rome with the message of God's love and salvation.

Calling Phoebe "a succorer of many," he placed a most dangerous letter in her hands and sent her to a hostile city with little more than a prayer for success. Phoebe's boldness and firm faith must have sustained her because she didn't fail. The growth of the western church is true testimony to the fertility of the seed she planted.

Phoebe was ordained by Paul to be his messenger. She must have been an exceptional woman. The commendation he gave her (Romans 16:1–2) was not one he would give a silenced woman. She had his authority to teach and speak for him. Paul commanded the Christians in Rome to do whatever she asked, knowing that many of them had small reason to obey him. As Saul of Tarsus, he had persecuted them and driven them to Rome.

The message Phoebe carried is timeless. Its meaning and thrust are just as strong today as they were then. The moral conditions of our society reflect those of ancient Rome. The fiber of our faith is weak, and once again, we need the bravery of Phoebe. Let us share the adventures of this noble and wonderful woman.

Max Call
Garland, Texas

DEADLINE
IN
ROME

Phoebe's Voyage

Asia Minor

Cenchrea

Corinth

Achaia

Malea

Crete

Mediterranean Sea

Africa

CHAPTER I

I commend unto you Phoebe our sister, which is a servant of the church which is at Cenchrea.

ROMANS 16:1

Anxiously scanning the southern horizon for any possible adverse change in the weather, Phoebe's nerves were taut with excitement. If this good weather held she would be sailing for Rome in the morning. Twice her departure had been delayed by sudden spring storms, and one more postponement could bring disaster. She had a deadline in Rome and it was only 34 days away.

The second story balcony of her quayside villa overlooked Cenchrea harbor where the six ships of her fleet had been anchored throughout the seemingly endless winter. *Odessey,* her flagship, was now tied to the quay taking on a cargo of hard Eygptian wheat. By sailing early—two weeks ahead of all other vessels—that cargo would bring a handsome profit in Puteoli. But the richest cargo of all was already aboard, safely stowed away at the bottom of her great sea chest, under the beautiful wardrobe she'd assembled for the journey.

Twelve copies of the apostle's letter, each in its own tallowed canvas bag, were sailing with her. She, Phoebe of Cenchrea, had been chosen to deliver them to the Christians in Rome. Drumming her slender fingers impatiently on the carved marble balcony rail, she took a deep breath and considered the incredible string of events that had led her to this point in time.

Four months earlier, standing in this very spot, she had watched Marcus Paetius, the emperor's centurion, disembark from the *Odessey's* crowded deck. Seeing him for the first time, she had felt a shiver of foreboding. The gold medallion, swinging free on a chain around his brawny neck, set him apart from the other Romans in Greece. It meant that he was immune from all authority except that of Nero himself. The pennant, bearing the imprint of the medallion and flying from *Odessey's* mast, had alerted them to his coming while the ship was still at sea.

It's remarkable, she thought, *how time can change so many things. Marcus came here to destroy Paul and his ministry. Now, he's to become one of us.* He would be baptized that very afternoon and sail with Phoebe the following day as a follower of Jesus. She felt a flush of happiness as she remembered how Paul had helped her turn Nero's centurion away from the pagan delights of Aphrodite. She knew it was the teacher's wisdom and her charm that had first attracted Marcus. But in the end, it was the true gospel of Jesus that impressed him.

The sea-freshened wind that would carry her to Rome ruffled the long skirt of Phoebe's pale green gown as she watched Captain Castor direct the loading of *Odessey.* He was the youngest of her captains, and she often wondered if he'd accepted Christianity simply to please her. Being a young widow, only 23, she had been subjected to many romantic advances. She knew her wealth was immensely attractive to ambitious men, and she regarded Castor as ambitious. At Castor's baptism, Paul had privately observed as much. "He's an ambitious man, and whatever you ask of him, if it serves that ambition, he'll obey."

Simon, her steward, walked with his familiar limp into Phoebe's view. He conferred briefly with Castor and then haltingly made his way back to the warehouse that was beneath her feet. Simon and Paul were the same age, and together, they had helped reconcile her to the death of her husband. As a Roman citizen, Phoebe had inherited her husband's estate, but Simon's knowledge of shipping and the sea had saved it for her. Each of her ships carried a carved dolphin on its bow—the well-known symbol of her fleet and business. In the management of the Dolphin, Simon was second only to her in authority. While she was away, he would be in charge.

Am I being foolish in making this trip? she asked herself. The question had occurred to her several times during the past two weeks. Brushing back an errant strand of her long, black hair, Phoebe shielded her fine-boned face from the warm, Greek sun and seemed to search the choppy, white-capped waters of the Saronic Gulf for an answer.

When Paul first came to her, knowing she had a ship scheduled for an Italian voyage, she had listened with high interest. That was almost a month before and now on the eve of her departure she found herself questioning the wisdom of that conversation and the decision that had been reached.

Phoebe had readily agreed to schedule the sailing as early as possible. She understood the importance of Paul's letter arriving in Rome before the Nones of April. Nero was planning to have himself declared a god on that date. Marcus had brought them this news. The centurion had been brutally honest with both Paul and Phoebe after receiving a pledge of secrecy from them. The terrible impact of his news became more apparent to her when Marcus explained the reason behind his voyage to Greece.

"My emperor has sent me here to find Paul. I've been commanded to bring the apostle to Rome so that he can lead the Christians in the worship of Nero when he proclaims himself a god. If he refuses to come, I'm to kill him."

Those words had sent a chill down Phoebe's spine. The cold-blooded way they were spoken reflected the absolute power of Nero. Marcus had continued with an even greater complication.

"However, Seneca, my adopted father and Nero's key advisor, has given me additional secret instructions. He wants Paul to remain away from Rome, and if he insists on coming, then Seneca wants him dead." Marcus had smiled and added, "I've chosen to obey my father."

All through this brief exchange Phoebe had watched Paul's craggy face. The teacher had shown no emotion or alarm. He had remained silent, waiting for the centurion to say more.

"The choice is up to you, Paul," Marcus had said. "The only way I can obey both my father and my emperor is to kill you, but if you agree to remain here, I will hold my sword."

At first, in spite of Marcus' statement, Paul had felt compelled to go to Rome. He knew the Christians there would be the first to suffer Nero's wrath when they refused to worship his self-proclaimed deity. He felt they would need whatever strength and faith he could give them to resist the emperor. Telling Marcus he'd give him a decision soon, Paul withdrew to pray. The chill of that cold, winter day had reminded Phoebe, and she'd told Marcus, "No one will sail for Rome until spring, so there's still time for all of us to reconsider our options."

Marcus had granted them the time, and they hadn't wasted it. After much prayer, Paul admitted, "I can't go to Rome. If I do, and anger Caesar by refusing to worship him, I could become the spark that would ignite a persecution that might never end."

Phoebe had been using a copy of Paul's letter to the Corinthians to acquaint Marcus with the principles of Christianity. Seeing this, Paul had decided to send a letter to Rome. Out of the strange, three-way friendship that had developed, Marcus agreed that a letter would do no harm and wouldn't violate either of his orders. Paul rejoiced over this, and one evening confided to Phoebe what he felt was the true will of God in this matter.

"As you know, my dear lady, I've prayed and agonized over going to Rome. I have no fear of death as long as I am walking in the will of the Lord. But every time I've prayed, I've seen a vision of Jerusalem. I've long planned on going to Spain, but my ministry to the Gentiles is in dispute. I feel

God wants me to have it confirmed by the council of the apostles in Jerusalem before I go any further west. Once that's done, I'll go to Rome on my way to Spain."

"There are also the funds that we've collected for the relief of our brothers and sisters in Jerusalem," Phoebe reminded. "You promised Timothy in Macedonia that you'd take them yourself."

"True," Paul had admitted. "That, too, is in the will of God." Phoebe remembered the roughness of Paul's work-worn hands as he gently held hers, saying, "All of this makes my letter of extreme importance. It must clearly state the ministry Jesus gave me on the road to Damascus. It must establish, once and for all, the supremacy of the New Covenant over the Old. And above all, it must condemn the heresy that Nero is planning to create. Our problem now is to find the right person to deliver it."

Phoebe had contracted with Gaius of Corinth, Paul's employer, to provide new sails for her fleet during the winter layover. When this was completed in mid-January, Paul had returned to Corinth to compose his epistle. From time to time, Marcus would visit him there and report back on the letter's progress. When Paul came to her in mid-February concerning the sailing date of her flagship, he again brought up the subject of who should actually deliver the letter to Rome. The two of them were seated at the long cypress table in her dining hall, and after being assured that *Odessey* would sail as early as possible, he asked for additional help.

"Phoebe," he thoughtfully said, "the pledge of secrecy we gave Marcus regarding his mission here has caused me some concern."

"How?" she asked.

His eyes swept the dining hall and the entry to the adjoining kitchen to be certain they were alone. "I need a messenger to deliver my letter, and it seems, there may be a breach of that promise no matter whom I choose."

"I'm certain Marcus would agree to one other person knowing our secret," Phoebe speculated.

"Perhaps he would," Paul softly replied. "But that's also part of my dilemma. The man I select would have to be one the centurion could trust."

"Paul, on your recommendation, I'm sure Marcus will accept anyone you choose." She smiled encouragingly at the apostle and asked, "Whom have you considered?"

"That, too, is part of my problem."

Phoebe voiced her puzzlement. "I don't understand."

"When I wrote my letters to the Thessalonians and the Corinthians, I was writing to people and places where I'd already ministered. They knew of me and had heard my witness, but I've never been to Rome. My messenger will have to speak for me. He may have to explain my teachings. He may face hostile men, both Christian and pagan."

"I can understand the danger of pagan hostility, Paul, but you can't be serious about the Christians."

"Oh, but I am," Paul sadly replied. "The Christians in Rome are all Jews. They still cling to the old laws and traditions. To them, Jesus is the Jewish Messiah, and a Gentile must become a Jew before he can worship our Lord. He must submit to the old sacrament of circumcision." Paul leaned forward as he added, "As a result, in all of Rome there are fewer than 500 Christians. Our number is so small that Nero considers us nothing more than a sect of the Jewish faith."

The apostle fell silent for a moment. Phoebe watched his face fill with anguish. Her heart went out to the old man. She loved him as if he were her father. When he resumed speaking, his voice contained a note of pain.

"I'm not important to Nero; he doesn't even know me. As Marcus has told us, it's the Sanhedrin in Jerusalem that wants me punished. Through their ambassadors in Rome they are using Poppaea Sabina, the emperor's mistress, to force either my death or my denial of Christ. They have never forgiven me for turning to Jesus." He raised his eyes toward the ceiling. "As Christians, we're no threat to Nero; nor is our ministry of love a threat to the Sanhedrin, but they're a proud and stiff-necked people and they want my blood."

Phoebe wanted to reach out and wipe the tears from his

eyes, but wiped her own instead. She was beginning to understand.

"Everywhere I've preached, since meeting Jesus on the road to Damascus," Paul said, "I've found fear and hatred in the eyes of some people. I've had to go to them and ask their forgiveness." His eyes locked on Phoebe's. "They're the ones who fled from my persecutions when I served the Sanhedrin. It's the same look I saw in the faces of the Christians when Stephen was stoned in Jerusalem."

He stopped again. She could hardly hear his voice when he finally asked, "Oh, Phoebe, can you feel the pain I feel, remembering how they laid Stephen's garments at my feet?"

His pain was real, and she felt it. No answer was necessary; her tears spoke for her heart. This was a side of Paul she'd never seen before. She prayed for him. After a few minutes, the strong fiber of the Holy Spirit was back in his voice.

"The man I send to Rome to speak for me will have to face many of the people who fled from my persecution of them or their families. He will have to teach the truth of the New Covenant. He will have to have a youthful spirit and be firmly founded in the faith. He will have to be conversant in both Greek and Latin. He must have the ability to negotiate the traps and snares of a pagan emperor and a doubting people."

"Have you considered Gaius?" Phoebe asked.

"Yes, but he's uncircumcised and might be suspect by those who are."

"What about my steward, Simon?"

"He meets all the qualifications except one," Paul admitted. "He's needed here and because of his injured hip, I fear the voyage would be too much for him."

"Would Tertius, your scribe, be willing to go?"

Shaking his head, the Apostle observed, "His Latin lacks polish, and he clings to the old ways. While writing the letter, he wanted to debate almost every word." Paul laughed softly. "I truly believe Tertius thinks Gaius is still a heathen. You should have seen and heard his reaction when my Roman host offered us a noontime meal that contained boiled pork!"

"If he were baptized, would Marcus serve?"

Paul smiled and asked, "Would our centurion submit to the Jewish knife?" He held up his hand to stop her reply. "And even if he would, our friends in Rome would probably reject the word of God if it came from the lips of an officer of the Praetorian Guard. The final straw is that he's the adopted son of Seneca, Nero's right hand."

"But his natural father stood at the foot of the cross when our Lord died. Would they discount the word of the son of that centurion?" Phoebe pressed.

Paul sat in silence for a moment before he answered. "I can't risk it, Phoebe. Nothing must stand in the way of my letter. The only hope they have in Rome is for my letter to be received and believed. Nero fears only the power of the people, so their safety depends on their ability to convert large numbers of Romans. The Jewish knife must be removed and replaced by the circumcision of the heart! In some small measure," he softly added, "I pray that my letter will touch the heart of Nero. It will be a miracle of God if it does!"

"Paul," Phoebe asked, "could I take your letter to Rome?" The startled expression on the teacher's face told her not to wait for his reply. "I'm fluent in both Latin and Greek. Circumcision will not be a problem with me. I'm young in spirit. I understand your ministry to the Gentiles. I've led every member of my household to the Lord. I understand the truth of the New Covenant. I have the ship for the trip and can afford the journey."

"But you're a woman!" Paul protested.

"Does that really matter?"

"And there's the danger," he added.

"I have no fear of Rome," Phoebe flatly stated.

"No, you can't go!"

"Why?" Phoebe demanded.

Paul took a deep breath. "Phoebe, you're a woman." His voice contained love and gentleness. "They wouldn't allow you to speak. They worship in the old manner. Their women can't even sit with the men, and they're commanded to silence in the churches. I can't ask you to take a message to them that might not be believed. I'm not too sure they'd accept my teachings if I took them myself!"

Bowing her head, Phoebe silently prayed. She felt the Holy Spirit urge her on. Without raising her head, she spoke. "Let me take the letter to Aquila. He's now in Rome."

Paul's silence told her she'd hit the mark. Aquila and Priscilla had returned to Rome when Nero lifted the Jewish banishment of the Emperor Claudius. Phoebe knew them both from the days they had spent in Corinth, seven miles from Cenchrea. They had gone to Ephesus with Paul. He had worked for them and knew them well. They had been greeted in his letter to Rome. Paul's answer stunned her.

"I'm not sure Aquila will accept my letter." Phoebe looked up. "He has never totally agreed with my stand on the Gentiles." A slow smile formed on his lips. "Having a woman deliver my letter might confound them. It would certainly get their attention, but they still might not believe."

"That didn't bother Jesus," Phoebe firmly said.

Paul's expression asked the question.

"When our Lord had an even more unbelievable message, He gave it to a woman. He sent Mary of Magdala into a hostile city to find terrified men and tell them of His glorious resurrection!" Once again, Phoebe knew she'd hit the mark. "When Jesus sent the woman of Samaria into the city to proclaim the coming of the Messiah, He even chose a Gentile."

Reaching across the table, Phoebe covered his hands with hers. "Paul, can you deny me the honor of serving our Lord in the same manner?"

She saw admiration in the teacher's eyes. She knew she'd won. His words confirmed it. "This, too, is of God and you shall go to Rome. I'll commend you in the letter and ask them to receive you with love."

A flash of reflected light caught the corner of Phoebe's eyes before the cadence of metal-reinforced half-boots striking the quay stones reached her ears. In perfect formation a five-man squad of Roman soldiers turned the corner of the villa's west

21

wall. Marcus was in the lead. His gleaming helmet, polished breastplate and crimson lined palla—or cloak—represented the glory of Rome. Each man, including Julius, the decurion, carried a sea chest on his shoulder. She watched them march smartly to the bottom of the *Odessey's* gangplank.

"Squad, halt," Marcus shouted. The emperor's medallion caught the sun as the centurion turned to speak to Captain Castor who was standing on the ship's quarterdeck. "Captain, may I have my luggage brought aboard?"

At Castor's nod, Marcus spoke to his decurion and watched as Julius led the other men up the gangplank. The sun once again flashed from their polished helmets when they turned toward the small cabin on the ship's port side under the quarterdeck break. Marcus and Julius would occupy that cabin while Phoebe and her maid, Debra, would take the great cabin to the starboard.

The commanding presence of the centurion held everyone's attention. As an officer of the Praetorian Guard, he was a prime example of Roman manhood. His were the classic proportions any sculptor would have been proud to reproduce; broad shoulders and narrow waist were carried erect on muscled legs.

With his possessions stowed aboard the ship, Marcus dismissed his men and strode toward the villa. He noticed Phoebe standing on the balcony and called out.

"Good morning, my lady." Waving toward the soldiers returning to their barracks, he added, "As you can see, Julius and I are ready to sail. Can I or my men be of any service to ou?"

Phoebe acknowledged his greeting with a slight bow. "Thank you, but my servants have already attended to my preparations. May I offer you the hospitality of my house until we sail?"

Marcus nodded his acceptance and walked toward the gate to the villa's inner courtyard. A sudden movement on the deck of the *Odessey* caught Phoebe's attention. Castor had whirled away, scowling, after witnessing their friendly exchange. Glancing quickly at Marcus, she saw the captain's actions had gone unobserved by the centurion.

CHAPTER II

Nay, in all these things we are more than conquerors through him that loved us.

ROMANS 8:37

AS PHOEBE watched Marcus disappear under the archway, she fought down the feeling of excitement his presence always stirred in her. At first both she and Paul had seen him as the enemy. But his openness had intrigued them, his quick understanding had charmed them, and his driving energy had stirred Phoebe. Now she found herself having to struggle to get her emotions under control. She hoped he would take at least a few minutes to reach the balcony where she waited.

Phoebe raised her eyes to the sparkling Saronic Gulf beyond the harbor. She traced the low-lying, western shoreline, now highlighted by the morning sun, to a rock outcropping about a mile south of Cenchrea. There, nestled against the sea, was the fabled Bath of Helen.

It was an idyllic place with a crystal pool and aromatic cedar trees where the legendary Helen was said to have often come. To Phoebe it was a site of poignant memories. For it was there that she had last seen her father and mother together.

Her father, like Marcus, had worn the uniform of Rome. In memory Phoebe could still see the love in his eyes for her mother, Exelophene of Sparta. Her noble blood traced back beyond the immortal "300 of Thermopylae." They had gone to Helen's bath for a farewell outing on the eve of her father's departure for Egypt with the XXI Cohort which he commanded. Four months later her mother was a widow with two daughters: the baby, Kyria, and five-year-old Phoebe.

Remembering that long-ago outing brought fresh pain. Phoebe and her husband had gone to Helen's bath on the afternoon before he sailed on his last voyage. It had been a happy time. They'd been married only a few months, and that was to have been their first separation. Then, three months later, she'd received word of his shipwreck and death in the Strait of Messina. Phoebe had vowed never to go back to the Bath of Helen again. However, Paul had overcome her superstitious fear by baptizing her in that very special pool.

Behind her, Phoebe became aware of voices drifting out from the interior of her house. Marcus was talking with some of her servants. She sensed he was enjoying the conversation; the delay gave her memories more time to continue back over the years.

As a Roman citizen she had inherited her husband's estate. Her pagan religion offered no solace for her sorrow, and she found herself exposed to the greed of the temple priests at every turn. In desperation she had gone to the Christians, and they had taken her to Paul. His patience, kindness and love had guided her to Simon, now her steward, who had become a Christian. She came to trust Simon, and his advice regarding her fleet and business affairs proved well founded. Paul had then introduced her to the gospel of Jesus of Nazareth. It was through his teachings about Jesus that Phoebe discovered she wasn't alone, that she had no reason for superstitious fear. Under Paul's guidance, she had made the decision to become a Christian. Then she had asked for, and received, the infilling of the Holy Spirit. In that instant, her life had changed, and she had never looked back.

Her sister, Kyria, had followed her example and was now happily married to a Christian merchant in Ephesus. The modest warehouse Phoebe had inherited from her husband was now the dominant, two-story building on the Cenchrea waterfront. Her villa occupied its upper floor. She had over a hundred people in her employ and most of them, too, had become followers of Jesus.

Now, she was going to Rome with Paul's letter. As she and Paul had become closer to Marcus he had revealed to them a great deal about the inner workings of the imperial court. They discovered that Marcus was the adopted son of Seneca who was Nero's principal advisor and the second most powerful man in the Roman Empire. The centurion was truly a man with high connections.

The intrigues, bloodletting and depravity of the Roman court, as described by Marcus, shocked them deeply. Nero was the nephew of the Emperor Caligula and the adopted son of the Emperor Claudius. Agrippina, his mother, had married Claudius after Claudius had his third wife, the Empress Messalina, killed. When the Emperor Claudius died suddenly, there was private speculation that Agrippina had poisoned Claudius, but there was no proof. Nero, whom Claudius had named his heir, then ascended to the throne over Claudius' natural son, Britannicus. At his mother's insistence Nero had married Octavia, Claudius' daughter by Messalina, when they were both 16. A year later he had become emperor and was now in the second year of his reign.

Fighting off the domination of his mother, Nero appointed his boyhood tutor, Seneca, a Spaniard, as his chief advisor in civil affairs. Burrus, the prefect of the Praetorian Guard, was his chief military counselor. Most palace watchers knew that Nero had become emperor as a result of his mother's design and ambition. Agrippina fully expected to rule the empire through her son, but Seneca and Burrus encouraged Nero's independence and balanced her influence. But all three—Agrippina, Seneca and Burrus—had overlooked the negative influence of Octavia, Nero's wife.

Octavia was prim and proper, and Nero disdained her as a prude. As empress, she was the leading patron of the College of Vestal Virgins, and she held that chastity was a virtue. Octavia refused to participate in the free-swinging orgies Nero loved so well. This attitude led the emperor to look elsewhere for his sexual enjoyment. Now, at the age of 19, Nero craved uninhibited sensuous pleasure, and this insatiable appetite found satisfaction in the wives and families of the men around him.

Phoebe shuddered as she remembered Marcus' exact words. "When the emperor sees a woman who excites him, he simply orders her husband or father to send her to him. In some families this type of personal service to the emperor is considered an honor, and the women comply willingly. That was the case with General Otho's wife, Poppaea."

According to Marcus, General Otho had happily traded the favors of his wife for a high-ranking army command in Gaul. To Poppaea, bored with being a military wife, being Nero's mistress offered an exciting opportunity.

She desperately wanted power and now possessed a means to gain it. Endowed with a voluptuous body and a sensual mind schooled in the arts of passion, she soon held sway over the emperor. She was, in fact, the driving force behind Nero's desire to deify himself. If this happened, Poppaea felt she could gain the ultimate power she craved.

Because of Nero's wife, Octavia, she couldn't become empress. But if Nero were declared a god, she would become his chief high priestess. Then, she alone would hand down his divine decrees. Thus all who stood in her way—Seneca, Burrus, Agrippina and Octavia—would only be able to approach the emperor-god through her.

But this wasn't the end of Poppaea's shrewd plan. She also was friendly with the Jewish high priests of the Sanhedrin in Jerusalem. Since many Roman Jews were wealthy and in high civic favor, the Sanhedrin also represented power. And Poppaea lost no time in ingratiating herself with its leaders. She dispensed governmental favors to them and, whispered gossip had it, her favors with some of the Sanhedrin ambassadors became quite personal.

Before his conversion, Paul had served the Sanhedrin as a persecutor of Christ's disciples. But since he had accepted Jesus as the Messiah, they considered him a betrayer and had desperately sought his conviction and humiliation on the charge of Jewish heresy. In this they had failed. Now, through Poppaea, they hoped Nero would do what they could not. If Nero could command Paul's worship, it would openly prove that he didn't believe the gospel he was teaching. If Paul refused to worship the emperor, he would be tried and convicted of treason. Either way, the Sanhedrin would win and Paul would no longer be a thorn in their sides.

When Paul heard from Marcus of Nero's plans to declare himself a god, he had been quick to point out that Jews, believing in one God, would be subject to the same imperial pressure. But Marcus had reminded him that an accepted precedent already had been established by the Jews for their own self-preservation. The previous Roman caesars who had deified themselves, Julius and Augustus, were honored at the Jewish temple in Jerusalem by blood sacrifices offered in their names as an accommodating gesture by the priests of the Sanhedrin. Marcus had argued that Nero could simply be honored in the same manner. Even Caligula was so honored after he declared himself a god.

But Paul stressed that this accommodation was denied to the followers of Christ. When God allowed His only Son to die on the cross, He had made the final, perfect sacrifice for the sins of all men. Blood sacrifices were no longer necessary. Jesus had commanded His continued sacrifice through the sharing of His body and blood. And the breaking of the bread and the sacramental cup could only be shared in Jesus' name.

Hearing footsteps along the balcony, Phoebe shook off her somber thoughts and watched with quick interest the approach of the centurion. Marcus was carrying his helmet in the crook of his muscular left arm. His short, curly, blond hair resembled spun gold in the morning sun. A wide smile and sparkling blue eyes highlighted the deep tan of his face. The blood of his Saxon mother and Roman father blended perfectly in him. Phoebe felt a kinship with Marcus. They were both children

27

of the empire whose fathers had found their mothers while serving outside Rome. His paternal parent had died in Jerusalem while in the service of the procurator, Pontius Pilate. Seneca was his father's patron and had claimed Marcus through adoption in place of the son he couldn't have.

The centurion's baritone voice contained a playful note. "Phoebe, you look so reflective this morning." He took her extended hand and pulled her away from the balcony rail, studying her carefully. "I've just made a new discovery. The green of your gown perfectly matches the color of your eyes." Bowing slightly, he raised her hand to his lips.

She liked the cool touch of his lips on the back of her hand, and she matched his mood. "You do have a way with words, don't you?"

Still smiling, Marcus straightened and looked down at her. "The truth is, my lady, that I have not seen anything in the women of Rome that can match your charm and grace." He lowered his voice to a confidential whisper. "Paul has told me of your mission. This afternoon I will take the step that will enable me to share it with you."

Phoebe understood his meaning. All through the winter, she and Paul had been explaining to Marcus the meaning of the gospel of Christ. He had admitted that since the age of 10 he had questioned the divinity of the old Roman gods. He had prayed to them and offered sacrifices without results. When he arrived in Greece three months earlier, he had concluded that all religious faith was just another tool of civil government. He had seen the ruling class use religion as another means of controlling and pacifying the people. In his opinion, the only god with any meaning was the sword he wore at his side.

However, after long talks and much prayer, Phoebe and Paul together had led Marcus to a greater consideration. As a result, the centurion whom Nero had sent to drive Paul to Rome was going to be baptized himself that very afternoon. Phoebe was convinced that it was the Spirit of Jesus in her that made Marcus feel she was so different from the other women he'd known. She doubted that Marcus, as yet, knew this, and she prayed that he would come to understand as he matured in his new faith.

Allowing him to hold her hand as a gentle breeze washed over the balcony, she murmured, "Marcus, are you sure you are ready to accept the love of Jesus?"

The centurion's face lit up. "You and Paul and the others around you reflect a peace and joy that I haven't found anywhere else in the empire. You say your Lord gives you this great gift and I know I want it too."

"Then I pray you shall have it," she declared.

Phoebe told him of the preparations she was making for the reception that would follow his baptism. Christians from Cenchrea, Corinth and Lechaeum had been invited, and more than 200 were expected. Gaius, Paul's employer, was coming, as were the members of her ships' and their families. She suspected that Marcus would be amazed by the number of Roman soldiers among his troops who had accepted Jesus as their Lord and who would be attending. In addition to celebrating his baptism, the party would also mark the beginning of the sailing season and her departure for Rome. Most sea commerce didn't start until the Ides of March, but *Odessey* was sailing early and would chance the late spring storms. The Nones of April wouldn't wait, and she had to be in Rome before Nero's proclamation.

Crossing the portico at the east end of the balcony, she and Marcus brushed past servants busily setting up tables for the reception. They entered the villa's great hall, which was filled with the heady aroma of roasting fowl and calf. The scent of freshly baked bread and stewing leeks intermingled with the pleasant odor of simmering sauces laced with wine. Her steward, Simon, was directing Marcus' sergeant, Julius, who'd volunteered to help in setting up casks of wine for the expected guests. Seeing them enter the hall, both the steward and decurion stopped working and looked expectantly toward them.

As the elder of her household, Simon would perform Marcus'

baptism. Phoebe met his expectant glance with a look of affection. A lock of his unruly gray hair hung down over his left eye as he squared his narrow shoulders and limped toward her. He'd been beached years before by a severe hip injury suffered in a shipwreck, but his knowledge of the sea made him invaluable to her. He had earned great respect on the waterfronts of the empire and, as the steward of her enterprise, he was second only to her in authority.

Brushing the gray locks from his face, Simon smiled at Marcus and said, "This is going to be a marvelous day. I predict that your baptism will mark the beginning of a glorious adventure for you." Turning to Phoebe, he added, "Captain Castor has reported the *Odessey* ready to sail, and your maid Debra says all your chests and bags are aboard." Nodding his head toward Julius, he observed, "And I can't tell who is happier, the sergeant or the maid, over the fact that they'll be traveling with you."

Phoebe was aware of the budding romance between Marcus' decurion and her maid. Julius had become a Christian recently and while they were packing for the trip, Debra had mentioned the possibility of a future marriage. Phoebe's smile widened when she remembered Debra's veiled observation that Marcus would also make some fortunate lady a fine husband. The thought of marrying again had entered Phoebe's mind, but she had pushed it aside. Although Castor was close to her in age, and as the youngest captain in her fleet, the brawny dark-eyed man would seem to qualify, Phoebe still doubted his intentions. She suspected that the handsome, Greek captain was more interested in her shipping enterprise—the Dolphin— than in her as a wife and companion. Watching Marcus stride across the room toward Julius, she considered him as a husband.

As Seneca's adopted son, the centurion was already wealthy. Thus he was not likely to pursue her for money. Phoebe acknowledged his physical appeal. She knew he was interested in her, but she suspected that his conversion to Christianity was more an attempt to become attractive to her personally than because of in-depth convictions. Marcus would have to prove that he loved God first and her second before she could seriously think of him as a possible husband. Other than that, she admitted, Marcus was ideal. He was attentive and considerate. And, most important, he had told her he intended to resign from the army after reporting back to Nero.

Remembering the close relationship of her mother and father, Phoebe felt certain she and Marcus could achieve the same happiness. Free of the army and Caesar, he would make a fine master for the Dolphin. They could work together and create a life for each other in mutual service to the Lord, but she again reminded herself that his commitment to Jesus would have to be complete first. *Perhaps,* she thought, *I can resolve my doubts concerning the depth of his faith during the trip to Rome. If Marcus is accepting Jesus only to impress me, then I must trust the Lord to reveal it to me.*

With his arm on Julius' shoulder, Marcus winked back at her and declared, "My sergeant is a true son of Rome; he has come, he has seen and he has conquered."

Phoebe flinched at his words. They were the statement of a proud centurion of Caesar who would feel justified in using any and every means of gaining her favor. Julius perceptively corrected Marcus' misconception.

"Oh no, sir," he happily admitted, "I'm the one who has been conquered."

Looking around the room, Phoebe could see that all preparations for the reception were nearly complete. With Marcus helping, Simon and Julius finished arranging the wine casks. Goblets of pale blue Corinthian pottery, emblazoned with a white dolphin, were neatly arranged on a long table in front of the casks. Two other tables were awaiting the mountains of food that would pour from the kitchen. All the other furniture had been pushed back against the walls. From the angle of the sunlight streaming down through the translucent marble windows, Phoebe knew it was time to start her personal preparations.

Asking Simon to find Debra for her, Phoebe excused herself

from Marcus and Julius and made her way down the long hallway toward her private suite of rooms. Pausing at her door, she looked back and saw Julius lead Marcus into one of the guest rooms where the centurion's baptismal tunic had been laid out for him. After his baptism Marcus would change again into the purple-bordered white toga praetexta which she was giving him as the first gift for his new birth in Jesus Christ.

Her own white silk stola with the purple border was lying across her bed when she entered the room. Sitting down at the dressing table, she studied her reflection in the polished silver mirror while waiting for the maid.

The bone structure of her face, inherited from her mother, projected a proud beauty. High cheekbones framed her delicate, slightly upturned nose and seemed to support her large, shining green eyes. Slender eyebrows matched the black of her hair. Full lips outlined her small mouth. The gentle curve of a firmly formed chin blended perfectly with the contour of her long, graceful neck.

Standing, she slipped her shoulders free from the open neck of her gown and allowed it to drop from her slender shoulders to the floor around her tiny feet.

Debra joined her as she stepped out of the fallen gown. The girl's dark brown eyes sparkled with excitement as she announced, "Paul and his scribe Tertius have arrived from Corinth along with Gaius, the sailmaker." The maid picked up Phoebe's gown and laid it on the bed, adding, "Gaius wanted to see the new sails Paul had designed for the *Odessey,* so Simon's taken them all down to the ship."

"Have many others arrived?" Phoebe asked while seating herself once again at her dressing table.

"Several are already in the garden and others are milling about on the quay," the maid replied as she started brushing Phoebe's hair.

"Then we must hurry," Phoebe said. "I don't want everyone waiting on me."

The girl laughed softly. "We have plenty of time. Paul wants to talk with Marcus before the ceremony. Gaius wants to see the new sails on all the ships and Tertius has gone to the taverna with Captain Castor." Between brush strokes she continued. "And all the others are catching up on the news each has brought with them."

Phoebe frowned at her maid's statements. She could understand Paul's wanting to visit with Marcus and Gaius wanting to see the sails his company had made, but what were her captain and Paul's scribe doing at the taverna when free wine was available at the villa? They certainly had never been friends. The one thing they had in common was their frugality, and she had never observed any interest between the two men.

She tried to recall all she knew about Tertius. He was wiry and explosive. As Paul's penman he had written the letter she was taking to Rome. As Paul had dictated the letter to him, she wondered if the teacher had impressed upon Tertius the need for secrecy. Was Tertius breaking this secrecy by talking to her captain?

A chill came over her as she recalled a statement by Marcus. The centurion had commented that he believed Poppaea had prevailed upon Nero to select him for the mission to Greece because of his relationship with Seneca. By having Nero send Marcus after Paul, it would appear that Seneca was supporting Poppaea's plans. Phoebe shuddered. If word got back to Poppaea of the contents of Paul's letter and of Marcus' conversion to Christianity, the evil woman could bring them all down. Poppaea would twist all their actions into a conspiracy against the emperor. Paul's only importance to Nero was the importance Poppaea and the Sanhedrin placed on him. Thus, if she learned of Paul's letter, she would turn it into a document of treason. Everyone, even those remotely associated with it, would fall within the so-called plot. Even Burrus, Marcus' commanding officer, and Seneca would be incriminated. With them out of the way, Poppaea could then rule supreme through her sexual influence over the soon-to-be-proclaimed emperor-god.

As Debra interlaced her upswept hair with long strands

33

of pearls, Phoebe's thoughts darkened as she thought of her journey beginning tomorrow. Most of the Christians in Rome were converts from Judaism. Paul's ministry to the Gentiles hadn't as yet reached there. In fact, that was the main thrust of his letter. He wanted to show all Romans, including Nero, that Jesus' salvation was available to everyone without first having to become a Jew. But as a woman, Phoebe knew she was still faced with the restriction of Jewish tradition. In going to Rome she would have to violate this tradition.

Paul had told her that his scribe Tertius vigorously opposed her selection as the messenger. Like all Messianic Jews, Tertius demanded the silence and segregation of women in the worship of God. In railing at Paul, he maintained that women should never have authority over men nor be allowed to teach the new faith. Yet in delivering the letter, Phoebe knew she would have to teach and explain some of the things Paul had written.

In view of this, Paul had commended her in the letter, hoping to generate a degree of acceptance for her among the believers in Italia. In the letter he had asked that they treat her fairly and welcome her warmly in love, as Christians, and do whatever she asked of them. The teacher had reminded Phoebe that his commendation might have little or no effect in Rome because of his reputation as the one-time persecutor. Only Aquila and Priscilla, he noted, whom Phoebe had known in Corinth and who had gone to Ephesus with Paul three years earlier, could be depended on to receive her in the imperial city. The couple had returned to their home in Rome after Nero lifted the Jewish ban imposed by Claudius.

As Phoebe thought about Tertius, a cold feeling of anxiety crawled up her spine. Irrational as he could be, Tertius could throw the whole enterprise into jeopardy by breaking their fragile security. That was why she was so troubled by the knowledge that he was now meeting with Castor at the taverna. The captain always had been loyal to her. But after Paul's observation about Castor's obsessive ambitions, she had begun to doubt that loyalty. If Tertius inadvertently gave him too much information, it could greatly increase the risk of her mission to Rome.

Standing before her mirror, Phoebe allowed Debra to lower the stola over her carefully arranged hair. She exchanged the green slippers she was wearing for pearl-trimmed white ones and studied the drape of the gown as Debra circled her waist with a silken cord that matched the stola's purple border. Smiling with satisfaction at her completed reflection, she thanked Debra for her help and sent the girl off to get herself ready for the reception.

Once Debra was gone a feeling of total inadequacy swept over Phoebe. Every direction she looked there was danger and uncertainty. Who did she think she was to go against Paul's common sense evaluation of her mission? Why did she think that somehow she alone could break down the historic and cultural barriers against women? But she wasn't alone, she suddenly remembered.

Phoebe knelt beside her bed. "Dear Jesus, I have given my life to You and now I submit my journey to Rome for Your glory. I humbly ask that You accept my love and devotion and guide my footsteps in the path You have chosen. Give me the wisdom and discernment to follow Your will. Touch those around me with Your love and bless us all with Your strength. Let our feeble hands do Your great work. If any of us stray from the task, pull us back. Bless Marcus at his baptism and let the Holy Spirit fill him with Your power and understanding. Guide me in my relationship with him, and if it's Your will, let us serve you together. I pray in Your holy name. Amen."

She remained, eyes closed, kneeling in silence as Paul had taught her, waiting on God. A thought formed in her head: *I am with you.* A feeling of warmth settled over her. Her tears were of joy. Behind closed eyes she could see a glowing golden light that seemed to touch the very core of her soul.

Certain that God's hand had touched her, she waited for further divine assurance. Phoebe's heartbeat quickened as her mind recorded an awesome command that came to her consciousness in audible words: "My message must be delivered to the pagan emperor." She was about to gasp her inadequacy, but the Holy Spirit assured her that He would be with her,

35

and she meekly submitted to His will. God was with her, she knew. But she also knew that man was still free to rebel against Him, and the danger of such rebellion was rampant in Rome.

Drying her eyes, Phoebe stood and walked slowly toward the door. She realized that her mission to Rome was already beginning, and when she passed through that door, her life would never be the same again. Trusting in God, she opened it and stepped into the hallway.

CHAPTER III

. . . his servants ye are to whom ye obey . . .

ROMANS 6:16

HAVING dismissed Julius to make his personal preparations for the reception, Marcus paced back and forth before the open window in his room. Paul had sent word for him to wait. The apostle wanted to talk to him before his baptism. He felt light on his feet and attributed it to the simplicity of his dress. He was naked except for the knee-length linen tunic and cross-strap, canvas sandals.

Turning his back on the uncluttered room, Marcus paused in front of the window and viewed the increasing activity in the courtyard below. He recognized some of the people. The others were strangers. The number of Roman uniforms surprised him. Phoebe had said that only Christians were being invited. He spotted Simon limping through the crowd with Paul and Gaius in tow. They were stopped by several clusters of people obviously wishing to talk to the teacher, and Marcus knew it would be some time before Paul got up to him. Resuming his pacing, the centurion reviewed all that had happened.

He'd spent three months in close contact with Paul and Phoebe. They had patiently instructed him in the principles of their faith. Inwardly smiling, he recalled again the orders he'd received from Nero. The depth of Caesar's voice once again echoed in his head.

"Marcus Paetius, it's my command that you search out and find a Jewish tentmaker named Paul. He's a teacher of the Christ and preaches there is only one God. This man was once known as Saul of Tarsus, highly regarded by the Jewish Sanhedrin in Jerusalem."

The centurion remembered Nero kept referring to a scroll which he held in his hands as he spoke.

"This Jew was brought before Seneca's brother, Gallio, for trial in Corinth by the Jews of that city. He was charged with teaching the worship of their single God in a manner contrary to Jewish law. Gallio released him because he'd violated none of our laws."

Nero's sardonic smile filled Marcus' memory.

"But that will change," Nero had declared. "On the Nones of April the Roman Senate will be commanded to declare me a god, and unless this Paul proclaims me *his* single god, his teachings will become treasonable." The emperor's voice had risen almost to a scream. "And I want him here in Rome where I can make him worship me! I want him to lead all the Christians to the foot of my throne!"

Marcus remembered Nero's voice dropping to a whisper as he went on with his discourse.

"It would please me greatly, Marcus Paetius, and would make you a tribune, if you can convince this Paul to come to Rome and bend his knee to me of his own accord. Use any means you desire to accomplish this," Nero had hissed. "If Paul refuses to worship me, and you can't drive him to Rome with fear, then kill him!"

Pausing once more in front of the window, Marcus watched Paul enter the ground floor of the villa. The subdued hum of conversation coming from the great hall told him that it would still be several minutes before the apostle reached him. He retreated into his reverie and recalled Seneca's reaction to Nero's orders.

"Damn," the imperial advisor had exploded, "this business of Nero's becoming a god is Poppaea's doing! That slut and her Jewish friends are using the emperor to accomplish what the Sanhedrin has failed to do!"

The sensuous image of General Otho's wife drifted before Marcus. Poppaea was a devilish creature. Just watching her walk could cause good soldiers to forget their duty. The fact that Otho had left her in Nero's care when he departed for a legion command in Gaul had earned her the barracks title of "Otho's whore." While Seneca, together with Burrus, the prefect of the Praetorian Guard, actually ruled the empire in Nero's name, Poppaea was corroding their influence in seeking power for herself.

"Marcus," Seneca had angrily declared, "by having Nero send you after Paul, Poppaea has indirectly involved me in her plot to harass the Christians. As an officer in the Praetorian Guard and a member of my family, you have become her tool to make it appear that both Burrus and I are in league with her. She is using you and my deep friendship with Burrus to compromise us all!"

Marcus remembered asking why the Jewish tentmaker was so important.

"Paul is of no importance to Rome," Seneca had replied. "It's the Sanhedrin in Jerusalem that wants him destroyed. To do this they are using Poppaea to bewitch the emperor. Nero is still but a child. I've been his tutor since he was 11. Poppaea is corrupting him with sex, using her body to control him. His becoming a god is her idea. She will become his controlling high priestess and confound us all with his divinity."

"What can I do?" Marcus had asked.

"Go to Corinth and find Paul," Seneca had flatly replied. "Tell him what Nero intends doing, but don't let him come to Rome. You must give Burrus and me time to counteract the influence of Poppaea. Keep your actions in Greece a secret from everyone else. If word gets back to Rome that you're preventing Paul's coming, Poppaea will convince Nero that we're plotting against him."

"But, Seneca," Marcus had protested, "are we not plotting against Nero?"

"No!" the imperial advisor had thundered. "We're *not* plotting against the emperor. Our plot is against his mistress."

As he recalled the scene with Seneca, Marcus shook his head. "And now I'm about to return to Rome having obeyed my adopted father and disobeyed my emperor," he thought aloud. But he smiled wryly as he considered how both men had underestimated Paul. He was sending a letter to Rome, and Marcus was certain it would be effective. Phoebe had used Paul's letter to the Corinthians when she was teaching him about Jesus. It had become a book of faith. Even without reading Paul's Roman letter, the centurion knew it would be more than just a greeting. It, too, would become a book of faith.

Hearing the door latch pulled, Marcus turned and faced Paul as he entered the room. Physically, the apostle wasn't imposing. His thinning grey hair didn't cover the crown of his head. He was short in stature and seemed to roll on his thin, bowed legs. The knee-length, rough woolen chiton he was wearing spoke of poverty in its dull grayness. But his light blue eyes contained a fire that matched the majesty of his nose, and a pointed beard and thick mustache added authority to his face. His eyebrows formed a solid, thick line that seemed to support his high, gleaming forehead, and anyone ever hearing Paul's deep rumbling voice would never forget it.

"Marcus," he chuckled, glancing at the open window through which could be heard the hubbub of the crowd, "I tell you, I've never seen such religious fervor as that generated by the prospect of free wine and food." Striding forward, he clasped the centurion in a manly embrace. "Phoebe's outdone herself. There are people here I haven't seen in months." Holding Marcus at arm's length, he grinningly added, "But then I'm not preaching today, and you're being baptized. That may have something to do with the turnout."

Normally Paul wasn't this light in his manner, and Marcus sensed that he was being prepared for some very heavy conversation. Looking the teacher directly in his blue eyes, the centurion felt a kinship with the man. Paul had taught him that they were brothers in the Lord, but Marcus considered the older man more of a fatherly figure. Trying to keep their conversation light, the Roman laughingly replied, "No, Paul, it's the prospect of a possible Roman drowning that's brought them out in such numbers."

Paul smiled, then his eyes turned serious. "We shouldn't be joking about your baptism," he said. "When you make this outward sign of your commitment, you must leave everything else behind. We have a jealous God, and He must be first in our lives."

Marcus watched Paul settle on the edge of the bed and pat the space beside him in invitation. The centurion shook his head and remained on his feet. "I've a feeling that I'll receive what you're about to say better if I remain standing."

Extending his bowed legs before him, the apostle studied his worn sandals. "Perhaps you're right," he murmured. Looking up, he caught the centurion's eyes and held them. "Marcus, in a worldly sense, you have a fine future ahead of you. As Seneca's son, you can gain power, fame and wealth. As a Christian, you may lose all of that and earn the anger of your emperor in the bargain."

"I'm willing to take that chance." Marcus observed.

"But for what reason?" Paul questioned.

"Because I've come to love the Lord."

"Have you?" Paul asked. "Those are easy words to say, but they're hard to live by. Do you love the Lord your God with all your heart, body, mind and soul?" A fire crept into the apostle's eyes. "Have you surrendered everything to Jesus?"

Marcus turned away toward the open window, saying, "I think I have."

"Are you sure?" Paul pressed. "What about your career: will you sacrifice that if the Lord commands it?"

"Yes, of that I'm sure," Marcus firmly answered.

"What about Phoebe?" Paul demanded. "I've seen the feelings grow between you two this winter. Do you love her?"

Marcus whirled on the apostle and declared, "Yes, I love her."

"Could you sacrifice her to the Lord if He asked?"

"He'll never ask that," Marcus replied.

Paul lowered his eyes and studied his sandals once again. Silence filled the room, and Marcus turned back to the window. Neither man spoke for several minutes.

"Marcus," Paul softly said, "God asked Abraham to sacrifice his only son, Isaac, as a test of the old man's love."

Without looking at Paul, Marcus answered, "But He'll not ask me to give up Phoebe. He couldn't be the God you've taught me He is and do *that.*"

"Our God," the apostle solemnly observed, "will not ask any man to do more than He is willing to do Himself. And God so loved the world that He sacrificed His only Son that it might be saved. Marcus, you cannot say that God will not ask you to give up Phoebe."

"Must I love God first and Phoebe second?" Marcus turned and waited for an answer. It came quickly.

"Yes."

"Can't my love for Phoebe be the same as my love for God?"

"No."

"But why? I can surrender myself to both in equal measure," Marcus pleaded.

"Marcus," Paul countered, "would you sacrifice yourself for God?"

"Yes."

"And for Phoebe?" he asked.

"Yes."

"Then why can't you sacrifice her if God commands it?"

Marcus stood at the window and studied the sea for a long moment, then turned and sat down next to Paul with a sigh.

"When—and if—I ever receive such a command," he answered, each word an effort, "I suppose I could obey it if it truly came from God. In such a case," Marcus reasoned, "I'd have little choice, but I wouldn't like doing it."

"Good man," Paul roared, slapping his knee. "Now you can be baptized!" He rose from the bed and strode toward the door, saying, "Let's join the others on the portico and rejoice in your victory." With his hand on the latch, he stopped, faced the centurion and his voice lowered. "We'll talk more of this before you sail, but on your voyage to Rome, don't place too much trust in Captain Castor. I may have inadvertently caused you trouble three days ago when I told Tertius that Phoebe was carrying my letter to Rome. When he learned that you were sailing with her, he exploded: 'At least Castor will know what must be done when that centurion betrays us all!' " Paul tried to smile. "I'm afraid my secretary doesn't have much confidence in your conversion nor in Phoebe's ability as a messenger and teacher."

Following the apostle down the hallway and into the great hall, Marcus was once again aware of Paul's power. The teacher's discernment gave him insight into the motives of men. As a military commander, he'd always considered himself endowed with this gift, but it was nothing compared to that of Paul. Marcus intended to take Paul's warning seriously.

While allowing their eyes to adjust to the bright sunlight, both men stood in the portico doorway for a moment. Marcus recognized the men clustered around Phoebe near the head of the garden stairway. Polax, the tall, red-haired, Persian giant was standing slightly away from the others. He was the leader of *Odessey's* galleymen, a former cavalry officer for an eastern potentate, but now a convicted thief serving out his sentence at a galley oar. Marcus trusted the man because of his unquestioned devotion to Phoebe. She allowed her galleymen limited liberty while in port and paid them a small wage while at sea. Polax was dressed in polished sea boots and a yellow, ankle-length robe with a green sash that matched his stylized turban.

Next to the Persian was Sextus, the *Odessey's* mate and a man wise in the ways of the sea. He was the same age as Simon, and his conservative, gray, woolen, knee-length chiton spoke of years of wear. Gaius, Paul's Roman employer, was standing at Phoebe's right, pointing toward her fleet anchored in the harbor. He was in contrast to all the others in wearing a blindingly white toga that had been treated with fuller's chalk to achieve its brilliance.

Tertius and Castor completed the group. Paul's secretary

was wearing a dark brown chlamys, or cloak, over a single-girdled, undyed, rough wool chiton. Both garments reflected the scribe's reputation of frugality. Castor's sun-bleached pantaloons were topped by an open-necked shirt of blue linen and a scarlet bandana. He carried a sheathed dagger in his red sash.

Seeing the captain's weapon reminded Marcus that he was wearing none. Looking around the crowded portico for additional familiar faces, the centurion was impressed with the size of the crowd. He spotted Julius, in full uniform, standing off to the side sharing a goblet of wine with Phoebe's maid. Paul raised his arm in the air and shouted for attention. "Brothers and sisters!"

As conversation died and eyes turned toward the apostle, Paul led Marcus to the head of the stairs. "We've come here today," Paul continued, "to witness the baptism of Marcus Paetius." He raised the centurion's arm in the air. "Phoebe and I are his sponsors and Simon, as elder of this household, will be the baptizer." Marcus became aware of the crowded garden below as a great cheer went up and Phoebe took his other arm.

He'd never seen her look lovelier. Her gentle hand nudged him down the stairs toward the waiting Simon. At the foot of the stairs, she placed his hand in Simon's and the elder man led the centurion toward the garden beach and the gleaming waters of Cenchrea harbor.

The water felt cold around his ankles and the skirt of his tunic wanted to float as he went in deeper. Using his free hand, he pushed it under and it clung to his legs and body. Marcus experienced a momentary flash of embarrassment, but this passed when Simon faced him as they both stood waist deep. Simon smiled and solemnly asked, "Do you, Marcus Paetius, renounce all other gods and swear fidelity to our Lord Jesus Christ?"

"I do," the centurion firmly replied.

"Then I pray that God's grace descend on you in full measure and I baptize you in the name of the Father for the salvation of your soul." Simon placed his right hand in the small of Marcus' back, closed his nose with the other hand and pushed him backward under the water. Marcus felt himself lifted back to the surface and heard Simon continue. "And I baptize you in the name of the Son for the forgiveness of your sins." Once again the centurion was submerged and resurfaced. Blinking back salty water, Marcus caught a breath as Simon cried out, "And I baptize you in the name of the Holy Spirit, empowering you to love and serve the Lord, your God." He went under for the third time, and when he finally stood free facing his baptizer, Marcus was suddenly aware of the people singing their praises to God.

Experiencing a feeling of elation, the centurion helped Simon from the water. The steward's limp was noticeable to a greater degree after the chill of the sea. Phoebe's eyes sparkled with joy as Marcus accepted her embrace and followed her through the crowd up the portico stairs and into the great hall. Julius was waiting to help him change when he entered his room.

The high point of the reception was when Gaius, with his hand on Marcus' shoulder, announced the distribution of the gifts he'd brought to honor his fellow Roman. Servants carrying baskets mingled with the crowd handing out small leather bags. Gaius shouted special instructions concerning the gifts.

"Please," he cried, "don't open your bags until they've all been handed out."

His request was greeted with laughter and amused agreement. Turning to Marcus and Phoebe, he reached inside the neck of his toga and withdrew two bags tied with twisted silver cord. The murmur of the crowd died as the merchant surveyed the empty baskets in the servants' hands. Holding those in his hands aloft, he announced, "Dear friends, this is a great day for the Lord." Gaius turned, displaying the bags to everyone. "Our Lord Jesus once said, 'He that takes not his cross and follows after me is not worthy of me.' Each of you has a cross to bear." He presented a bag first to Phoebe and then to Marcus, saying, "Open your bags and wear your crosses with honor."

Not a sound came from the crowd as everyone pulled the drawstrings of their bags. A delighted female cry signaled the start of a murmur of pleasure that rose to a buzz of grateful satisfaction. Every bag contained a small silver cross suspended on a fine silver chain. Phoebe held hers in the air and then lowered it over Marcus' head. The centurion returned the favor and beamed his happiness to the men around him. Paul stepped forward, holding his cross in his hand.

"I pray," the apostle shouted, "that today marks the beginning of a Christian tradition—that each of us will bear our crosses with the love of God in our hearts."

Paul led a prayer and everyone joined in the "amen." This was followed by Phoebe's invitation to dine, and she led Marcus, Paul and Gaius to a table on the harbor side of the portico. Once they were seated and served, she smiled at Gaius and thanked him for his great kindness. Caressing the cross at her throat, she murmured, "I shall wear it always and remember the reason it was given to me."

In Marcus' eyes, she was an angel. Every movement of her delicate hands pulled at his heart. Remembering the question Paul had raised before his baptism, and seeing her now, he wasn't sure he'd been truthful with the teacher. Phoebe's beauty was supreme in his most tender thoughts. The way her lashes framed the glory of her eyes filled him with desire. She was worthy of any sacrifice and Marcus knew God would never ask him to give her up. She was too precious for that, and Marcus silently pledged his body and soul to her. His thoughts raced on to the coming day. *Tomorrow,* he thought, *Phoebe and I will sail for Rome, and when we return, I'll spend the rest of my life loving and serving her.*

A flash of red across the portico caught Marcus' attention. It was Castor's sash as the captain started down the stairs toward the Athena gate of the villa. Tertius was following close behind. The centurion momentarily caught the wiry scribe's eyes and saw a flare of fear in them before the man turned away and disappeared down the stairs. Glancing at Paul, Marcus saw that he too had seen the fear in his secretary's eyes.

"They make an odd pair," Paul observed quietly. "It's unlike Tertius to leave a party before all the food is gone."

Marcus stood and searched the crowd for Julius. Not seeing the sergeant, he excused himself and made his way into the villa. Debra caught his arm just inside the doorway.

"Sir," she whispered, "Julius said to tell you that he's gone to the Bow and Bell Taverna." She lightly touched the centurion's lips for silence and added, "He suspects that Captain Castor is plotting against you."

"Did he say anything more?"

"No, sir," she replied.

Marcus stepped back into the sunshine and slowly walked to the portico railing overlooking the harbor. Paul joined him and together they watched Castor and Tertius cross the quay in the direction of the taverna. Acting slightly drunk, Julius wasn't far behind them. The centurion chuckled at his sergeant's antics and spoke to Paul.

"He's a good man and I passed your warning on to him while I was changing. He'll keep an eye on our friends until we sail."

Turning his back to the quay, Paul leaned against the railing. "Perhaps we should ask Phoebe to replace Castor for your voyage."

"No, Paul," Marcus flatly stated, "if he means any danger to Phoebe, I want him where I can find him."

"What harm can he do if you sail without him?"

"That's just the point," Marcus answered. "We'll never know what's really going on if we leave him here." Shrugging his shoulders, he added, "And leaving him here wouldn't stop him from sailing in another vessel and following us to Rome."

Paul agreed with the logic and led the way back to Phoebe's table. Simon had joined the group and he and Gaius were discussing the merits of the *Odessey*. Marcus remained standing and looked down to where the ship was moored, keeping an eye on the taverna at the end of the quay.

The *Odessey* was 72 feet long and the newest ship in Phoebe's fleet. Fifteen oars on both the starboard and port sides were manned by convicts from the prisons of Asia Minor. Phoebe's policy of limited freedom for such men gained her their loyalty, and the fairness of her treatment helped many of them to accept the Christ she served. The balance of the *Odessey's* crew was composed of six men; the captain, first mate and four watchkeepers, one of whom was a boatswain's mate. These men handled the sails, steered the ship and tended to the needs of the passengers.

Unlike the war galleys of the Imperial Navy, *Odessey* was wide in the beam. Her best speed, under ideal conditions and with combined sail and oars, was 12 knots. This could only be maintained for a couple of hours. Under sail alone and with favorable winds, she could achieve nine knots. Without sail, the galleymen could hold her to four knots for hours on end by alternating the stroke and spelling a third of the oars regularly. With all these variables, her average cruising speed was set at six knots and voyages were planned accordingly.

In addition to her crew, *Odessey* could accommodate six passengers, four in the large cabin and two in the small. Both of these were located aft under the quarterdeck with only five feet of headroom. The captain and mate were berthed in bunk lockers located just under the quarterdeck break. Galleymen slept on their rowing benches and the four watch-keepers slept forward in the boatswain's locker.

The *Odessey* carried double steering oars and 1,200 square feet of canvas on a single yardarm and mast. The hold, which ran the length of the ship under the main deck, could carry 240 filled amphorae—clay wine jars—or 30 tons of solid cargo. The amount of freeboard now showing above the waterline told Marcus that she was loaded to capacity. He'd come to Greece in the *Odessey* and knew she was a sound vessel.

With the setting of the sun, guests were beginning to visit Phoebe's table to wish her well on the voyage to Rome and to thank her for the grand reception. Marcus found himself being included in their farewells and for the first time since arriving in Greece, felt that he was no longer an outsider. These Christians expressed their love for each other with a freedom he was just beginning to understand. He discovered a new feeling of affection for each one and was beginning to learn that one must give affection in order to receive.

With the exception of Gaius and Paul, who were staying the night to see them off, all the guests had left within an hour. The imperial dispatch bag from the governor arrived as the sun was setting. Marcus was to carry it to Rome. The final preparations for departure were completed, and Castor reported *Odessey* ready for sea. Julius was spending the night aboard ship and Marcus walked to the quay with him.

"Did anything happen in the taverna?" the centurion asked.

"No sir," the sergeant answered. "They drank together at a corner table. The scribe seemed agitated over something, but the captain reassured him, and they parted on what seemed like friendly terms."

It was a soft, warm, spring evening and after watching Julius enter the small cabin, Marcus turned to walk along the quay. He turned as Phoebe called to him from the villa's courtyard gate. She was wearing a long, white palla over her gown and appeared to glide toward him over the uneven paving stones. To Marcus her voice was like music.

"Paul and Gaius have retired, Simon is checking the *Odessey's* manifests with Castor, and I'm too excited to sleep." She linked her slender arm through his, and he shortened his stride to match hers as she murmured, "My heart is so full tonight because of what you did this afternoon."

Marcus wanted to tell her of his love but realized he must first clear himself with Nero and the complications in Rome. Having her next to him was enough for now, and he sensed that she knew of his love. Instead, they talked of the coming voyage as they walked along the quay.

They planned to sail at daybreak. As the first ship out for the new season, almost the entire village would come to the harbor to see them off. Marcus' imperial pennant would fly from the masthead under the bold Dolphin banner. Their route would take them south around the Malea and then west before the fingers of the Achaia. Their first port of call would be

Syracuse, then on to Rhegium and the dreaded Strait of Messina. Once beyond the toe of Italia, they'd sail north past the volcanic islands to the principal port city of Puteoli. From there, they would travel by land to Rome.

Phoebe's agents in the various ports would assist them, and Marcus' banner would guarantee them priority treatment by the authorities. It should be a swift passage in spite of the danger of late spring storms.

Marcus walked Phoebe back to the villa knowing they would be at sea before they talked privately again. Bidding her goodnight in the great hall, he gently kissed the palm of her hand. She then reached up and lightly touched his lips with a slender finger before turning away and disappearing down the dark passage to her suite.

CHAPTER IV

So then every one of us shall give account of himself to God.

ROMANS 14:12

FAVORABLE winds so blessed the *Odessey* that she turned the Malea at noon on the second day. By nightfall the ship was out of sight of land and Castor used the stars for direction. It was Phoebe's first time this far at sea, and she was filled with wonder. The phosphorus-colored wake was fascinating, and she began to understand the mystery and superstition so many sailors attached to the sea.

During the day she could see huge, gray sharks, their dorsal fins cutting the water, keeping pace with the ship's progress. The water would turn from a translucent green to a deep blue. Every hour spent on deck revealed a new experience and gave her a deeper respect for God and His creation. Giant fish, larger than the *Odessey,* had sounded nearby and sent clouds of stinking spray whooshing into the air from small holes in their backs.

Knowing that these terrors were still around her in the night gave her an extra reason for prayer. How could men, she wondered, go to sea so bravely when almost everything around them seemed independent of human control? Surely their courage must come from God. How else could they survive the terrors they must face? Standing on the quarterdeck, with only the tillerman on watch, her eyes beheld a beauty that transcended every mental image of the sea her mind had ever conceived. Each wave and wavelet was capped with silver. All her fear was suddenly gone. The gentle roll of the ship held her in awe. It was if the Lord had placed His hand under them and was pushing the *Odessey* through the water. The rise and fall of the bow seemed a response to the nodding approval of God.

Phoebe watched the silhouetted figure of Marcus emerge from the small cabin and lean against the well-deck rail. The Roman also seemed engrossed in the magic of the night and totally unaware that Castor had slipped from his sleeping locker behind him. A flash of silver light caught Phoebe's glance, reflected from something held in the captain's right hand.

Castor stood, swaying with the movement of the ship. Creaking timbers obscured all other sound. His head moved forward slightly. Phoebe watched as though frozen, feeling the same degree of fascination she experienced while watching a snake crawl in her garden. The captain's glance took in the sleeping galleymen on their benches. He cocked his head to one side until he heard the splash of the single steering oar. The tillerman's eyes were fastened on the North Star.

Knowing her pale blue gown was aglow in the silver light, Phoebe silently glided forward to the quarterdeck rail. She was standing directly above and behind Castor. Marcus hadn't moved. With the roll of the ship Castor stepped toward him. The centurion's deep voice caught the captain off balance.

"With so much beauty around us, it's no wonder the three of us can't sleep."

Castor hesitated in his step. Catching his balance with catlike quickness, he smoothly sheathed his knife as Marcus turned away from the sea. The captain's eyes followed the centurion, then moved to Phoebe standing above them. Phoebe relaxed the tight grip she'd taken on the quarterdeck rail while a shiver ran up her spine. Her mind refused to accept what she had just seen. Castor had been about to kill Marcus! The realization of it filled her with revulsion. Her throat was too dry to speak. As the Roman passed the captain and started up the ladder, Castor found his voice.

"My lady, I thought you were abed."

Stopping at the top of the ladder, Marcus added, "So did I." He looked down at Castor. "But it is too beautiful a night to be inside."

"True," Castor replied as he started up the ladder, "but looking at the moon and sea isn't my purpose in being away from my bunk."

With Marcus standing beside her, they watched the captain ascend the ladder and head for the tillerman's position. She knew why Castor wasn't asleep, but she listened to his explanation.

"I'm up to check the position of our guiding star." He pointed into the northern sky and added, "That unmoving spot of light must be kept directly off our starboard side in order to maintain our westerly course. If I find it off our stern quarter, we'll be sailing southwest and away from our destination. If it's off the bow quarter, we're traveling northwest toward the heel of Italia. By keeping the star abeam of us, where it is now, we're on course to Syracuse."

Knowing how the star, Cynosura, was used by ship's captains, Phoebe was unimpressed. She understood that all the stars in the heavens moved except that one. Her father had explained years ago when she was a little girl how Cynosura was used to guide armies in the desert and ships at sea. Every seaman in her employ knew its meaning. The tillerman was aware of the star's importance; she had observed his constant attention to it. No, she decided, Castor had a more deadly objective than his explanation suggested.

"How often do you check the star?" asked Marcus.

"At the end of every night-time watch," the Captain replied.

"But, captain," Phoebe imposed, "the sand clock is still a quarter full."

"It's of no importance," Castor said walking toward them. "I'll rouse Sextus for the next watch before I turn in again."

Pausing before them, he added, "In the meantime, I'll check the rest of the ship."

They watched him continue on to the ladder and descend to the well deck. Rolling with the ship, he made his way forward between the rows of sleeping galleymen. Castor stepped up onto the forecastle deck and stood in *Odessey's* bow. The bosun's locker, and the balance of the sleeping crew, were located directly below him.

Gripping Marcus' arm, Phoebe whispered, "You must have eyes in the back of your head."

"No, Phoebe," he chuckled, "there's a squeaky hinge on Castor's cabin door."

"He was going to kill you," she exclaimed in a hushed voice.

"We don't know that for certain."

"Oh, yes we do," she insisted. "His knife . . ." He put a finger to her lips.

"I know about the knife," he confided, "but many men check their weapons when they awaken. It's a habit I have myself when I'm in the field."

"But Castor's not a soldier."

"Every seaman aboard," Marcus reasoned, "carries a knife. It's a tool of their trade. It would be natural to check it before making an inspection of the ship."

Doubt of Castor's intentions began seeping into Phoebe's thinking. What Marcus said was true. The captain could have been getting his bearings while standing behind Marcus. But Castor didn't sheath the knife until Marcus turned on him. The knife was still in his hand when he took that first step toward the centurion.

"Marcus, are you trying to shelter me from the knowledge that Castor's a threat to you?" she asked, her voice shaking now. "Are you really unaware of what almost happened tonight?"

A slow smile formed on the centurion's face, but the sound of his voice was most serious. "Dear heart, I pray you know me better than that. I'm very aware of what almost happened, but I'm puzzled by one thing. If he intended to kill me, how did he expect to get away with it? What reason would he

54

use to justify the act?" Nodding his head toward the ship's bow, Marcus paused.

Phoebe turned in time to see Castor descend the four steps from the forecastle to the well deck. The captain stopped at the first galleyman's bench on the starboard side. She and Marcus watched as Castor stooped and shook the sleeping man's shoulder. It was Polax; when the giant sat up, the captain pointed into the bow and said something to the Persian. Polax nodded his head and lay back down.

Standing up, Castor surveyed the rest of the sleeping men and started aft. Phoebe looked up to see the centurion scowling with perplexed interest.

"Marcus, what is it?" she whispered.

"I can't understand," he answered in hushed tones, "why the captain would wake a man to tell him something that didn't require his immediate attention."

Castor stopped at the base of the mast amidships and inspected the lashings holding the sail's spar aloft. Taking Phoebe's hand, Marcus led her aft, past the tillerman, to the very stern of the ship. It was only the distance of a few feet, but because the quarterdeck rail was a closed, solid surface, and the deck itself was five feet higher than the well deck, Castor couldn't see them. *Odessey's* phosphorescent wake reminded Phoebe of the tail of a shooting star. She was fascinated by the path they were tracing in the sea; but Marcus stood beside her with his eyes forward toward the billowing sail. Phoebe wondered if he were thinking of Castor.

"What motive could he have for wanting me dead?" he asked again. "The death of a centurion aboard his ship would be difficult to explain to Roman authorities. How could he expect to get away with it?"

"Regardless of the Roman authorities," Phoebe observed, "he'd never be able to explain it to me!"

Speaking to himself almost as much as to her, Marcus murmured, "We cannot let Castor know we suspect anything. His actions will tell us more about his motives than all our speculation if he believes we're not watching him.

"If this weather holds," Phoebe said, "we'll be in Syracuse

in three days. You have 'til then to discover what you feel we must know." Her voice tremored as she continued. "My only concern is for you and I'm convinced he means you harm."

"If all else fails," Marcus replied. "I'll confront him and demand some answers."

"Answers or no," Phoebe concluded, "I'm tempted to relieve him of his command and put him ashore at Syracuse."

Turning her back to the sea, she linked her arm around the Roman's and leaned back against the stern rail. She could feel the hardness of his muscles through the fabric of the tunic he was wearing. In the silver light the healed scar of an old battle wound seemed to glow along his right forearm. Gently tracing it with the tip of her finger, she asked tenderly, "Does this ever give you pain?"

"Not any more," he murmured. "And the man who gave me that mark feels no pain either."

Phoebe knew what he meant. Death was part of a soldier's life. She found herself praying for the soul of the dead man to whom Marcus referred. She leaned her head against his shoulder. *He's so much like my father,* she thought. Memories pulled her back in time. She remembered when she was three and was allowed to snuggle down between her parents in their great bed on holiday mornings. She would put her curly head against his shoulder and feel the vibrations of his voice when he spoke to her. It was best when he laughed, she recalled, and the morning she found his ticklish ribs was delightful. Suddenly Phoebe wondered if Marcus were ticklish. As if it had a mind of its own, her free right hand found the spot and she had her answer in Marcus' sudden gurgle.

They were still standing together, content with each other's company, when Sextus came on deck to relieve the watch. The mate was older and shorter than the captain. His gray hair and slight frame belied the true strength of his body. Sextus had been a sailor since he went to sea as a boy. His education was limited to ships and the men who served in them. When he took the steering oar and sent the other man forward, one could see him become a part of *Odessey*. He was barefooted and wore an old chiton.

Greeting Phoebe and Marcus as he settled into position astride the oar, he glanced at the star and sniffed the air. His eyes seemed to search the surface of the water and then rest on the horizon beyond the bow. Phoebe watched him tilt his head back and followed his line of sight to the top of the mast. The sail flapped loose for a moment and then filled again with a snapping crack. Seeing it happen told her she'd been hearing it for some time. Reaching forward to the binnacle, Sextus turned the sand clock and took a small pebble from a box on the left and placed it in a box on the right. Another pebble would be passed when the clock was turned again.

Setting his feet against the mark carved in the deck, he straightened to his full height and fixed his eyes on the guiding star. He moved slowly to his right and Phoebe watched the rigging of the ship swing slightly closer to Cynosura. Sextus moved back to his original position. He had corrected the course, but his body remained stiff as his eyes returned to the distant horizon.

Sensing something was wrong, Phoebe moved away from Marcus and called out to the mate. "What's happening? Is it the wind?"

Glancing back at the star, Sextus answered, "The weather, my lady. I think it's changing."

"In what way?"

Marcus joined her as the mate replied. "The wind is gusting and shifting to the west. If it continues, I'll have to rouse the galleymen to maintain our course and speed." Pointing out over the bow, he indicated a dark mass on the night horizon which she had thought was an island. "Those low clouds could mean a storm."

Marcus entered the conversation. "Then we'd best go below and get some rest while we can."

"Aye, sir," Sextus agreed. "We may be in a tempest by daybreak."

57

Taking a last look at the cloudless sky overhead, Phoebe felt a stir of cool air. The sail hung limp for a moment and then quickly rippled with bulging strength as a gust of wind caught it. The sharp snapping of suddenly filled canvas became the dominating sound of *Odessey*. Limp lines would suddenly draw tight and hum in the sporadic wind.

With Marcus to steady her against the slightly increased roll of the ship, she made her way down the ladder to the well deck. Looking out at the rising sea it was apparent that a dramatic change was taking place. Phoebe's eyes opened with wonder as the silver crowns on each wave appeared higher, grander and ever more majestic in their rolling splendor.

Having no skylight or opening of any kind, Phoebe's cabin was pitch black when Marcus closed the hatch behind her. She dreaded this kind of close confinement; it was the reason she'd gone on deck when Debra retired and the single candle was snuffed out. There were four bunks in the compartment, two on each side. Debra was sleeping soundly in the lower bunk on the starboard side. Phoebe's bunk was opposite with a small table bolted to the deck between them. Under the table in a waterproof leather pouch was Paul's letter, plus the extra copies. On a sudden impulse she picked up the pouch and placed it under the blanket at the end of her bunk.

Groping her way in the pitching darkness, she painfully bumped against the table, then grabbed it to steady herself. With a possible storm coming, Marcus had suggested that she not undress. He told her it was next to impossible to even find your clothes, let alone put them on, with the ship pitching and rolling. Phoebe couldn't bring herself to put her feet under the covers wearing sandals so she removed them and carefully placed them on the table where they could be found in the dark.

She was kneeling beside her bunk, praying for the ship's safety when the sandals hit the deck and skittered away. Her first reaction was to grab for them; but after bumping the table again, she gave up and crawled into bed, her feet resting against the leather pouch. It would be safe, even if she weren't.

Curling up on her right side to steady herself against the ship's movement, she tried to sleep.

The bulkhead at her back had a voice of its own. The creaking seemed to grow louder the more she tried to ignore it. The air was too close to pull the covers over her head, so she grimly waited for drowsiness to come.

In her half sleep she dreamed of a silver ship sailing on a silver sea with silver galleymen pulling her through the shimmering water with silver oars. Even the stroke drum was silver and each beat was like a note of ethereal music. As reality came back to her, she realized it was the *Odessey's* stroke drum she was hearing. The measured, dull thud of the drum told her the oars were out and the thrust of the ship through the water came to her through the rhythmic sensation of forward motion.

Fully awake now, her ears picked up other sounds. Muted voices were relaying orders. The soft sigh of the wind had become a full-throated roar. Suddenly she felt herself lifted in the air only to be slammed back firmly in her bunk. Debra was awake, and her startled scream added to the growing terror Phoebe was beginning to feel.

"Stay in your bed," she shouted to the girl. "I'll try to open the door and get some light in here."

"What is it?" Debra yelled while Phoebe swung her feet to the deck.

Once again Phoebe was airborne. Pain shot through her shoulder where it struck the wall next to her bunk. Struggling to gain control of her body, she ignored the girl's question. Gripping the bunk timber above her, Phoebe firmly found the deck with her feet. With uncertain steps, she moved slowly toward the hatch. The heaving deck beneath her created confusion in her mind. Being slammed first against the bunk and then hurled away from it made the short distance to the hatch seem endless.

With determined effort, she made it and threw her full weight against the panel. It didn't budge. The hatch was locked! Still clutching the bunk, she called out for help, but even as she yelled, she knew no one could hear her. Water was crashing down on the deck above her and the wind was now a constant howl. Closing her eyes against the darkness, she prayed. She dimly heard Debra's frightened voice.

"Phoebe," the girl screamed, "water's coming through the walls. We're sinking!"

With a strange calm, Phoebe turned back toward the sound of the girl's voice. She was afraid to let go of the bunk until she reached the table. *Thank God,* she thought, *this cabin isn't any larger or I'd never make it.* Finding the table with her right hand, she slowly moved toward the sound of Debra's sobbing.

Water was ankle deep around her bare feet when she finally fell on the soaked blankets of the girl's bunk. Debra was sobbing fearfully when Phoebe's probing hand found her. The girl clung to her mistress with all her might. Breaking the girl's grip, Phoebe pushed Debra down in the bunk and told her sternly, "It's only a storm. If we were sinking, the ship wouldn't be pounding like this!"

No sooner had she spoken than both of them were flying through the air. They came down on the deck and slid under the table. Cold water on the floor sloshed over them. Clinging together and gripping the table legs, they slowly and painfully pulled themselves toward Phoebe's bunk. Finally, they wedged themselves together under Phoebe's relatively dry blankets, shivering and clinging to the bunk, their feet pressed against the leather pouch as if seeking the security and strength of Paul's words.

Debra seemed to gain strength from Phoebe's sense of calm. They gradually became aware of other things. The rise and fall of the howling wind allowed them to hear some of the frantic activity going on outside the cabin. They could only guess at what was happening, but Phoebe knew *Odessey* was in God's hands, and again she began to pray.

At first, Debra joined her timidly, but as the prayer continued, both voices gained volume. Knowing their fate rested with God, they surrendered themselves to His will with total love and trust.

From time to time Phoebe thought she could hear Marcus shouting on the deck above her. Once she recognized Castor's voice screaming an order. She knew the ship was being damaged but kept the knowledge to herself. Many of the crashes she heard were from solid objects as well as the wind and raging water.

The locked hatchway bothered her. If the *Odessey* were to sink, she and Debra would be trapped. They both knew they could do nothing topside to help the men; but at least, if they were free, they could swim for their lives if they had to. Remembering the sharks she'd seen the previous day, Phoebe seriously doubted anyone's chances of survival in the water. Still she didn't like having no obvious means of escape.

Even while praying, she resolved to learn who had locked the door and why. She wondered if Marcus could have done it to keep her from harm. If the ship were sinking, she knew he would rescue them. The thought seemed to mollify her, but her anger rose again when she realized it might have been Castor. Then panic began to bore in on her. Castor would want her locked away where she couldn't witness the terrible things he could do to Marcus during the storm. With everyone desperately fighting to save the ship, no one would notice the violence of one man against another. Catching her breath, she realized Marcus could already be lost in the sea. His body could be torn apart by those terrible fish. Phoebe's fear for Marcus' safety became a living thing; she wanted to claw her way out of the cabin.

CHAPTER V

*. . . the judgement of God is according to truth against
them which commit such things.*

ROMANS 2:2

SLEEP had evaded Marcus and Julius. Their small cabin was
barely larger than the captain's bunk locker. It accommodated
two passengers whose bunks ran fore and aft. In rising seas,
this meant any occupant would be feet down one instant and
head down the next. Having taken all that they could, both
Romans got up and dressed for heavy weather.

Wearing uniform tunics of unbleached wool and forsaking
footgear, both men reported on deck and volunteered their
services to Castor. In times of stress at sea able passengers
would often submit to the authority of a ship's captain. Castor
immediately assigned Julius to the second steering oar with
orders to follow the motions and directions of Sextus. The
clouds which the mate had earlier pointed out to Phoebe on
the distant horizon were now boiling overhead.

As Castor ordered Marcus forward to the forecastle, the
centurion noticed that a stout timber had been placed in the
locking brackets of the large cabin's hatch. The women were
locked in! Pointing at the timber, he shouted over the wind.

"Why?"

"We don't need a couple of useless, frantic women running
loose in a storm," Castor shouted back.

62

Seizing the man's shoulders, Marcus faced him and yelled, "How will they get out if we start to go down?"

"I'll release them," Castor roared and turned away. Marcus continued to stare at the bar across the hatch as he followed Castor forward.

Leaning into the rising wind, Castor led the way along the walkway between the rowing galleymen. The sail and spar had been lowered and tied down, running fore and aft, sloping down from the top of the quarterdeck break to the lower forecastle beam. Rigged this way, the spar provided a solid lifeline between the bow and stern section of the well deck. It was needed because when *Odessey* plunged down from the crest of the growing waves, green water broke over the forecastle peak and cascaded down on the rowing men. Passage along the walkway would have been impossible in the rolling, bucking ship without the secured spar for support. The galleymen had tied themselves to their benches.

Stopping amidships, Castor patted four coiled lines which were lashed to the base of the mast. These were auxiliary ropes to be used in the event any of the guys or stays supporting the mast broke during the storm. Marcus' eyes followed the captain's finger as it traced the auxiliaries to the tip of the swaying mast. Castor's voice rose above the wind.

"I want you to stay here and watch the mast. If any of the existing lines snap, you'll have to run one of these to the proper outboard quarter-stanchion and secure it as a replacement." He waited for the centurion to nod his understanding before continuing. "If you fail, the mast will come down on the galleymen and we'll lose our stroke. If that happens, we'll broach and capsize!"

The steady throb of the bosun's stroke drum set the tempo of shipboard activity. Glancing at the rowing men, Marcus appreciated the importance of their pulling together. A falling mast would indeed break their effort; the ship would then turn and, caught sideways in the waves, the *Odessey* could easily roll over and sink.

In the half light of the cloud-shrouded rising sun, Marcus

knew the next few hours could be the last for *Odessey* and everyone aboard. The seas were becoming monstrous. One moment they would tower over the ship and its stubby mast; in the next instant, *Odessey* would fly upward and seem to soar over the raging sea. Screaming wind and pounding water made further conversation impossible.

With his back to the bow, Marcus watched the captain make his way aft along the spar. *Odessey* broke over the crest of a gigantic wave and started its headlong slide. Polax and his mates pulled away, increasing the ship's descent speed until she buried her bow at the bottom, hurling tons of water into the air. Clinging to the mast, the centurion lost his footing as solid water passed over him. Gasping for breath, he shook the water from his eyes and looked for Castor. The wave had swept the captain from the spar and slammed him against the quarterdeck break. He scrambled to his feet and frantically clawed his way up the ladder to relative safety at the binnacle.

Odessey was once again climbing to the crest of a mountain of water. Marcus quickly surveyed everything around him. He caught the flash of the starboard oars from the corner of his eyes while watching two seamen manning a leather bellows pump. It was sending a small unsteady stream back into the sea. Marcus entwined his right arm through the four auxiliary lines and set himself for the next wall of water. From his position amidships, he could make out the tops of Julius' and Sextus' heads. They were struggling with the steering oars under the baleful glare of the captain. The wave struck and the process began all over again. Ascending each wave, *Odessey* would try to free herself of the water through cascading scuppers, only to be deluged on the next plunge.

The wind increased and the seas heightened. Slanting rain joined the flying spray in sheets of stinging torment. When *Odessey* lunged down the slope of each wave, Marcus felt certain she would continue to the bottom of the sea. Mass after mass of green water struck his back and tore at his arm, trying to hurl him into oblivion. Each time the ship shot upward, he would blink away salty water and search the vessel for damage.

The weather clothes on both sides had been torn away and the toiling galleymen were even more exposed to the raging sea. The bosun, struggling with his own footing, was managing to maintain the beat. With the oars dipping and pulling in unison, *Odessey* was keeping her bow to the storm. The lines to the mast were holding, but every wave was taking a toll. Soaked with water, the new ropes were stretching and each roll of the ship was straining the upside lines while those on the downside were hanging loose.

Knowing these loose lines would have to be tightened to prevent the slack from causing a snap break, Marcus debated about leaving his position to tighten them. He glanced around for help but seeing none decided to remedy the danger himself. Working his way forward on the starboard side, he left the security of the spar during an upswing and fought his way to the outboard stanchion just a few feet beyond Polax's bench. The straining galleyman grinned encouragement to the centurion as he thrust his oar forward in preparation for the next stroke. Marcus grabbed the stanchion and hung on as *Odessey* plunged into the next wave.

Waiting for the ship to roll his way and give slack to the line, the centurion realized he'd made a mistake. If this or any of the other lines snapped, he'd be out of position to make repairs. He'd have to work his way back to the base of the mast and get the auxiliary line and then come back to the stanchion. It would take twice as long and twice as much damage would be done. The ship rolled, and he looped the line twice around the spike securing it firmly in place. He was waiting for the next upswing to go back to the spar when he saw Castor literally clawing his way toward him through the rowing galleymen. "Get back to your post!" he screamed at Marcus, his face black with rage. Marcus understood the captain's anger over leaving his post, but before he could explain, Castor attacked him furiously.

In the split second remaining he braced himself for the double onslaught of the raging sea and the captain by wrapping his left arm around the line he'd just tightened. Castor and the sea struck simultaneously. His arm felt as if it were being torn from its socket by the force of the water plus the impact of Castor's charge. Polax had tried to stop the captain but was helplessly tied to his bench.

The target of the captain's fury was Marcus' arm. The flash of a blade blurred before the centurion's eyes as he hung on, trying to fend off Castor with his right hand. He knew if he lost the battle Castor could claim his death was justified because he had imperiled everyone's life by abandoning his post.

The shining blade stung his arm like fire and Marcus released his grip on the line to fight back. However the battle had destroyed the steadying cadence of the oars and the *Odessey* swung sideways to the waves and began to broach. As she rolled on the rising side of a wave, the centurion lost his balance and tumbled backwards into the sea.

Water closed in around Marcus and his sense of direction became confused. Opening his eyes he could see the dimness of surface light high above him. His lungs were bursting when he finally took his first stroke. It seemed endless. He had to fight the pull of the wave's undercurrent. The water felt soft, as if he were trying to pull himself through a bottomless cloud of choking feathers. Something huge and gray appeared over him. The ship! Madly, he tried to swim from under it. The ship and he were going in the same direction. Marcus stopped. He had to breathe. His brain refused to let him inhale. He saw the ship slide away from him and the light increased. He could hold his breath no longer. With one final thrust toward the surface, his head broke free of the sea, and he sucked in air.

The ship was wallowing in the trough of a massive wave. Without a miracle, Marcus knew he and the *Odessey* were lost. Desperately trying to get back to the ship, Marcus felt something hard strike his side. Throwing his arm over the object, he gripped it with all his strength. The ship rolled away from him and at the same time he was lifted clear of the water. He was on the very tip of Polax's oar. The galleyman was trying to fight off the enraged captain and at the same time pull Marcus in. The centurion started over-handing himself along the oar's shaft toward the ship. With a desperate lunge, he got his fingers on the ship's rail and fell onto the deck.

In frustrated hatred and rage, Castor turned from attacking the galleyman, to Marcus, slashing at his throat. The centurion ducked his head and lunged forward. Bent low, his left shoulder struck the captain's stomach and Marcus' momentum threw Castor the length of the rower's bench. The crack of the Greek's head against the tied-down spar could be heard above the storm. He fell unconscious on the walkway.

The broached ship had miraculously survived one wave and was beginning to rise on another. Only seconds separated them all from disaster. Reacting with a natural instinct of command, Marcus ordered an immediate push stroke by the port oarsmen. The ship had to be properly headed or they'd capsize on this next wave.

Aware of their danger, Polax ordered a pull stroke from his mates on the starboard side at the same time. Retying himself to his bench, he joined the effort halfway through the stroke. Slowly the bow began to swing toward the oncoming waves. Ordering a second thrust on his side, while Polax countered with his own pull, Marcus watched the crest approach. They were three quarters turned when *Odessey* started her downward plunge. Marcus shouted the order that saved them.

"Starboard oars, pull away!" The port bank of flashing blades halted. *Odessey* was straight at the bottom of the wave, but the added momentum drove her deeper into the onrushing sea. Locking his legs around Castor, Marcus seized the spar in both arms and held on while shouting, "All oars, pull away!"

The crashing water around him was massive. This was the largest and most frightening wave that had hit so far. Marcus feared its power would destroy them, that the water would never recede. Suddenly, he could see clearly again.

Quickly looking to the rest of the crew, Marcus saw the two men at the pump were gone. Julius and Sextus were also nowhere in sight. Fear for the sergeant and mate rose in the centurion until he saw them emerge from behind the quarterdeck rail. Sextus cupped his hands to his mouth and yelled, but the wind carried his voice away. Julius frantically waved both arms as if he were swimming under water. Both men had made no effort to return to their steering oars. Marcus ordered the galleymen to maintain their stroke thereby controlling the ship.

This wave was smaller and seemed less intimidating. The wind also seemed to have fallen off. Following the ship's plunge from its crest, Marcus ordered Polax and his mate in the port side sweeps to ship their oars. Putting them to work at the pump, he dragged Castor aft and threw him in the small cabin, dropping a locking bar across the hatch.

Every man's eyes followed the centurion's actions. When he stepped to the center of the well deck, he looked up at Sextus and called, "You're in command of this vessel; give us your orders." All eyes turned to the mate.

Standing into the wind, his tunic whipping wildly, Sextus quickly surveyed the ship and shouted back to Marcus. "Take in the mast lines as you intended!" Leaning forward, he roared a second order to the galleymen. "Continue to pull away together, but stand ready to break stroke on each side. We must steer with the pull of your oars!"

Sextus sent Julius forward to help Marcus. The two Romans made the needed adjustments in the lines. The sea had lost some of its harshness and the mate's excellent seamanship served them well. He kept the ship headed into the storm by stopping the stroke drum from time to time and signaling which side of oars should pull away. All sweeps went into action at the sound of the drum.

After trimming the mast lines, Marcus resumed his station at the foot of the mast, sending Julius to relieve Polax at the pump. The storm was slowly abating, but still contained enough violence to imperil the ship. The Persian cautiously made his way to the centurion's station.

Marcus marveled at this magnificent man. The galleyman had saved his life, and the Roman wanted to express his appreciation. Clinging to the spar, they embraced each other with their free arms. The wound Polax had received from Castor's knife wasn't deep, and the almost constant washing with raw sea water had kept it clean. Acting as an astringent, the salt in the water had stopped the bleeding. The slight wound on Marcus' forearm had received the same treatment.

"I'll not forget what you did," Marcus said. "My life was gone but for your quick action. Your days on the rower's bench are over."

Polax was grateful but disclaimed any undue credit. "All our lives were gone if you hadn't turned the ship in time." He grinned and added, "Besides, I enjoyed fighting the captain. Castor took great delight in doing little things to bother me. Last night he woke me to ask if I were asleep."

Watching the Persian return to the pump, Marcus considered the man. His confident boldness at other times was indicative of something more than an average man. Resolving to learn the Persian's history, the centurion returned to his attention to the welfare of the ship.

The storm continued to moderate. Brief squalls would temporarily heighten its fury, but the worst was past. *Odessey* had suffered heavy damage. The binnacle, with its sand clock and watch stones, had been swept away. The steering oars and their mountings were gone. Part of the port rail had collapsed. The bowsprit was torn from its moorings and had swept the forecastle deck clear of its anchor mountings. Marcus' eyes swept the choppy sea, recalling the two lost men. Had it not been for Polax and his oar, he too would have shared their fate.

Feeling it safe to leave his post, Marcus hurried aft to release the two women. Castor was protesting his confinement by pounding on the small cabin hatch when Phoebe and Debra hurried on deck. Sextus reported the status of *Odessey* to his mistress and detailed what had happened to the captain. Her eyes never left Marcus during the report and when the mate finished, she climbed the ladder to the quarterdeck and addressed the ship's company.

Her hair hung limp on her head and shoulders. Bruises showed on her arms and forehead. The damp gown she was wearing clung to her body, but her face was composed as she spoke.

"We must first thank God for our safety and pray for the souls of the two brothers we've lost." Bowing her head, she led them in a prayer. "Dear Father, we are Your loving children and we praise Your divine majesty for seeing us safely through this terrible storm. We offer our thanks to You for Your great love and humbly beg that You receive our lost brothers into heaven with that same love."

A loud chorus of "amens" joined hers as the mid-day sun broke through the clouds and gleamed on them. Calling down to Julius, Phoebe ordered the captain released.

Blood was streaming down the side of Castor's head when he emerged from the cabin. He looked pale and drawn with fear as he stood between Sextus and Julius. Looking up at Phoebe, he started to protest his treatment but remained silent when her eyes met his. Her voice was low and controlled.

"You're relieved of command." Pointing at Polax, she added, "You'll replace the Persian at his bench until we arrive at Syracuse. Your wound will be washed and bound, and you'll be fed." Her eyes swept every person in sight. "But no one is to speak to you." Phoebe's gaze returned to Castor. "If Marcus Paetius wishes to bring charges against you, you'll be turned over to Roman authorities for trial and punishment. You've betrayed my trust. You're no longer one of my captains."

"My lady," Castor pleaded, "the centurion had abandoned his post during the height of the storm. After volunteering to serve, he refused to obey my orders. He placed the entire ship in danger and resisted when I tried to force his obedience."

Directing an angry look at Marcus, he continued. "If it were any other man, he would be tied to the mast and flogged for cowardice." Then, turning to Sextus, he implored, "You saw him leave his post; tell her that I speak the truth."

Marcus stepped forward. "Part of what Castor says is true. In ignorance, I left my post but quickly realizing my mistake, I intended to return . . ."

Polax interrupted. "My lady, the ship broached when Castor broke the stroke on my side by attacking the centurion. He continued to press the attack even after the ship was endangered." Lifting his voice so that all might hear, he ended the captain's appeal. "It was Marcus who came back from the sea, assumed temporary command and saved the ship!"

"My judgment stands," Phoebe declared. "Sextus is now the captain of *Odessey.*" Turning away to hide the tears beginning to crowd her eyes, Phoebe led Marcus to the stern of the ship. Out of Castor's sight, she began to weep from the long night's ordeal. Lifting Phoebe's face up toward his, he brushed away her tears and said, "It is done. We'll put Castor ashore at Syracuse and sail on without him."

Sextus coughed as he topped the quarterdeck ladder and his set, grim expression didn't change when they turned and faced him. His voice had a rough and husky quality when he tried to speak softly and it was apparent he didn't want the others to hear him.

"My lady, there is another problem." Stepping closer he continued, "We were blown off course during the storm and with the sun in its present high position, I can't even tell you which direction is west."

Marcus' eyes swept the horizon before he looked up at the sun. It was directly overhead, and the sea which had been so wild was now a series of slowly rolling swells. There wasn't a breath of wind nor a cloud in the sky. *Odessey* was lying becalmed in an empty sea. Sextus went on with his summation.

"I've put the men to work making repairs. With your permission, I'll promote the bosun to mate, and I'd like Polax to take the drum."

"It's your ship, Captain," Phoebe replied. "Make whatever assignments you feel are best. What about replacements for the two seamen we lost?"

"I'd like to take them from the galleymen," Sextus answered. "They're a loyal crew, and it might make their lives easier if they knew promotion could come to the bench."

"Do it," Phoebe agreed. "But what about our position?"

Marcus cleared his throat and asked, "How long will the repairs take?"

"Sundown," was the captain's brief answer.

"That will tell us which way is west," Marcus observed, and waited for the captain's nod. "Tonight you can set course on a star slightly north of the setting sun. We're bound to sight land within four days."

Sextus' grim expression changed to a wry grin. "Aye, sir, if we weren't blown more than 50 miles south during the storm."

"What then?" Phoebe asked.

The captain's rueful laugh told her more than his spoken answer. "The first land we'd see would be the Pillars of Hercules near the end of the earth."

The centurion offered a solution. "At sunset tonight, set a course due north. In the morning, put the rising sun at our backs and sail west. It may add a day to our journey, but we'll sight either Italia or Sicily within three or four days."

"Is that reasonable, Captain?" Phoebe inquired.

"Aye, my lady."

"Then do it," she ordered, feeling her spirits lift.

Watching Sextus return to the well deck, Marcus made an additional suggestion. "When we arrive at Syracuse, I'll obtain the release of three men from the local prison to fill the vacancies on our galley benches. Polax can pick the men."

A note of deep sadness was in Phoebe's voice when she said, "The two men we lost were both married. I'll take their families into my household when we return, but it will be difficult to tell them what happened."

Five days later, the island of Sicily broke the horizon. Sextus identified the landfall as the island's barren south coast. Ordering a more northerly course, he anticipated making Syracuse within a few hours.

By early afternoon, they'd sailed past the statue of Poseidon erected at the end of the harbor jetty and tied up at the mole. Castor was allowed to pack his personal property. Phoebe, with Marcus at her side, met him at the gangplank and paid him off in gold coins. Nothing was said between them; but watching the man go ashore, Marcus knew she had valued Castor's service and regretted the end of it.

CHAPTER VI

Owe no man any thing, but to love one another . . .

ROMANS 13:8

Syracuse was founded by Greeks and theirs was still the common language. The Roman masters spoke Latin. Being proficient in both, Phoebe was amused at the compliments she overheard concerning her beauty as they walked through the busy streets. Marcus was delighted with her laughter and change of mood. They were one block away from the waterfront when Polax nudged his arm and indicated, with a nod of his head, the doorway of a nearby taverna. Castor, drinking mug in hand, was lounging against the door jam watching their progress. The stocky Greek disappeared inside when he saw Polax staring at him.

Phoebe's flowing peplos gown and pearl-trimmed sandals did as much to indicate her station as Marcus' uniform did for him. Polax, however, outshined them both. Having been promoted to bosun, his appearance reflected the change. The moment *Odessey* was tied to the mole, the Persian had disappeared into the waterfront shops of Syracuse which transformed him into a man of high stature. His muscular frame was clothed in a Greek tunic of fine yellow linen, a soft brown palla which was bordered in gold and handsome metal-faced sandals. A broad scimitar hung at his side from a wide leather belt.

Stopping to shop, Phoebe ordered fresh fruit sent back to the *Odessey*. This identified her to the people and word spread fast that she was the famous mistress of the Dolphin. A crowd started to gather and follow them as they walked on toward the Roman barracks.

At the barracks gate, Marcus' rank and medallion gained them immediate admittance. The decurion of the guard ran across the compound ahead of them and the commanding tribune welcomed them himself.

Marcus presented Phoebe and Polax to the officer and accepted his invitation for refreshments. Following the tribune, Licinius, through his office, they emerged in the atrium of his villa. A small statue of Mars stood before the pool in the center of the room. At Licinius' order, a slave scurried toward the rear of the house to summon the tribune's wife.

While waiting for his wife to appear, Licinius offered his arm to Phoebe and showed her his home. The old soldier was also a scholar, and his library was quite extensive. Marcus was startled when Phoebe asked, "Have you heard of the Lord, Jesus?"

The tribune didn't hesitate, but answered with a question. "Wasn't he the man who claimed to be King of the Jews and was crucified in Jerusalem several years ago?"

Before Phoebe could answer, Livia Licinius entered the room. Following the introductions, she led them through a rear door from the library into a colonnaded peristyle, or interior garden. The gracious woman was somewhat older than her husband, which indicated he had married for advantage. Her short, soft, gray hair was set in tight curls around her aristocratic head. She had the figure of a young woman, but the lines around her neck and brown eyes revealed her true age. The tribune was dressed in the toga of his rank and Livia's gown was a deep purple, high-girdled chiton. She wore it off her shoulders in a style that accented her body rather than her face.

While waiting for the servants to prepare refreshments, Marcus explained the purpose of their visit. The tribune readily agreed to release three prisoners for their galley oars, and Polax was dispatched to select them. When the Persian withdrew, he indicated he'd meet Marcus and Phoebe back at the ship.

While enjoying wine and fresh fruit, Phoebe told them of the storm and the needed ship repairs. They'd be in port two days and Livia invited them to stay at the villa. Phoebe accepted with delight.

"Oh Livia, I was praying that you'd ask us to stay." Holding out the skirt of her gown, she explained, "Except for this single dress, all my clothes were soaked during the storm, and my body is crying for a bath."

Their hostess laughed with understanding, and servants were sent to the ship to fetch Debra, Julius and all their belongings. Phoebe eagerly followed Livia from the peristyle with the promise of a hot tub and massage.

With the women gone, Licinius and Marcus raised their goblets for a refill and the tribune dismissed the servant. Turning to Marcus, he asked, "What is your relationship with the lady, Phoebe?"

Sipping his wine, Marcus paused before answering. "I hope to marry her after I report back to Caesar."

"Did you find the Jew you were seeking when you were here last fall?" Licinius inquired.

Crushing a grape between his teeth, Marcus nodded his reply.

"Marcus, can you tell me the reason for your search?"

The centurion shook his head and swallowed. "Why do you ask?"

The two men were seated side by side on a marble bench. Licinius leaned forward, placing his elbows on his knees. With his goblet held in both hands, he stared at the tiled floor for several minutes before answering. His voice was soft and confidential.

"I understand your history and know of the relationship your father had with Seneca. You have the favor of Nero and wear his medallion. Your future is assured, but mine died with the death of the Emperor Claudius." He turned his head sideways and studied Marcus before continuing. "Claudius made me a tribune and now his natural son, Britannicus, has been poisoned."

Marcus was shocked by this news but succeeded in keeping his emotion from appearing in his expression or voice. "When did this happen?"

"During Saturnalia, about 80 days ago."

"What has this to do with me," Marcus questioned, "and my mission to find Paul?"

Licinius stood and looked down at the centurion. "After Nero poisoned Britannicus, Seneca and Burrus equally divided the dead man's estates." A note of pleading entered the tribune's voice. "I need to know what's going on in Rome in order to protect my own small advantage."

"It's obvious," Marcus observed, "that you know more of what's going on in Rome than I do. But I can assure you that my mission in Corinth had no connection with Britannicus' death."

"I'm relieved to hear it," Licinius sighed. "When the guard reported a galley entering the harbor today flying an imperial pennant, I expected to be replaced."

"Why?"

"Because I'm of the Claudian party." The tribune sat down again before adding, "I'm also loyal to Nero, but he doesn't know that."

Marcus knew what Licinius wanted to hear, so he said it. "I'll make certain that both Burrus and Seneca know of your loyalty."

The look of relief that swept over the tribune's features was confirmed by his next words. "My dear Marcus, is there anything on the island of Sicily that you'd like for a wedding gift?"

Understanding the offer was a bribe, he answered, "Your hospitality today is a gift beyond price." Marcus put his hand on the tribune's shoulder and laughingly said, "I'm sure Phoebe considers her bath to be heaven-sent."

"Is she a Christian?"

The tribune's question caught Marcus off guard, but he

answered it honestly. "Yes, and I've received their baptism."

A prolonged silence followed his answer and Marcus feared his frankness had been a mistake. Then the older man smiled and expressed a personal conclusion. "Only a brave man can be loyal to his god, his emperor and himself, because each of the three can be a jealous master."

They were interrupted by the discreet cough of a servant who whispered a message to Licinius. "I'm afraid I must leave you alone for a little while," he said to Marcus. Gesturing toward the table of food, he added, "Please help yourself and consider this your home." He suddenly struck himself on the forehead as if he'd just remembered an important detail. "Please forgive me, Marcus. Would you like a bath?"

Fifteen minutes later the centurion was luxuriating in deliciously caressing hot water while his uniform was being cleaned and polished. Mentally, he was beginning to sort out the news of Britannicus' murder.

It's strange, he thought, *how so many of my old values have changed since leaving Rome.* Three months ago, Britannicus' death wouldn't have shocked him the way it did when Licinius conveyed the news. As Claudius' natural son, the young prince was a constant threat to Nero's claim on the throne. Though his sister, Octavia, was Nero's wife and empress, she had little love for her brother. Seneca had said that it was only a matter of time until Britannicus must die.

Murder had long been a favorite means of establishing imperial succession. Augustus, the first emperor, had been poisoned by his wife after she had killed every favored successor other than her son Tiberius. He in turn was poisoned after selecting Caligula as his successor. Caligula was murdered by his own Praetorian Guards, who then put the crippled and stammering Claudius on the throne. Following the scandal and divorce from Messalina, his third wife, Claudius sealed his fate by marrying Agrippina, Nero's mother. It had been rumored she poisoned Claudius after Nero was named his successor. Now, Britannicus, the best of them all, was dead. His murder proved that Nero would stop at nothing to protect himself and his advantages.

The news that Seneca and Burrus had shared in the dead prince's estate caused Marcus great concern. *Is it possible,* he wondered, *that Nero could have given them this great wealth simply to make it appear that they were involved in the murder?* By doing this had the emperor compromised the honor of both men? Would either of them be able to come to his defense when he appeared before Nero and confessed his failure?

Realizing that he might have to stand alone before Nero, a cold shudder of foreboding ran through his body. Marcus called for more hot water. Even after it was added to his bath, the chill remained. He and Phoebe were planning to enter the capital city of an empire ruled by a murderer. Nero possessed absolute power. His most perverted whim or desire was catered to and encouraged. The life or death of a centurion and a single lady from Greece would mean nothing to the emperor. If it gave him pleasure to see them die, Nero could laughingly order it.

There are 24 days remaining before the Nones of April, he mused. *Is that all that remains for Phoebe and me?* The emperor and Rome had seemed so far away from Cenchrea. *Was I right in allowing Paul to escape?* Closing his eyes, Marcus thought of Phoebe. *She's beautiful beyond reason. There's a light in her that is irresistible. I've laid my life and career at her feet. I've even been baptized in the hope of gaining her love. But does she love me?*

Later, while dressing, his brain continued to probe the problems surrounding him. He loved Phoebe, of that he was certain. She, on the other hand, had never made a clear, unmistakable indication of her feelings for him. Pondering this with one sandal on and the other still off, Marcus frowned over the possibility that Phoebe didn't love him. Paul had told him that he would have to learn to love God first and Phoebe second before she would accept him. "But that just doesn't make sense," he told himself while jamming his foot in the other sandal. "I've never known a woman who didn't want to be loved above everything else!"

Marcus was completely dressed when he reached for the emperor's medallion, hanging by its gold chain on the dressing room wall peg. The beautifully carved imperial eagle, surrounded by raised laurel leaves, symbolized Nero's power. Holding it in his hand, the centurion was suddenly aware of a different power it represented: the power to destroy without thought or reason. The entire history of the imperial family reeked of this power. It was a history tainted with madness.

Why hadn't he seen it before? he wondered. How could any sane man order the cold-blooded murder of his stepbrother? How could a wife murder her husband? Other evidences of Nero's madness began seeping into his mind. The sexual abuse of other men's wives, the flaunting of his homosexuality. Rumors of incest within the royal family were rampant. It was common history that Agrippina had enjoyed intimate relations with her brother, Caligula. Claudius was Nero's uncle before he became his stepfather. The empress, Octavia, had been his cousin before she became his stepsister and later his bride.

At night the streets of Rome reflected the moral character of the emperor. It was unsafe for a man, even a senator, to take his wife out without an armed escort. Women were gang-raped while their husbands were forced to witness the scene. Roman authorities winked at such things because the emperor himself was known to participate in similar activities. *It's plain and simple madness,* Marcus concluded, *and I'm taking Phoebe right into it!*

"All this because of a letter," he muttered. "No document, even by someone as great as Paul, is worth risking Phoebe's life." The thought of Phoebe's delicate beauty being bruised and violated by a sex-crazed mob raised the hackles on the back of his neck. *She's going to Rome with only her faith to protect her, and if Nero comes down on me, she'll be alone.* A cold chill swept up his spine as another thought crossed his mind. The Christians in Rome might be of little help to her. Paul had said that they had small reason to trust him, and they'd have even less reason to trust Phoebe.

CHAPTER VII

Be not overcome of evil, but overcome evil with good.

ROMANS 12:21

PHOEBE was torn between a need and a desire. The storm had cost them valuable days, and time was slipping away. She was aware of the crushing need for speed, but when Captain Sextus sent word to the villa that four days would be required to repair *Odessey,* she nevertheless was secretly pleased. It would allow time for the complete restoration of her wardrobe, and she was enjoying the company of Livia and Licinius.

The tribune it developed, knew a great deal about Jesus. As a young centurion, he'd served in Jerusalem. He had never seen the Lord, but he'd been to many of the holy places Phoebe had only heard about. Livia, too, had been there. When Licinius told of being stationed at the Tower of Antonia, where Jesus was tried before Pilate, she had closed her eyes and tried to picture how it must have been on that fateful day. Phoebe's heart was stricken when the tribune showed her a small, bloodstained portion of a paving stone taken from the tower's courtyard. The stone, he told her, was one of several which had to be removed because the stain couldn't be washed away. Livia explained how it came to be in their possession.

"I needed something heavy for a door stop and one of the

soldiers brought it to me. When we left Jerusalem and came here, it was included in our baggage."

"For some reason," Licinius had added, "I've never been able to throw it away."

"Would you let me have it?" Phoebe had asked.

The old soldier had pressed it into her hands, saying, "I know what you're thinking. It could be the stain of your Lord's blood. But my dear child, it could also be a forgotten dyer's stain made when he crimsoned the governor's draperies."

On the evening of the third day, Licinius and Livia hosted a banquet in honor of Marcus and Phoebe. The governor attended in addition to all of Licinius' officers and their wives. It was near the end of the evening's activities when Phoebe's Syracuse agent, who was also a guest, approached her.

"My lady, I must report that two days ago Castor signed as a bosun aboard a ship bound for Puteoli."

Phoebe replied that she was pleased that he had found employment so soon, but Marcus was concerned.

"You say he accepted a bosun's berth?"

"Yes, sir," the agent replied, "after refusing the command of a vessel bound for Alexandria. My informant tells me that Castor carries a letter from Corinth proving that you're a traitor. He says he must warn the Christians in Rome against you."

"How does your informant know this?" Marcus demanded.

"He overheard Castor say so in a tavern before he sailed," the man answered.

"Did he say who the letter was from?" Phoebe asked.

The agent shook his head.

Both Phoebe and Marcus were puzzled, but after the agent had departed, the centurion revealed to Phoebe that such a letter could explain Castor's blatant actions.

"How else could he murder me and expect to get away with it?" Marcus reasoned.

Phoebe was forced to agree, but she couldn't think of anyone in Corinth with enough of a reason to write such a letter. Marcus knew it wasn't Gaius, and, other than Tertius, no one knew of their proposed journey in time to accomplish such a betrayal. Phoebe carefully went over every possibility. She momentarily considered Simon as the author but quickly discarded such thoughts. Recognizing this additional need for haste, she sent word to Sextus ordering *Odessey's* repairs completed by torch light. *Odessey* would sail at dawn. If Castor's letter could justify murder, it could destroy her mission.

Phoebe ordered their packing done that night. She informed Licinius and Livia they'd be leaving for the ship before the first light and explained truthfully the need of their being the first ship in Puteoli with a cargo of wheat. Their hosts bid them farewell before they retired for the night.

The *Odessey's* oars flashed in the morning sun as the ship left a creamy wake in Syracuse harbor. It was 60 miles to Rhegium at the toe of Italia, and Phoebe intended to be there before dark. Her desire to pass through the Strait of Messina by night was overruled by Sextus. He refused to risk life and ship in those narrow confines with only moonlight to guide him.

Once away from land, the sail was raised, but Phoebe insisted the drum continue to beat. She prayed for favorable winds, and her prayers were answered. It was a record passage and with the sun still high in the heavens at Rhegium, she ordered the port bypassed. Marcus supported her desire for haste and everyone aboard caught her fever for speed.

When Captain Sextus realized she was intending to press on through the dreaded Strait of Messina, he was shocked. "It's too late in the day, dear lady," he implored. "It's madness to attempt this passage now."

"When do you suggest?" she asked.

"In the morning," he urged. "We'll then have time for a careful passage."

Phoebe's jaw tightened. "No," she stated resolutely, "we have no time to waste." She ordered the ship onward.

As they surged into the 12-mile-wide southern entrance of the strait, Phoebe recalled the sailors' tales of its horrors. The Siculum Fretum, as the Romans called it, was 20 miles long with a narrow, northern entrance containing strong currents and rugged rock formations. It was vital they pass the Rock of Scylla and the whirlpool of Charybdis before sunset.

It was here in this strait that her husband had been lost, and now she was pressing against disaster in the same waters. For the first time Phoebe saw apprehension in Polax's eyes. She knew it wasn't superstition that made him afraid; he had seen what lay ahead and held these dangers in great respect. The whirlpool of Charybdis could suck the *Odessey* down into a bottomless sea, or they could be dashed against the Rock of Scylla and smashed like grapes in a winepress.

These were the challenges faced by Ulysses in ancient Greek legend. The list of brave sailors who had died here was almost endless, and yet Phoebe was crying for greater speed. Standing at the quarterdeck rail, her eyes searched whitecapped seas ahead for the first sign of Charybdis. The drum beat faster. Marcus was steering with the port oar while Sextus manned the other. Debra fled to the cabin as Julius stood watch in the bow. The four deckhands were anxiously watching the sail lines and awaiting orders from Sextus.

Phoebe's eyes widened as she beheld the spectacle ahead. There, 100 yards away on the port bow, was the outer edge of a gigantic concave dish of madly swirling black water. The wind died in the rigging. Every galleyman's back was knotted with straining muscles. Phoebe could hardly breathe. Her chest felt constrained in the grip of a monstrous hand. With sail limp, the ship was slipping toward the vortex of oblivion. A new, terrible sound entered her senses. It was a horrible sucking sound, as if a demon were inhaling an endless dying breath.

Screaming the prayer within her, Phoebe asked God to push them through to safety. She couldn't pull her eyes away from the howling hole in the sea. There was a loud cracking noise as the sail filled with wind and the ship surged forward. It wasn't until she was looking astern at its whirling madness that she understood they'd passed Charybdis.

Now Sextus frantically pointed to the starboard. Assuming the shape of a mad, pagan god, the Scylla rock loomed ahead of them. The wind-swollen sail, which aided their passage past Charybdis, was now driving them straight to destruction despite the herculean efforts of the steersmen. Ordering the sail dropped, Sextus and Marcus threw both steering oars to the starboard. *Odessey* heeled to the left and all oars pulled away. Weak from tension, Phoebe watched grim Scylla fall astern.

The gentle swells of the Tyrrhenian Sea welcomed a gliding *Odessey* as the galley oars were shipped and the sail raised to bear the soft wind of victory. Silence descended on the exhausted crew. Galleymen, chests heaving, were stretched out on their benches. Sextus lashed the steering oars in position and slowly settled beside Marcus at the base of the quarterdeck rail. Julius came aft from the bow and brought Debra on deck. Together with Phoebe, they served full cups of unwatered wine to all hands. With the setting sun sinking behind Vucano Island to the west, Marcus accepted his cup from Phoebe.

Looking into her eyes, the centurion shook his head in disbelief and softly chuckled. Her eyebrows peaked. "What's so amusing?" she asked.

"You are," he sighed. "With your hair streaming in the wind, you were a fearsome sight. How could you drive us to such extremes?"

Smiling, she answered, "It was the only thing we could do. We've gained a day on Castor. With God's help we'll arrive in Puteoli just a few hours behind him."

"No, my lovely one," Marcus corrected, "it wasn't the need to do it that got it done. You inspired us. You led us and replaced fear with bravery." He laughed joyfully and continued. "You should have seen yourself praying to God and defying the terrors of Ulysses. We'd have sailed *Odessey* over the edge of the earth with you leading us."

Phoebe handed Captain Sextus a cup of wine and sat down between the two men. Leaning back against the deck rail, she seriously studied each of them. When she spoke, her voice had a slight tremor in it.

"I was terrified. Just thinking of it now fills me with panic, but God filled our sail with a powerful wind." Turning to

Sextus, she asked, "Is it like that every time you sail through the strait?"

"No, my lady," he sighed, "as I said, we normally take our time and try to slip quietly between Scylla and Charybdis." He sipped his wine and visibly relaxed with a nervous laugh. "But today was special." Sextus closed his eyes and lowered his voice. "We were in the hands of the Lord and He let us briefly feel the glory of His power with the speed of His wind at our backs."

That night the wind was steady and *Odessey* sailed in serene majesty past the volcanic Aerolian Islands. Once again the full moon edged the sea with silver, and the distant 3,000-foot peak of Stromboli caught flashes of brilliant grey in its smoking crest. Phoebe was still feeling the exhilaration of the day and couldn't sleep. She silently shared the early watch with Polax.

Her mind was drawn to the letter she was carrying to Rome. Paul's words regarding the people of God and their destiny took on new and clearer meaning. Paul had written, "And we know that all things work together for good to them that love God, to them who are called according to God's purpose."

The storm before Syracuse had exposed Castor's treachery. The delay with Livia and Licinius had revealed the letter of betrayal. Their successful passage through the Strait of Messina had confirmed God's support for their mission. Looking down from the quarterdeck, Phoebe's eyes swept over the sleeping galleymen. Her "Dolphiniers," as they called themselves, were called to God's purpose. Marcus, Julius, Debra, Sextus and Polax served the same goal. Paul had said it many times: "Bear all things, believe all things, hope for all things, and endure all things, for all things are of God." She could remember his gentle voice as he spoke those words in Corinth.

Additional phrases from Paul's letter sprang up in her mind. "The Spirit itself bears witness with our spirit, that we are the children of God. And if children, then heirs; heirs of God, and joint heirs with Christ; if so be that we suffer with Jesus, that we may be also glorified together."

Through this new understanding, Phoebe felt a deep peace. Turning to Polax, at the steering oar, she bid him good-night and went to her cabin.

Odessey was becalmed the next day and the sun bore down with intense heat. The beat of the stroke drum was slow and measured. Every pull of the galley oars took its toll, and the ship's progress was reduced to bare headway. The low, unbroken, rolling sea was the color of dull pewter. By day's end, Sextus estimated they were still a hundred miles southeast of Puteoli.

Phoebe called for silence in the ship and prayed for wind, but God seemed not to hear. With darkness, the air cooled around them and the drum beat was increased. The flapping sail had become a drag in the dead air and had been lowered earlier in the day. Marcus and Julius took turns at the oars as did all the men. The two Romans learned a greater respect for those who sat at the benches. Phoebe couldn't explain her need for speed to the men without revealing that she knew Nero's plan to deify himself. But to them, her desire seemed reason enough.

At midnight, the wind stirred and the great sail was hoisted. *Odessey* heeled over and showed her teeth to the sea. In gratitude Phoebe led them in songs of praise which refreshed their tired bodies. The wind's song then gave them sleep.

The sun was just past the mid-point of its daily arc the next day when the Island of Capri was sighted off *Odessey's* starboard forequarter. An hour later, the ship was abreast of Capri to the seaward side, and Phoebe was enchanted by its lush green vegetation. Marcus pointed out the location of the Emperor Tiberius' former summer palace. As *Odessey* drew past the island, Sextus changed course a few degrees to the north, and they entered a beautiful blue bay. To the northeast, Phoebe could see a smoking volcano which Julius identified as Vesuvius.

Sextus pointed out the island of Ischia on their port side and then directed Phoebe's attention to a smaller bay which lay dead ahead.

"There is the Bay of Puteoli. We'll be tied to the quay before sunset."

Phoebe could detect a note of pride in the captain's voice. Their daring, and some would say reckless, charge through the Strait of Messina had cut two days from the normal sailing time. Bypassing Rhegium had gained them an additional day. Their haste had not been wasted. The Nones of April was 19 days away.

Watching the bay and city grow in her view, Phoebe asked Marcus about various buildings. He directed her attention to the temple of Augustus and pointed out the Sarapeum on the waterfront which was the city's administration building. Higher up in the city was the amphitheater. Marcus explained its unusual feature.

"As the most important port city in Italia, the Puteoli arena can be flooded with water and sea battles fought for the entertainment of the people. It has seats for 30,000, and they're filled six times a year for bloody contests."

Phoebe knew of the brutal Roman games and asked, "Have you witnessed these spectacles?"

Marcus nodded and replied, "I watched 60 men die in that arena on a sunny afternoon last summer. They fought bravely, but the waste of good fighting men sickens me. I've not attended a game since." He pointed off to the left and said, "Cicero owned a villa just a short distance outside the city. It now belongs to Seneca. That's where we'll spend the night."

"Why can't we leave immediately for Rome?" Phoebe asked.

"For two reasons," Marcus answered. "I have to call on the local Roman commander and arrange for our transportation."

"And the second?"

"The roads aren't safe at night."

"But what of Castor?" she demanded.

"He'll not travel at night either. And I must learn what I can about the latest activities in Rome before we proceed."

"Why?" she asked.

"Because I still have to face Nero. Licinius told me some

startling news that may affect my status. Nero has murdered Britannicus and Seneca's involved. My commander, Burrus, is also implicated and I may not be able to depend on either of them for support when I confess my failure before Nero. I didn't tell you about this because I didn't want to worry you."

"Then you should not go before Nero," she stated. "You should remain here in Puteoli until I return. Then we'll sail back to Greece and forget the emperor."

"No, Phoebe. With Castor in Rome, you can't go there without me." He smiled and added, "And I can't return to Greece still obligated to Nero."

Knowing it was pointless to argue with him, Phoebe turned to Sextus and instructed him to keep *Odessey* in Puteoli until their return—hopefully no longer than two weeks. He was to sell the cargo of wheat and take on a cargo of iron products from the smelters of the city plus bronze and copperware from Capua in the north. These industrial items would bring high prices in Egypt.

When the *Odessey* docked at the quay, an honor guard of soldiers met them because of the imperial pennant flying on the mast. In the reception party was Phoebe's agent. Marcus gave instructions to him where they would spend the night and then marched off with the soldiers.

From the agent Phoebe learned that Castor had already arrived. "Castor told me he no longer commanded the *Odessey*," he said.

"Did he tell you why?"

"No. But he did say that he represented an important man in Corinth and was on his way to Rome. He also said the centurion traveling with you was not to be trusted."

"Did Castor name the Corinthian?" she asked.

"No, my lady, but he did claim to have documents that prove that the Roman is dangerous."

"When's he leaving for Rome?"

"He's departing with a freight convoy in the morning. It's going as far as Capua; from there he'll travel alone by horse."

The agent added one further bit of information. "Castor said the centurion plans to turn you over to Roman authorities as a traitor and seize control of the Dolphin."

"There's no truth in what he told you," Phoebe declared, "and I don't want you to repeat what you've told me to anyone."

"Yes, my lady."

Phoebe didn't feel it necessary to tell the others what the agent had said. She warned him against any further dealings with her former captain and sent him back to Puteoli with Polax to obtain the supplies needed for their trip to Rome.

Arriving at the villa, Phoebe, Debra and Julius were welcomed by the major-domo and shown to their rooms. Sitting alone in her room, Phoebe began evaluating all the information she had received. Castor's actions were the hardest to sort out. His attempt to kill Marcus didn't make sense. And why would he lie to the agent, telling him that Marcus intended to betray her as a traitor? Surely, she thought, Castor knows he could gain nothing from this except revenge.

The news of Britannicus' murder was troubling. Phoebe wasn't certain she understood what the possible involvement of Seneca and Burrus would mean to Marcus' future. Her only concern was for the centurion's safety. If he had to face Nero without support, could he escape with his life? Would Poppaea allow him to go unpunished?

Then she wondered about her own feelings toward Marcus. "I think I love Marcus," she told herself aloud, "but has he truly accepted Jesus as his Lord?" Closing her eyes, she tried to visualize what her life would be without him. She was certain God had sent Marcus to her, and she prayed that he would be able to give himself without reservation to the Lord.

Thinking of Marcus brought her thoughts back to Castor. Neither he, nor his mysterious Corinthian friend, could be committed Christians and still pursue their dastardly course of action, she reasoned. What possible document could Castor have that would prove his statements against Marcus? Who could have prepared such a document? Suddenly, she remembered that Paul had warned her that Castor had accepted baptism in the hope of making himself more acceptable to her. As her husband, he would control the Dolphin. Now Castor was charging Marcus with similar motives. Realizing that he'd lost any hope of gaining his desire, was Castor now simply trying to destroy Marcus to prevent his success?

That has to be it, she concluded. But what effect would his charges against Marcus have on the reception of Paul's letter in Rome? Remembering Paul's reluctance to send it to Rome because of possible hostility toward him as a result of the years he had spent as a Pharisee persecuting Christians, she sadly shook her head. If Castor succeeded in creating a cloud of doubt in Rome about Marcus, it could become a big problem. The people might reject Paul's teaching, fearing the letter was merely a means of drawing them out for Roman persecution.

She hoped that Aquila and Priscilla wouldn't be influenced by Castor's story. Paul knew them well but was certain they'd see to the distribution of the letter. Phoebe recalled them from their days in Corinth. They were refugees then, and now, having regained their Roman property, would they risk possible further trouble for Paul? Phoebe remembered Tertius making this same point with the teacher when she overheard their discussion one day at the Dolphin.

Thinking of the wiry Tertius made her realize he could be the author of the documents Castor was carrying! The two men had spent a great deal of time together. Tertius didn't think a woman should be Paul's messenger. He had told Paul he was mad to trust Marcus. *That's it! Tertius is the Corinthian!* "What would Paul have me do about all this?" she wondered audibly. The answer came quickly. Paul would have her submit it to the will of God.

Kneeling beside her bed, Phoebe asked the Holy Spirit to illuminate her mind. Closing her eyes, she saw the stigmata— the nail holes in Jesus' wrists. She heard a gentle voice call her name. "Phoebe, look at the hands of the Son of Man."

Tears of joy flowed down her cheeks. The strong carpenter

hands of Jesus remained. She felt his love flow from them and understood their meaning. Jesus had suffered for man's sins. He had faced obstacles in His ministry, but He continued in faith. God used His suffering to teach man. Conditions were created to accomplish specific results. God could use Castor just as He had used Judas. She was to continue on as before, and Jesus would justify the results of whatever happened. Once again, she knew God wanted Nero to hear Paul's letter. Marcus was to be her key to the Imperial Court. Phoebe thanked and praised God for His answer.

Marcus arrived from Puteoli with Polax. The supplies they'd need were loaded in a cart with three seats: one for the driver, Polax, facing forward, and one on each side for Phoebe and Debra. There was plenty of room for their baggage, and Marcus felt the cart would be faster than a wagon and more practical and comfortable than a chariot. Besides, it required only one horse, and with the two that Marcus and Julius would ride, they'd only have to worry about caring for three.

Phoebe told Marcus her conclusions about Castor and Tertius. She made no mention as to what she'd decided about Castor's motives but listened intently to Marcus' speculation.

"If Castor discovers that Poppaea wants to have Paul discredited and humiliated," the centurion sighed, "he can become a wealthy man by naming you as Paul's authorized representative. Fortunately, I don't think he or Tertius is aware of Poppaea's involvement. We can only pray that Castor doesn't learn of it when he gets to Rome."

Eager to be on the road to Rome before sunrise, the travelers turned in early so they could be rested for the climax of their journey.

CHAPTER VIII

Know ye not, that so many of us as were baptized into
Jesus Christ were baptized into his death?

ROMANS 6:3

THE TENDRILS of dawn filtered through a grove of cloaked
ilex trees on the east side of the villa's courtyard when Julius
and Polax finished loading the cart. Smoke, with the scent
of pine, hung in the dew-laden morning air. As she had done
throughout the journey, Phoebe kept the weatherproof pouch
with Paul's letter close to her. She wedged it securely under
the seat herself, then she and Debra were helped up to the
two, back-to-back passenger seats. Though facing opposite directions, conversation between them would be easy because
their heads were almost touching.

Both women wore gray, knee-length tunics under dark
brown, ankle-length, hooded capes. Marcus and Julius, in Roman imperial uniforms, mounted their horses while Polax
climbed up to the driver's seat wearing seaman's pantaloons
under a short black tunic with a sheathed, curved knife tucked
into a bright yellow sash.

Rome was 130 miles to the northwest, and they planned
to travel up the coast to Sinuessa where they'd join the Appian
Way. Knowing that Castor was going by way of Capua, they
hoped this shortcut would put them on the Roman highway
ahead of him. Leading the way, Marcus and Julius cantered

out onto the road. Polax clucked the horse into motion, and the cart creaked after them.

An hour from the villa they crested a low, wooded hill and saw a landscape of volcanic desolation. Polax stopped the cart and called out for the Romans to hold up. Marcus and Julius reined in their mounts and trotted back in time to hear the Persian tell Phoebe and Debra about the lake below them.

"This extinct volcano crater is supposed to be the place where Ulysses descended into Hades." Turning to Phoebe, he added, "On my last voyage to Puteoli, I was told that Jesus entered Hell here during His three days of death. My lady, could this be true?"

Phoebe was thoughtful. "Anything is possible with God, but do you believe Jesus needed a hole in the earth to reach the pit?"

"No," the Persian firmly replied. "He didn't need a hole in my heart to enter me, so this must be a place of myth and legend." Turning back to the horse, he laughingly snapped a loose rein across the animal's rump and concluded, "But as you say, anything is possible with God."

Phoebe winked at Marcus, and the party was once again on its way to Rome. Julius galloped ahead while Marcus rode beside the cart. The smell of sulphur was strong in the air and as the sun climbed higher, the day became warmer. Removing their capes, Phoebe and Debra used them to cushion their seats against the jarring impact of the cart's wheels on the lava-strewn road.

As they traveled north during the morning hours the landscape began changing from volcanic to farm lands. Olive groves, vineyards and fruit orchards, still budding, were interlaced with stately rows of open fields awaiting the spring plowing. Land owners were seen along the way directing crews of slaves in the repair of winter damage to roads, ditches and stone fences. Occasionally the stench of pig farms would fill the air. This, however, was an almost welcome change from the sulfurous odors nature had provided for most of the morning.

Stopping on the bank of a small lake, they lunched on cheese, hard-crusted bread and mellow, red wine. The horses were hobbled and allowed to graze on new grass. Phoebe's thoughts were on the letter she was carrying.

"Do you suppose," she asked Marcus, "that even after I deliver Paul's letter, it will be overlooked and forgotten by the Christians in Rome?"

Marcus leaned back against the cart wheel and sipped his wine before answering. "That could happen," he admitted, "but from what I know of Paul, there's little about him that's easily forgotten." He flashed her a reassuring smile, saying, "The success of the letter will depend entirely on how it's received. Does it call for any overt action on their parts?"

Realizing that Marcus and the others had never heard or read the letter, Phoebe asked, "Would you like me to read it tonight when we're camped?"

"Yes," he answered. "Perhaps then I'll be a better judge as to how it will affect people in Rome."

They spent their first night on the road at a legion campsite near the mouth of the Volturnus River a few miles south of Sinuessa. The camp was unoccupied and consisted of minor earthworks, but Marcus felt it would give them the accomodations they needed without the confusion of a public inn. He also knew there wasn't a decent inn available until they reached Tarracina where the Appian Way turned inland.

There on the banks of the Volturnus River, Paul's letter was first read in Roman territory. Marcus, Julius, Polax and Debra, with the light of their campfire reflected in their faces, listened in silence. Sitting cross-legged, sideways to the fire for light, Phoebe unrolled the scroll in her lap as she read. For more than an hour her voice filled their ears and minds with Paul's words. At times she would glance at them, trying to determine their reactions. On more than one occasion, she paused and expanded Paul's written words with some of the explanations he'd given her during that first reading in her office at the Dolphin. Phoebe could see understanding in each face, but Marcus' expression projected a dark mood. When she finished, he got to his feet and walked away from the fire. She feared that he might not have correctly understood what he'd heard. The others started discussing the letter as she put the scroll back in the waxed, leather bag.

Half listening to what they were saying, she watched Marcus walk to the top of an earthwork battlement and stand alone in the moonlight. His palla stirred in the soft breeze, and silver light reflected from the polished surface of his breastplate. Excusing herself, she joined the centurion.

"Marcus, I expected a different reaction from you." She stood beside him, looking up into his face. "The others are praising God for what Paul has written. Can't you accept the truth of his letter?"

Marcus turned and placed his two hands on her shoulders. "The letter fills me with fear for your safety, Phoebe. Three months ago I was a Roman the same as Nero. I heard Paul's words as the emperor will hear them." Phoebe started to speak, but he stopped her. "In his heart, Nero must know he is only a mortal man, and what you read tonight will chill his mortal bones. Paul's letter is for the Romans, yes, but God had it written particularly for Caesar."

"Then don't fear for me, Marcus. Fear for Nero instead because if he reads the letter and doesn't believe, he will stand against God and be eternally condemned."

"Phoebe," Marcus exclaimed, "I've concluded that our emperor is insane. The reasoned beauty of Paul's words will find small hope of understanding or acceptance in Nero's twisted brain. With you as Paul's messenger, the emperor can have you killed just to prove he's greater than God!"

"If it's God's will that I die, so be it," Phoebe replied.

"God's will is one thing," Marcus said, "but Nero's will is another, and I don't want to lose you to the whim of a madman."

Phoebe felt a surge of affection for Marcus. His deep concern for her safety and the sincerity she heard in his voice stirred her emotions in a way she hadn't felt in several years. "Marcus," she asked, "have you really considered the extent of God's power?"

"I think I have," he replied.

"Do you agree with Paul's assessment of that power?"

"If you mean, that everything on the face of the earth is of God, I'm not sure that I do agree." He paused before continuing. "How could Britannicus' murder be of God? How could Nero's planned proclamation of divinity be of God?"

"Marcus," Phoebe declared, "I believe those things *are* of God. He will judge them. Remember what Paul said in his letter, 'Dearly beloved, avenge not yourselves, but rather give place unto wrath: for it is written, vengance is mine; I will repay, saith the Lord.' If you feel the evil of Nero isn't of God, how can you claim the good that's between you and me is of Him?"

"It's simple," Marcus answered. "One is bad and the other is good."

"The fact that one is bad doesn't mean that it's not of God or that He approves of it. God made man and allows him to exist. If man is evil, then God will judge him accordingly for the misuse of the gifts He's given him." She held his eyes in hers and added, "We're commanded to love the Lord with all our heart, all our soul, all our mind and all our strength. This is our first obligation to God. We cannot love Him that way if we claim that only some things are of Him. That's why the love you claim for me has to come second to the love you owe the Lord. The second great commandment we received from Jesus is that we must love our neighbors as we love ourselves." Phoebe reached up and gently touched his cheek. "You and I, Marcus, fall in that second category."

"But how can I love the Lord more than I love you?"

"By surrendering everything to Him, even your love for me."

"Phoebe, could you love me then?"

"Oh, Marcus, I've already given my love for you up to the Lord. He is waiting for you to do the same."

She could almost feel his eyes searching her face. He was silent for a long time. A night owl hooted in the distance, and Marcus turned away from her. "I hope the time will come when I can do that," he whispered.

The travelers joined the Appian Way at Sinuessa the following morning. Phoebe was impressed with the road. Its paved surface was 18 feet wide with traffic flowing in both directions. The lava paving-blocks were smooth and in many places worn with almost 400 years of continuous service. It was a ribbon of history. It had felt the tread of Hannibal's elephants, Sulla's plunder wagons, Pompey's legions and the victorious home-comings of Julius Caesar.

"This section of Via Appia is part of the first road built by the great censor, Appius Claudius Caecus," Marcus explained. "He designed the roadbed the same way our military engineers design walls. In fact," he added, "underlying every-thing, including the walkways on both sides, is a wall of crushed stone and lime. The paving stones are set in this rock-hard mixture so the rain and melting snow will drain to the gutters on each side." Standing in his stirrups, Marcus pointed behind them to the southeast, saying, "This first section runs from Capua, 20 miles back, to Rome." Settling back in his saddle, the centurion added, "It's an all-weather road for the army."

Marcus was riding beside the cart on Phoebe's side. He pointed to a mile marker beside the road, and Phoebe called a halt while she read its Latin inscription.

"Marcus," she exclaimed, "we're only 98 miles from Rome!"

"Yes," he agreed, "an entire army can travel that distance in three days of forced march. We'll do it in four and be fresh when we arrive."

Counting each milestone they passed, Phoebe's excitement grew. The glory of Rome was becoming more evident by the things they saw as they drew closer to the imperial city. Substantial country homes of powerful Romans flanked by great farms and vineyards indicated their owners' wealth.

The milestone announcing Tarracina caught Phoebe's attention. An almost obscure icthus symbol was crudely scratched at the top. She remembered Paul telling her of the symbol's meaning. The sign of the fish indicated there were Christians in the village. Christian travelers, upon meeting a stranger, could readily identify themselves with safety by simply drawing a curved line in the dust or sand. If the stranger completed the symbol with a second curved line to form a fish, then both knew each other's faith.

Turning to Polax driving the cart beside her, she pointed to the symbol and asked that he watch for any houses or buildings bearing the mark. Once inside the town, Phoebe called out to Marcus, asking that he lead them away from the highway. He turned right at the next intersection and led the way into a residential trade section of the village.

Phoebe explained her intentions to Marcus, and he sent Julius ahead to look for the sign of the fish on any door. The sergeant returned a few minutes later saying, "There's a house around the next corner with a bake shop in front that has the symbol over the entrance."

Stopping at the shop, Phoebe climbed down from the cart and went inside. The aroma of fresh bread and displays of sweet cakes and other confections delighted her senses. A lovely young woman with her hair neatly bound was busy adding new items to half-empty trays when Phoebe spoke.

"We're travelers from Greece, and we noticed the icthus over your door. Are you a follower of Christ?"

The woman silently nodded her head, and Phoebe immediately identified herself as a Christian. Explaining that her party was on its way to Rome, she mentioned they were carrying a letter from Paul. Hearing this, the woman called her husband from the kitchen and excitedly introduced Phoebe. They were of the Urbanus family, and the man's father had worked with Paul in Cyprus. When Phoebe told them that Urbanus was saluted by Paul in the letter, their interest became more intense.

Then when Marcus appeared in the doorway there was bewilderment. His uniform meant pagan authority, but Phoebe's introduction of the centurion removed all doubt from the faces of the baker and his wife. With the entrance of Debra, Julius and Polax, all restraint fell away and the travelers were invited to stay for supper. Phoebe accepted and then asked Polax to find the inn and arrange for rooms. The Urbanuses wouldn't allow it, and the man extended the supper invitation to include lodgings for the night.

While the meal was being prepared, their host asked Phoebe about the letter. She told him she was commissioned by Paul to deliver his letter to Rome. When he asked if the Christians in Tarracina could hear it, she paused a moment for any inner warning signal. Receiving none, she agreed. He left immediately, saying, "I'll send out word, and we'll meet in our garden."

Phoebe now anticipated reading the letter to a group of interested strangers. She could not only evaluate their reactions but also have a chance to polish her presentation and delivery. Uncertain whether Aquila and Priscilla would accept the letter in Rome and see to its delivery, Phoebe wanted some first-hand experience in delivering it herself.

Small groups of people started to arrive just as supper was ending. Their host ushered them through the house to the garden in the rear. Marcus and Julius had changed from their uniforms to the traditional togas while Polax remained dressed in his seaman's garb. Phoebe and Debra wore simple peplos gowns of sheer, unbleached linen accented with colored belts. Most of the guests wore their working clothes as did their host and hostess.

It was obvious these people had met in the garden before. Benches were arranged among the flower beds and a small table was set at the far end. Counting 52 people, Phoebe followed her host to the table carrying the canvas bag containing the letter. The murmur of general conversation faded, and he explained the purpose of the meeting. With pride in his voice, he introduced Phoebe and asked that she introduce her companions, Marcus, Julius, Polax and Debra who had found seats in the back. Looking at the crowd, she remembered Paul's warning. All of the women were seated in back, the men up front.

She stepped forward and asked each member of her party to stand. Announcing their names, she asked each in turn to testify to their faith. Polax was first. When he gave witness to being a thief serving out his time in Phoebe's fleet and meeting the Lord through her teachings, he was cheered by the people. Debra was next, and her testimony was especially moving as she told of being orphaned as a child and sold into slavery. Phoebe had bought her freedom and led her to Jesus. Julius told of his love for Debra and how she had turned his eyes away from Aphrodite and Diana to the face of the living God.

Everyone seemed to be waiting for Marcus. When he stood, the people expected him to deliver and read the letter. Phoebe sensed their expectation and removed the scroll from its canvas bag, intending to hand it to him, but Marcus was of another mind. She watched him walk toward her, realizing that he, too, had sensed their feeling. She had introduced him as simply Marcus Paetius of Rome, newly baptized as a Christian and returning to the imperial capital. Other than their host and hostess, none of the others knew of his official capacity. His toga indicated he was of a patrician family but nothing more.

Phoebe's mind was in turmoil. This was a traditional Jewish audience. She knew that a woman had never taught here. Glancing at her host, she tried to read his expression, realizing that she hadn't made herself clear to him that she was to present the letter. Since Tarracina wasn't a seaport, her reputation and authority were not known here. The baker had assumed that Marcus was in charge of the party. With Marcus standing beside her, their host touched her arm and indicated the bench behind them as he sat down. This confirmed it. He expected her to join him while Marcus read the letter. Marcus, too, had seen the host's action, and his nodded smile told her to comply. Sitting down, she felt a surge of disappointment and fought down her irritation as Marcus started talking. Paul's letter was still in her hand.

"Friends and fellow Christians," the centurion began, "I come to you as a new man. I have been born again through the love of Jesus the Messiah. I have learned, like many of you, what it means to receive a love that is beyond human understanding."

Phoebe's spirits suddenly rose, and she felt ashamed of her petulant feelings. She had never heard Marcus address a group before, and his eloquence surprised her.

"I left Rome several months ago," he continued, "as the adopted son of Seneca and a centurion of the Praetorian Guard." Phoebe heard a gasp from the audience at the mention of Seneca's name. "But now I stand before you as a child of God. My natural father, who was also a centurion of Rome, stood at the foot of Jesus' cross and watched Him die. He was in Jerusalem when Jesus rose from the tomb."

The silence was now intense as every eye focused on the centurion.

"My natural father wrote me a letter in which he tried to tell me of the living God," Marcus continued, "but my ears and mind were attuned to more earthly things and I didn't understand. I went to Corinth in Greece wearing this." Reaching inside the neck of his toga, Marcus brought out the emperor's medallion. Holding it up for all to see, the people recognized it and knew its meaning. Letting it fall to his chest on its golden chain, Marcus resumed. "My mission was to find Paul, the apostle, and question him concerning the religion he was teaching.

"I found Paul and the teacher impressed me as a man, but it was this lovely woman," Marcus turned and touched Phoebe's shoulder, "who introduced me to Jesus. In her gentle, loving way she taught me the truth." Once again, he reached inside his toga and this time took out the cross Gaius had given him. "And now I wear the medallion of a truly great king." Holding it up for all to see, he cried, "Now I wear the cross of Jesus!"

In the back of the garden Julius, Debra and Polax were on their feet holding their crosses out before them. Marcus' right arm stabbed the air in their direction as he said, "The four of us wear the cross of Jesus because of Phoebe's Christian love and concern for us."

Watching the audience turn and look at the three standing behind them, the astonished Phoebe realized that Marcus had deftly established her right to speak. The centurion clinched it with his next words.

"I ask you now to pray with me." All eyes returned to Marcus. "Dear Father, let Phoebe clearly read the words Paul has written. Let the Holy Spirit guide her tongue and open our ears so that Your Word will be understood. Fill her with Your love and us with Your charity that we may listen with open hearts. We pray this in the name of Jesus, Your Son and our Lord. Amen."

The universal "amen" from the audience told Phoebe they would listen. The moment had arrived. Her heart was wildly beating as she got to her feet. Marcus gently took her arm and presented her to the people of Tarracina. Unrolling the scroll, she looked into their eyes and found the love which empowered her to speak.

Her voice at first seemed to tremble, but as the impact of the Word became evident, her strength grew. The letter became a living thing in that garden and Phoebe felt the Spirit surge within her. The words seemed to jump from the scroll with a new meaning for her and those who heard them. About three quarters of the way through, she felt a vibrancy to the words that held a personal meaning for her.

"Let love be without dissimulation. Abhor that which is evil; cleave to that which is good. Be kindly affectioned one to another with brotherly love; in honor preferring one another. Not slothful in business; fervent in spirit; serving the Lord. Rejoicing in hope; patient in tribulation; continuing instant in prayer. Distributing to the necessity of saints; given to hospitality. Bless them which persecute you: bless, and curse not. Rejoice with them that do rejoice, and weep with them that weep."

Reading on, she found new and additional meanings to every phrase. The Holy Spirit had so inspired Paul that every reading of the letter would provide a greater understanding for the reader. When she came to that part referring to her, she paused and studied the faces of the people for a moment. It was in her mind to bypass it, but one glance at Marcus' shaking head told her not to. She read on.

"I commend unto you Phoebe our sister, who is a servant of the church at Cenchrea: That you receive her in the Lord, as becomes saints, and that you assist her in whatsoever business she has need of you: for she has been a helper of many, and of myself also."

Looking up from the scroll, she saw nods of agreement from those before her. Reading the salute to Urbanus, she turned to the son and smiled. There were murmurs of approval from the group. Concluding with the last "amen," Phoebe bowed her head and prayed.

"I thank You, Father, for the inspiration of Paul and for allowing me to read Your Word to the people of Tarracina. I praise You for the goodness of their hearts and the openness of their ears. I thank You for the Urbanus family and ask that You bless them, and all the people, with Your great love. I pray in Jesus' name. Amen."

When she looked up, Marcus was beside her, and she accepted the embrace of the baker. As she rerolled the scroll, she turned to their host, saying, "This copy of the letter is for you and your people." Placing it in his hands, she added, "It's a gift from God in appreciation for your kindness and hospitality."

Tears welled up in his eyes. Scrolls of any kind were extremely expensive and to have one so completely detailing their faith was above any possible value. People would come from all over the province to hear it read. Wealthy Christians would beg for the privilege of having it copied. He tried to give his thanks, but his voice choked as the tears flowed down his cheeks.

As the people came forward to greet her Phoebe prayed the letter would be as well received in Rome. The Nones of April when Nero would proclaim his deity was only 17 days away.

CHAPTER IX

To all that be in Rome, beloved of God, called to be saints . . .

ROMANS 1:7

WHEN the good-bys were said the next morning, their host insisted they take several fresh loaves of bread and made a promise to Phoebe. "Paul's letter will be read in Circei, Astura, Fregellae and Volturnus before the end of this month. I will personally see to it."

As the travelers headed toward Rome, Phoebe couldn't understand the feeling of foreboding that pressed down on her. The sun was bright and warm even though it was still low in the eastern sky. Her first presentation of Paul's letter had been an unqualified success, and she felt the steady glow of Marcus' love. *Why then,* she asked herself, *do I feel so apprehensive?* As the village of Tarracina grew smaller in the distance, Phoebe, once again, began counting the mile markers.

The almost straight course of Via Appia was taking them away from the coast. Extending ahead of them, almost as far as they could see, it ran up the Campagna Plain and by nightfall they were seeing increased evidence of the imperial city. Traffic was heavier along the road; twice during the day they had to make way for southbound troops of the legion. On both occasions, Marcus had conversed with some of the officers, and his expression grew more grim with every mile they traveled. Riding back and reining his horse around beside the cart, Phoebe learned the reason why. It also solved the riddle of her day-long uneasiness. Unconsciously, she, too, had been worrying about Castor.

"According to the commander of that last cohort, he's about three hours ahead of us," Marcus said.

"Are you sure it's Castor?" Phoebe asked.

"Yes," Marcus growled. "He's riding alone and fast. He tried to trade his spent horse for a fresh one with the commander and was refused."

Looking at the low sun in the west, Phoebe's eyes narrowed. "Then we must travel tonight."

Marcus shook his head. "No, Phoebe, we've been at it all day, and the horses need rest and feed. Besides, it'll be dark within an hour, and there'll be no moon until almost midnight. I've told Julius to lead us off the road at the next farm. We'll camp and rest until the moon's up and then go on." He grinned and added, "Perhaps Castor will find a jug of wine and sleep until morning."

They didn't have to camp. The farmer made them welcome and with a gold coin pressed into his palm, he provided feed for the horses, and his wife set a bountiful table. Phoebe and Debra were helping her clear things away after the meal when she told them of her husband's earlier good fortune.

"He traded horses with a sailor," she laughingly reported. "We got a fine young mare for an old gelding. She was really lathered, but my man walked her out and rubbed her down. She's fine now, and the sailor gave us silver to boot."

Phoebe found the men in the stable where the farmer had just finished telling them of his trade. The look on Marcus' face told her that their situation hadn't changed. The horses still needed rest and a half-night's sleep for each of them would improve their dispositions. Polax voiced the only bright note in the news.

"Castor will not get far on the horse this man traded him."

Under any other conditions, Phoebe would have welcomed the opportunity to travel by moonlight. It was a perfect spring night, and they had the Appian Way to themselves. Marcus had given Polax his horse, and the centurion was driving the cart. They had left the farm a little after midnight and traveled almost three hours when they approached a small village. Marcus called to Polax and told him to scout around in the town and see if he could find the farmer's old horse.

They watched the Persian gallop ahead and about 10 minutes later they followed the progress of his search by the barking of the dogs he had disturbed. Marcus roared with laughter. It was the first time he'd laughed since the previous afternoon, and Phoebe was glad. Leaning toward him, she quipped, "I don't know which is worse, you or the dogs."

"That crazy Persian," he said between paroxysms of laughter, "I'll bet he's riding through every house in the town, checking the beds and shaking them all out." Catching his breath he added, "By noon today there'll be a new legend in that village about a giant, redheaded god on a horse breathing fire and searching for some lost soul named Castor."

They were well past the town when Polax rejoined them. Riding up beside the cart, his cryptic answer started their laughter all over again.

"Castor wasn't there," he said simply. Shaking his head at the outburst his remark had caused, he rode ahead to give Julius the same message. The decurion almost fell off his horse laughing when he heard the Persian's curt report. Still chuckling, he told Polax what Marcus had said. When Polax stopped laughing, he turned in his saddle and shouted back to the cart.

"That's exactly what happened, but I told everyone my name was Marcus Paetius!"

Polax's laughter echoed into the night air as Marcus roared back, "But did they believe you?"

Eleven miles further on, Julius rode back and reported that they had found a dead horse beside the road. "It fits the description the farmer gave us," he explained.

Polax was leading his horse back up the bank when they pulled even with him. "It's the horse all right," he said, "but it's cold." He remounted and started off, saying, "Castor's afoot now. I think I'll ride on ahead for a way and see if he's sleeping in a ditch."

Phoebe's feeling of apprehension returned with the rising sun. The road seemed endless. They passed the 35-mile marker and she was certain they'd passed it before. Marcus had been silent for miles and Debra was asleep, bundled up in a blanket. Blinking her eyes to be sure she wasn't dreaming, Phoebe stared at a huge structure along the side of the road that resembled a gigantic, arched wall. Touching the centurion's shoulder, he sat upright, and she saw the look of recognition sweep over his face.

"The aqueduct of Claudius. It's one of many that carries water to Rome." Turning in his seat, he leaned toward her and kissed her upturned lips. Then looking back over her shoulder, he came to full attention. She swiveled in that direction.

A lone horseman was riding to catch them. Phoebe tensed as the centurion reached for his sword. Then she saw his arm relax.

"It's Polax. I wonder how we got ahead of him?" Calling out to Julius, still riding in the lead, he ordered, "Pull off at the next farm road. It's time for breakfast and a planning session."

They'd turned into a grove of tall oaks. The burned out remains of what had once been a farmhouse stood in stark testimony to some man's dreams gone up in flames. There was water in the well, and Julius was lowering a bucket for the horses when Polax rode in. The giant seemed born to the horse. He was dismounting while the animal was coming to a stop. His report had a military precision about it that Phoebe knew pleased Marcus.

"I rode in a two-mile circle around the location of the dead horse. I woke every farmer and made him count his animals. There was a horse missing just west of here."

"What made you think of searching like that?" Phoebe asked.

Marcus answered. "The saddle and bridle were gone from the dead animal."

Nodding his head, Polax added, "And I knew Castor wouldn't walk to Rome even if his life depended on it."

Using the burned-out farmhouse's stone fireplace, Debra and Phoebe prepared a breakfast of eggs and hot wheat cakes. By heating a mulling iron in the fire, Phoebe served the men hot wine laced with honey and small chips of cinnamon bark. This last item was a new spice one of her ships had brought from the east, and she hoped to build a market for it in Rome.

The house's foundation stones served as a table, and when they were finished eating, Marcus summed up their situation.

"We have to assume that Castor is ahead of us, and we can't catch him. Second, we can be in Rome late tonight, but I advise against it."

"Why?" Phoebe interposed.

"For several reasons," Marcus answered. "We'd have to press ourselves and our animals too hard to make it. We'd be exhausted. It would also mean searching for Aquila's villa late at night, and on the streets of Rome that is a very dangerous thing to do. I suggest that we stay outside the city tonight and enter in the morning."

"Can we find an inn?" Debra inquired.

"That won't be necessary," Julius replied. All eyes turned on him as he continued. "My older brother is a grave digger. He and his family live outside the walls just a short distance from Via Appia. We can stay with them."

Debra's face brightened with the prospect of meeting someone from Julius' family. She asked, "Do you suppose we can have a bath?"

"Oh yes, Julius. We must bathe before facing Priscilla," Phoebe pleaded. Seeing the smiles of the men, she explained self-consciously, "Priscilla is so fastidious. I couldn't bear for her to see me as I am now."

"We'll all have baths," Marcus agreed, "even if we must take them in a horse trough."

Polax offered a suggestion. "Perhaps I should ride ahead, find Castor and silence him once and for all."

Phoebe objected, saying, "No harm must come to him. We must remain blameless if we're to put the lie to whatever message he carries."

Marcus nodded. "These final miles will be the most dangerous. Rome reflects the attitude of the emperor and almost any act, if it gives someone pleasure, is tolerated. Castor, traveling alone, may not make it even without your suggested interference."

The centurion's remark startled Phoebe. "Is Rome really ruled by such anarchy?" she asked.

"No," Marcus replied, "but the law is being twisted to accommodate the perversions of the emperor. Many people think they can follow his example, and in too many cases they get away with it. A woman without sufficient escort isn't safe on the streets of Rome, day or night."

As Phoebe watched Marcus walk to his horse, her brain suddenly reeled under the impact of a very dark thought. He was going to confess failure to an emperor who was so self-indulgent that his people's lives and safety had little or no meaning. What chance for justice would he have before the demented Nero? How could God give her love for this man and then allow Nero to take him away?

Her somber mood wasn't brightened as they drew nearer the city. Rome was surrounded by cemeteries. Monuments and tombs for the dead dotted both sides of the highway. The traffic was heavy. Wagons loaded with perishable food and building material crowded them, slowing their progress. Mounted columns of men skirted the congestion raising great clouds of dust, adding to the confusion. They were still several miles from the city walls and each mile marker heightened her fear for Marcus.

By early afternoon they still had not stopped to eat. Phoebe kept looking for a likely place to picnic, but couldn't bring herself to eat on someone's grave. In desperation, she, Debra and Polax shared the last now-stale loaf of the Tarracina bread.

Phoebe was about to call a halt to get the cheese from the bottom of the cart when Julius and Marcus turned off the highway. They waited for the cart to join them on a dirt road. Excitement showed on Julius' face.

"Emil, my brother, lives about a mile up this road." Pointing east, he added, "Shelta, his wife, will fix us a hot meal."

Marcus told him to ride on ahead. Other than a few cows, which grazed over the graves, and an occasional herder, they were alone on the road. They'd gone about three quarters of a mile when they saw Julius riding back. Seeing him slouched in the saddle, head down, they knew something terrible had happened. Marcus quickly rode out to meet him. They watched the two soldiers talk briefly and then Marcus took the decurion's bridle and led the horse off the road beside a gabled, marble tomb.

Driving the cart up beside the building, Polax leaped down and joined the two dismounted Romans. Debra and Phoebe watched Marcus put his arm around Julius' shoulder and force him to sit on the grass. Then Polax returned to the cart.

"He wants you, Debra," he somberly said and helped the girl down. She ran across the grass and knelt beside Julius as Polax came around to Phoebe's side of the cart.

"What happened?" she whispered.

Shaking his head with sadness, the Persian answered softly, "They're all dead. Julius is the only one of his family left. Emil, Shelta and their seven children died in a plague two years ago. He found their graves beside the burned remains of their little house."

Leaving Debra with Julius, Marcus slowly walked back to the cart, tears in his eyes. Seeing Marcus cry in sadness tore at her heart. She wanted to comfort both men but felt helpless.

Standing in front of her beside the cart, Marcus brushed away his tears. "He wanted to show off his new rank to them and introduce us as his friends. He wanted his brother to see Debra's beauty and come to his wedding. He wanted the children to be proud of their Uncle Julius."

111

Phoebe reached for his hand. "They'll know all of that in heaven and be proud of him."

Marcus shook his head. "That's what makes it so difficult for Julius. They didn't know the Lord."

"Help me down," Phoebe requested and Marcus gently lifted her to the ground. Hand in hand they went to where Debra and Julius were kneeling.

She knelt in front of Julius and raised his chin with her hand. "Emil, Shelta and the children are with our Lord," she said. "Paul could explain it better than I, but in his letter to the Romans, he spoke to this very thing. 'For when the Gentiles, which have not the law, do by nature the things contained in the law, these, having not the law, are a law unto themselves.' Don't you see, Julius? Jesus will judge them by the way they lived. In His great love for all men, He'll embrace them because they lived according to the gospel without knowing the gospel."

She saw understanding come into his eyes but could barely hear his choked whisper. "Thank you, my lady."

Debra remained with the decurion while Phoebe and Marcus rejoined Polax at the cart. They were about nine miles from the city walls and the sun was sinking below the tree tops.

On exploring the nearby tomb, Polax found it empty. "It doesn't have a bath," he said, "but we could stay here tonight. There's enough water in our jars for the ladies to clean themselves reasonably well, and someone before us had made a fireplace of grave markers in the back."

"Perhaps there's an inn nearby," Phoebe volunteered.

"If there is," the Persian answered, "it'll be crowded with grave robbers. From what I can see, there isn't a grave out here that hasn't been picked clean."

Marcus decided for them. Taking a purse from his girdle, he tossed it to the Persian, saying, "There's an inn called the Emperor's Cloak just inside the city walls near the Porta Naevia. Take Julius' horse and ride like the wind. Reserve rooms for us and wait until we arrive."

As Polax mounted, Phoebe called out, "And tell them to heat plenty of water."

The splendor of Rome became more apparent as they approached the city walls. Julius was driving the cart with Marcus leading the way. Even in the gathering dusk Phoebe could see torch-lit watchtowers extending above the walls, and the gate just ahead blazed with light. On her left the wall turned away in a northwesterly direction, and its detail became lost in the shadow of the hills. Lights could be seen beyond the walls which indicated the breadth of the city.

Her throat tightened as she realized that this was the center of the Roman Empire, seat of all imperial power. It was through the gates of this city that Rome's legions marched to extend that power. Kings, emperors and princes bowed to this city. And it was here that her ministry would be truly tested. Cleopatra had entered this city seeking to conquer an emperor and had failed. The city had killed him and driven her out. But the Egyptian queen had come without God, while Phoebe knew that she had a huge advantage through His presence. With God's help, she would succeed.

Then feeling a check in her spirit, she realized that it was pure arrogance to decide in advance what God would do in any situation. Who could know the will of God? Other Christians had died while holding fast to the faith. So could she.

The commander of the guard snapped to attention as Marcus dismounted. The emperor's medallion caught the torch light and flashed its authority as it swung from its chain on the centurion's chest. The two men exchanged salutes, and Marcus waved Julius forward with the cart. Bowing to Phoebe, the commander welcomed her to Rome. He was courteous, but his eyes were bold. Travel weary and dusty as she was, Phoebe recognized the spark of desire she created in his eyes. Julius was the proper soldier, looking neither right nor left. When Debra blushed under the commander's scrutiny, Marcus stepped between them and the guard and ordered Julius to drive on through. The centurion was angrily muttering to himself as he rode on ahead to lead the way to the inn.

The Emperor's Cloak was built into the city wall, and its common room was frequented mostly by off-duty guardsmen from the Porta Naevia. By no means a luxury hostel, it was clean and had a reputation for simple food served in large portions.

After a meal of roast goose, bread stuffing laced with leeks, boiled turnips and fresh, hard-crusted bread swimming in dark brown gravy, Phoebe and Debra followed the innkeeper's wife down the back stairs to the bath. An hour later, Phoebe found Marcus alone in the common room dozing in a chair. The snoring she'd heard along the hallway told her the other two men were in bed. Sending Debra on to her own room, Phoebe went in and sat down across from Marcus.

She could see he was exhausted and wondered why he hadn't retired. The tunic he was wearing indicated that Julius had taken his uniform for cleaning and polishing. Though he hadn't shaved in two days, the stubble of his beard, being blond like his hair, was hardly noticeable. It caught the flickering candlelight and seemed to soften his handsome features. Cocking her head to one side, she decided that with a neatly trimmed beard, he'd be a true likeness for the ancient Greek god, Adonis.

In this quiet moment, Phoebe realized how much she loved him. The beat of her heart quickened under the thin fabric of her white silk nightgown and heavier wool robe. Removing the slipper from her right foot, she extended her leg and playfully caressed his bare ankle. With her damp hair bound up in a white drying cloth, she smiled almost coyly, waiting for him to wake up.

Blinking his eyes, he jerked himself awake and his right arm shot to the seat of the chair beside him. The naked blade of his sword flashed in the candlelight as he whipped it out. Coming fully awake and seeing her startled expression, he apologized while placing the weapon on the table.

"I'm sorry, Phoebe, but I volunteered for the first watch, and you caught me sleeping."

"First watch?" she questioned.

Marcus nodded as he rubbed his eyes. "We're staying at a public inn, and I learned long ago that innkeepers make terrible guards." He smiled and asked, "How was the bath?"

"Heavenly," she replied, "and if you must stand watch, I'll stay with you. My bath has completely restored me."

The expression in Marcus' eyes told her how much she was wanted. Her hand crept across the table and rested lightly on his arm.

Marcus cradled her hand in his and lowered his voice. "I was hoping you'd stay with me for a little while; I've things to tell you which I didn't want the others to hear." He paused a moment to caress her fingers. "The Lord has brought us together, and I love you more than life itself. Please keep that knowledge foremost in your mind during the next few days." Leaning forward, with his elbows on the table, he lifted her hand to his lips and held it there as he softly spoke. "Tomorrow, Julius and I will take you, Debra and Polax to Aquila's. Paul told me his villa was located on the Tiber side of Aventinus Hill. After getting you established there, Julius and I will proceed to my stepfather's house on the Palatine." He lowered her hand to the table and straightened in his chair. "In all likelihood, I'll appear before Nero the following day."

Phoebe's feeling of foreboding returned.

"Seneca will advise me on the best way to report my failure to deliver or kill Paul," Marcus continued. "There's absolutely no way to predict what the emperor's reaction will be; if Poppaea is with him, I'm sure it will be disastrous. But under no circumstances are you to try to help me."

As she started to speak, he frowned and shook his head. "Your job here is to deliver Paul's letter. That must come first. Seneca and Burrus will do everything that can be done for me. You will only endanger yourself and your friends by getting involved in my problem. This is Rome, and I understand it better than you." He paused for a moment before asking, "Will you obey me?"

Phoebe nodded.

"Good. Now, there's something else you must understand. Seneca is the second most powerful man in Rome. He's feared and respected everywhere. There isn't a soul in this city who doesn't know of him and his power. Even in Tarracina, you'll remember, they gasped at his name. If the Christians in Rome have any fear of pagan power, it'll be reflected in their attitudes toward Seneca. He is the man who sets their taxes and sees to their collection. He's the one who decides how the laws will be applied to the people. Nero is emperor and he has absolute power, but Seneca and Burrus administer that power. Do you understand?"

Again Phoebe nodded.

"Tomorrow," Marcus continued, "will be the 14th day before the Nones of April. If Seneca has succeeded in neutralizing Poppaea's influence over the emperor, that date may have no meaning for any of us. But Poppaea is a seductive, older woman, and Nero finds her very appealing. I suspect Seneca and Burrus haven't been able to replace that appeal. God alone may be the only power left strong enough to stop the emperor from following her lead." Raising her hand again, he kissed her fingertips. "The Lord has placed His power in this slender delicate hand, and you must wield it for His glory."

"Marcus, what will happen to you?"

He smilingly answered, "Nothing fatal, I hope and pray. I intend to offer my resignation from the guard as tribute for my failure. If Nero is alone, and with Seneca's recommendation and Burrus' agreement, the emperor may consider that punishment enough. But if he's with Poppaea, she may demand my head—and get it!"

Phoebe gasped at the finality of his statement.

"Poppaea's friends, the ambassadors from the Sanhedrin, are already gloating over the expected humiliation of Paul. If that fails to occur, they know Nero has ordered his death. When they learn that Paul isn't coming to Rome, and that he's still alive, they will be enraged."

She silently studied his face, trying to memorize it. If this were to be their last night together, she wanted to remember him as he was now. She caressed him with her eyes and wished they'd been married in Cenchrea before they sailed. *At least then,* she thought, *I'd also have that tenderness to remember.*

"The rent on these rooms here at the Emperor's Cloak has

been paid for 30 days," Marcus continued. "Paul told me that Aquila may refuse to accept his letter. You may not be welcome there, and with Castor here ahead of us to muddy things, you may be on your own. If that happens, I want you to come back here and stay until Julius or someone brings you word of what's happened to me. If I can, I'll come to Aquila's for you. If you're not there, I'll come here. In any event, you must deliver Paul's letter." His grip on her hand tightened. "Otherwise, all of our efforts will have been wasted."

"I love you," she said. "The Lord is our shepherd, and He shall not let us become lost. I'll wait for you, darling, until the end of time if I have to."

CHAPTER X

Greet Priscilla and Aquila my helpers in Christ Je-sus . . .

ROMANS 16:3

THE TRAVELERS left the Emperor's Cloak two hours after sunrise. Phoebe was wearing a high-collared, sleeveless, mauve, silk gown under a hooded, blue cloak trimmed with white calfskin. Her hair, under the hood, was brushed to a high sheen and hung almost to her waist. Debra's dress was similar in style and cut but yellow in color.

Marcus and Julius reflected the glory of Rome in their crested helmets and gleaming uniforms. The red-haired giant, Polax, was resplendent in his Syracuse finery with the addition of large, golden rings in each ear. Even the horses were curried and brushed and their tails braided with crimson ribbon. The baggage in the cart was covered with new canvas and the wheels washed and oiled to a high polish.

As they passed through the streets, Phoebe noted that commerce was being conducted amid the constant clamor of human voices, barking dogs and the screech of greaseless wheels. Occasionally a covered sedan chair would pass, carried by a team of four or eight slaves. In almost every case these chairs were accompanied by an armed escort. Her own escort commanded sufficient respect to gain her the right of way, and every question for directions the centurion asked was promptly answered.

Now that she was properly dressed for the occasion, Phoebe

was looking forward to seeing Priscilla again. She remembered her as a strong-minded woman with definite opinions on almost every subject. Aquila's leather tannery in Corinth was the city's largest and their Ephesus firm also was thriving. The couple had established branches of their business everywhere they'd gone with Paul. Phoebe knew they were wealthy. The ships of her fleet carried many of their products.

They traveled in a northwesterly direction toward the point where the Probi Bridge crossed the Tiber. Aquila's villa, according to Paul, was up the slope of the Aventinus from there. She expected them to have a fine home, but when Marcus called a halt before the gates of an impressive, hillside estate, Phoebe thought he'd made a mistake.

Dismounting, Marcus handed the reins of his horse to Julius and strode to the closed iron grill gate. A servant was sweeping the paved courtyard and looked up as the centurion called out.

"Is Aquila the master of this house?"

The servant nodded his head and came running. Opening the gate, he bowed low and stated, "My mistress is at home, my lord. Can she serve you?"

Phoebe joined Marcus and answered, "Please tell Priscilla that Phoebe of Corinth and Cenchrea is at her gate."

The man stepped back and bowed again, saying, "Please come in, my lady. I'll inform my mistress at once."

They watched the servant hurry across the courtyard and into the house as Polax drove the cart inside. It was an impressive house, two stories high, with a balcony running across the front and around the side facing the river. Carved, wooden grills encased every window, and the red tiled roof gleamed in the late morning sun. Leading the horses, Julius joined Debra at the cart. Polax remained in his seat while Phoebe and Marcus stood in the center of the yard. The great carved doors both swung open, revealing a woman in her early 40s, dressed in a classic stolla of pale green.

"Phoebe, it *is* you!" she exclaimed, rushing forward with her arms extended in welcome.

Marcus watched as the two embraced. He snapped to attention when he was introduced and crossed his chest in a Roman salute. Taking Priscilla's hand, Phoebe introduced the rest of her party.

Graciously, Priscilla extended an invitation to each of them to stay at the villa. Marcus declined for himself and Julius, explaining, "Having been away in Greece for several months, Seneca, my father, will expect me to grace his table, and my decurion will be required there. Please accept my thanks, however, for your courteous invitation."

At the mention of Seneca's name, Phoebe observed a quick reappraisal of Marcus by her hostess. Then Priscilla bowed again.

"At least, my lord, you can stay for the noon meal. It would be a great honor for our house, and we have to thank you for bringing Phoebe to us."

"That, my lady," Marcus replied, "we can accept with joy."

Additional servants arrived, the baggage was carried into the house, the cart was wheeled to the side and the horses were led away for water and feed. As she followed her hostess inside, Phoebe studied her friend.

Priscilla still wore her golden, titian hair like a crown, and the planes of her delicate cheekbones seemed to support her beautiful, large, hazel eyes. In profile she strongly resembled the high-born features portrayed in the Corinth painting of the ancient Egyptian queen, Nefertiti. Her slim, willowy figure moved smoothly erect, on the balls of her tiny feet, and the graceful curve of her neck and shoulders blended perfectly with slender arms and hands.

Entering the villa, Phoebe was impressed with its size. The glazed tiles of the atrium floor reflected the sun's brilliance through the opening in the roof above the sparkling rain pool. Curving stairs led to the second floor on her right, and a large, Roman-style dining room was to her left. The couches used for reclining at the table were padded with yellow silk cushions and the walls were decorated with tile mosaics depicting harvest scenes. The library was off to the right, tucked under the top of the stairs. Through its open doorway, Phoebe could see a columned peristyle garden with a bubbling fountain surrounded by a blue marble patio framed with shrubs and ivies.

Two children were playing by the fountain. The boy looked to be about six and the girl, four. Both had their mother's flaming hair. They came running when Priscilla called them. "This is Abrum, our oldest, and Rebecca; she's my baby."

Phoebe had been unaware that Aquila and Priscilla had any children. She could see from the pride in their mother's eyes that a great deal of life revolved around them. The boy bowed and the girl curtsied at their introduction. They greeted the guests in Latin and then excitedly surrounded Marcus, admiring his uniform and sword. The centurion took his helmet from the crook of his arm and placed it on Abrum's head. The lad snapped to attention and crossed his chest in salute. Both Romans returned it with laughter.

Leading everyone into the dining room, Priscilla first served them goblets of wine and then ordered a sumptuous meal consisting of cold roast peahen, jellied gravy containing sprigs of mint, cooked apricots rolled in honey and crushed nuts, and slender shafts of celery filled with soft cheese. When she sent the children to eat in the kitchen with the servants, Marcus retrieved his helmet from Abrum as the boy whooped with joy and started for the back of the house.

Watching Priscilla and the children, Phoebe was suddenly aware that she had changed. They were now truly Romans. Latin was used in their home instead of Greek or Hebrew. She wondered if Aquila had changed as much. Was he still the staunch prayer warrior Paul remembered? Her hostess seemed intent on creating a favorable impression on Marcus, even to the exclusion of asking the purpose of Phoebe's trip to Rome. It wasn't until the meal was served that Priscilla turned her attention to Phoebe and asked about it.

"I've come to Rome with a letter Paul wants delivered to Aquila," Phoebe replied.

"Is it a personal letter?" Priscilla asked.

"Yes and no," Phoebe answered thoughtfully. "It's addressed to all the Christians here, and Paul hopes Aquila will see to its distribution."

At the word "Christians," Priscilla's eyebrows raised slightly, and looking at Phoebe, her eyes darted toward Marcus with the unasked question.

"Marcus was baptized in Cenchrea before we left, and Julius has been a follower for over a year."

Priscilla visibly relaxed. "Then he understands the delicate balance we Christians must maintain here in Rome. When Aquila and I returned to Rome from Ephesus, we shared the imperial welcome Nero had accorded to all Jews. The Jews here want nothing to do with us, but the government thinks we're part of them. Having regained our property and citizenship, we've come to an unspoken agreement with the Jews that as Christians we'll not cause any problems which might result in our second expulsion."

"Is your husband expected soon?" Marcus asked.

"He could be returning at any moment," Priscilla answered turning to the centurion. "Aquila was called away to a meeting early this morning by Rufus, one of our leaders in the northern part of the city."

Looking at Phoebe, Marcus inquired, "Could this be the same Rufus Paul mentioned in the letter?"

Having never met Rufus, Phoebe directed the question to Priscilla with a glance.

"He's the son of Simon, the man who carried Jesus' cross to Golgotha. He fled from Jerusalem with his mother and brother when Paul led the persecutions that killed his father."

Phoebe felt a chill crawl up her back. Fearing to ask but knowing she had to, she questioned, "Was Aquila told the reason for the meeting this morning?"

"Not completely," Priscilla answered. "It was something to do with future plans, but the messenger seemed very agitated." Concern entered her voice, "Why do you ask?"

They were reclining at the table, eating Roman style, and Phoebe twisted sideways and sat up. "I'm afraid a former captain of mine may have something to do with it."

She told Priscilla of the voyage and how Castor had raced them to Rome. The others went on with their meal, but their hostess stopped eating when Phoebe mentioned how they'd learned of the letter Castor was carrying.

"Do you have any idea who wrote this letter Castor's carrying?"

"I think it may have been Tertius, Paul's scribe," Phoebe answered.

"What sort of letter would he send?" Priscilla pressed.

"I suppose it's a letter warning everyone against Marcus."

A forkful of food stopped halfway to the centurion's mouth and slowly returned to his plate. "You see, my lady Priscilla," Marcus observed, "that delicate balance, which you spoke of a moment ago, may soon no longer exist. Poppaea, the emperor's current favorite, is close to the Sanhedrin. She intends, as Jesus said, to separate the sheep from the goats!"

"What exactly does that mean?" she queried.

"The Sanhedrin wants Nero to exclude from the pardon he granted to the Jews all Jews who have become Christians," Marcus replied. "Poppaea is the Sanhedrin's agent, and she's contrived a plot to accomplish that result."

"What kind of plot?"

"I'm afraid I'm not at liberty to say," Marcus answered. "But if Castor's letter damning me causes the Christians to mistrust Phoebe and Paul's letter, there's an excellent chance Poppaea will succeed."

"How can Paul's letter stop her?" Priscilla asked.

"It encourages the conversion of Gentiles in a way that might result in large numbers of Romans becoming Christians."

"I don't see how the conversion of many Gentiles would stop Poppaea. And angering the emperor could threaten Jewish security," she persisted.

"There's safety in numbers," Marcus reasoned. "The only power Nero fears is the power of the people. Over half the population of Rome is living on welfare. He encourages and sponsors the games to keep them entertained. He maintains power by keeping them pacified. Nero will not act against a large body of people, but as a small body, we Christians could become part of the entertainment."

"I'm afraid," Priscilla observed, "you'll have a difficult time convincing Aquila of all of this."

"Why?" Phoebe asked.

"Because Aquila believes Jesus was the Jewish Messiah and in order for anyone to receive His salvation they must become Jews first and thus be circumcised."

"Priscilla," Phoebe implored, "I'm a Christian, and I was a Gentile. And I wasn't circumcised."

"Of course not, you're a woman," she retorted. "God only commanded the men to be circumcised."

"Be that as it may. Jesus is my Lord, and I'm not circumcised," Marcus interjected.

"Nor am I," said Julius.

An uncomfortable silence settled over the group which Priscilla finally broke.

"I suggest that we wait for Aquila's return. He'll know what to do, and if your suspicions of Castor are correct, he'll know what's contained in Tertius' letter." Her smile didn't convey much confidence as she added, "My husband's a fair man, and he knows of Paul's feelings towards the Gentiles. He's bound to have the answer."

Marcus arose from the table and bowed toward Priscilla. "My lady, we thank you for your gracious hospitality. Phoebe, Debra and Polax will remain with you, and I pray that all our difficulties will be resolved." Julius and Polax left to make the necessary preparations. Debra forlornly followed after them.

When Priscilla discreetly withdrew, Phoebe fought back the tears, knowing that this might be the last time she would ever see Marcus. She arose and walked into his waiting arms. But the centurion had something on his mind.

"Phoebe, you know and I know that I have not yet completely given myself to our Lord. I've held something back. I've never been able to convince myself that it was really necessary to love God more than I love you. But now I feel I'm ready to do this, with your help."

Grasping his hand, she led him to a corner of the room where they knelt. "We'll pray together and ask Jesus to accept our love and submission to His will," she said. "Tell the Lord that you belong to Him, that you love Him above all else, and ask Him to fill you with His Spirit."

Quietly Phoebe prayed—first in words that Marcus could understand, then in words he did not.

The centurion started slowly, hesitantly; then the words began to flow. "Lord, I give myself to you again. This is difficult for me, Sir. I so want to run my own life, but I know now You can do it better. Take my love for Phoebe as an offering of my love for You. I want You to come first, Lord. I don't want to be deceptive with You any longer. I love Phoebe with all my heart, but I want my love for You to be even above this. Please bring this about, Sir."

Marcus stopped a moment, trying to frame his next prayer. "Lord, Phoebe has told me how Your Spirit gives us great love and joy. I want this now, please. Fill me with Your Spirit." He was quiet for a moment, then chuckled softly. "I feel Your joy beginning in me, Lord. Thank You. Thank You." Tears began to flow down the centurion's face, and his prayer moved into a new dimension of the Spirit.

As Phoebe held tightly to the centurion's hand, a passage from Paul's letter illuminated her mind. "The Spirit also helps our infirmities: for we know not what we should pray for as we ought: but the Spirit itself makes intercession for us with groanings which cannot be uttered."

Time slowed down and seemed almost to stop. Marcus now turned and took her tenderly in his arms, first kissing her hair, then her eyes, then her cheeks, then her mouth. As they clung together their tears seemed to merge. All the boyish uncertainty was gone from his face; now there was joy, peace, serenity, love.

Marcus helped her to her feet, but Phoebe could not let him go. She tightened her arms around his neck and melted against his body, trying to breathe in the very essence of him, sensing the pressure of his breastplate against her. When he kissed her again, she lost herself in the sweetness of his lips.

As they reluctantly drew apart and headed for the courtyard, Phoebe was overwhelmed by her longing for a physical union with Marcus. *What is this all about?* she prayed. She would certainly have to ask Paul to explain why a powerful experience of the Holy Spirit could relate so closely to one's physical desires.

Before they parted, Marcus gave her some final advice. "Phoebe, remember what I told you last night. Paul's letter comes first." His hands were on her shoulders drawing her eyes to his. "If Aquila will not accept it, you must deliver it. If you're not here when I return, I'll meet you at the Emperor's Cloak. Polax and Julius will look after you. I'll come as soon as I can." Gently kissing her forehead, he turned away. She stood in stunned silence and watched him cross the atrium. Opening the great doors, he stood framed in the outside sunshine and blew her a kiss. When the doors closed, he was gone.

Priscilla was waiting at the foot of the stairs. She smiled at Phoebe with understanding and led the way up the stairs to her room. The sunny, cheerful, airy room did much to brighten Phoebe's spirits. It contained a big bed and had a door which opened onto a balcony facing west that overlooked a lazy bend in the Tiber. Phoebe welcomed Priscilla's company as she opened the chests she'd brought from Cenchrea.

"Are you planning marriage?" Priscilla asked.

"If it's God's will," Phoebe answered.

"Seneca, his father, is a powerful man. Will you live in Rome?"

"I don't think so."

"Why in the world would you not want to live in Rome?"

Phoebe carefully removed a gown from the chest and spread

it on her bed. "Cenchrea is my home. It's where Marcus and I met, and the Dolphin is there."

"But Phoebe, do you realize who the centurion's father is? He's the emperor's right hand! Your Marcus has a brilliant future here in Rome. Can you ask him to turn away from all that and go back to Greece with you?"

"We'd have each other, and that's really all that matters."

Priscilla shook her head in exasperation. "Marcus could be the governor of Greece."

Phoebe didn't answer. Instead she turned away toward the view of the river.

"Why are you so sad?" Priscilla demanded.

As if she were outside herself, Phoebe heard her own voice answer. "By this time tomorrow Marcus may be dead." Whirling back on Priscilla, she added, "He's going before Nero to plead for imperial mercy because he failed to kill Paul! He's here to resign from the Praetorian Guard, hoping Nero will consider that punishment enough and allow him to live. He loves Jesus more than all the wealth and power of the empire. And there may be nothing his powerful stepfather can do to help him."

"Stepfather? What do you mean?"

"Seneca's not really his father," Phoebe explained, her voice lowering. "Marcus is an adopted son. His mother is Seneca's mistress. His real father died in Jerusalem."

"Real father? Who was he?"

"The centurion who stood at the foot of Jesus' cross and proclaimed Him the true Lord. Seneca became enamored with Marcus' mother and arranged it so that his father couldn't return to Rome."

Watching Priscilla assimilate all this information, Phoebe wondered if she had said too much. She waited for her hostess to press for more information about Marcus' failure, but Priscilla's mind was on a different track.

"Phoebe," she said, "in Rome an adopted son takes precedence over a natural son. It's an indication of higher favor in the eyes and heart of the adopting father. Marcus knows what he's doing, and Seneca will support him. Nero will do nothing more than reprimand Marcus. After all, Paul can't be that important to Nero."

Walking back to the chest, Phoebe could hardly believe what her ears had heard. Priscilla's primary concern was for the opportunities Marcus' position could gain him. She hadn't really heard or understood what he had said about Poppaea and the Sanhedrin. No, she concluded, this couldn't be the Priscilla whom Paul remembered. Suddenly she felt a need to know more about Aquila.

"I pray that a reprimand is all Marcus receives from Nero," she continued. "Once he's freed himself from his obligation to the emperor, and I've delivered Paul's letter to Aquila, we're leaving for home."

"You'd be a fool to leave Rome with the prospects Marcus has here," Priscilla stated flatly. "And if Paul's letter deals with the subject of circumcision in the manner Marcus described, then that's a piece of foolishness also."

Phoebe started to protest, but Priscilla stopped her. "No, hear me out. It's always been Aquila's opinion that Paul turned to the Gentiles because the Jews refused to listen to him in sufficient numbers. Yet Paul himself has always admitted that God considers the Jew first and the Gentile second. Therefore, Aquila is convinced that God intends the Gentile to become a Jew before becoming a Christian. Part of becoming a Jew is circumcision. It was commanded by God and cannot be bypassed."

When Phoebe smiled encouragingly, Priscilla continued. "Now for this business of Castor's and Tertius' letter. Aquila will remember that Tertius, like Paul, worked for us in Corinth. And that's another point; everywhere we've gone with Paul, he's been employed by us. It's never been the other way around."

Paul would be the first person in the world to admit to that, Phoebe thought. He's always been proud of earning his own way. Being in business herself, Phoebe couldn't resist asking, "Was his employment an act of charity, or did you benefit from Paul's labor?"

Priscilla continued as if she hadn't heard Phoebe's question. "And now to Paul's letter. If Paul were truly serious about the contents of his letter, he'd have sent it with a man as his messenger."

Slowly standing erect, Phoebe looked at her hostess and demanded, "What's *that* got to do with it?"

"Phoebe, you know as well as I do that Jewish men will not receive instruction from the lips of a woman. Paul is a Jew, and frankly, I'm amazed that he sent you."

"It's only common courtesy for them to allow me to be heard. Paul is requesting that much of them."

"No," Priscilla said, "I doubt they'd even listen to Paul if he were here himself. Rufus, for example, remembers Paul as the persecutor of Christians. So do most of the others. Aquila and I have testified to Paul's conversion and teachings, but it's had little effect on their opinions. Paul's not trusted in Rome."

"But his letter will change that."

"We can only pray that it will," Priscilla stated. "But a man will have to read it to them."

"Paul wants Aquila to do that."

A frown creased Priscilla's forehead and she avoided Phoebe's eyes. "I'm not sure we can afford the luxury of Paul's blessings."

"What do you mean?" Phoebe demanded.

"Please try to understand," Priscilla pleaded. "Aquila and I have given our lives to the Lord, and in doing so, we've accepted Paul as an apostle of Jesus. We've suffered with Paul and defended him. We love him as a brother, but he's been nothing but a problem to us. He's a troublemaker. He's been in and out of jails all over the world. You've seen the life we've finally found for ourselves here." Pausing, she took a deep breath. "We can't risk losing our peace and security for the second time. We're not as young as we used to be, and we have our children to consider."

"Priscilla, Paul is depending on you and Aquila!"

Shaking her head, Priscilla replied, "No, he's depending on *you*. You're his messenger."

"But what if God commands your actions?" Phoebe reasoned.

Smiling patiently, the hostess softly proclaimed, "If God commands our action, we'll obey; but Paul is not God. You're a Gentile, and Paul ministers to you; we're Jews and we have a heritage with God to follow. That heritage includes the law and the prophets." Smiling with total assurance, she added, "And Jesus is the Jewish Messiah."

"Priscilla," Phoebe asked, "would it be easier for you if I left your house?"

"Don't be silly," the hostess declared. "Where would you go?"

It was Phoebe's turn to smile with total assurance. "Marcus made arrangements for me, not knowing if I'd be welcome here."

"Well, you are welcome and that's that," Priscilla said. "You're welcome for as long as you wish to stay. The very idea of your staying any place else is ridiculous. If Aquila knew you had even asked such a question he'd have a fit." She glanced at the sun outside and announced, "He should be coming home soon. He'll know what effect your ship captain's letter has had, and he'll know what's to be done with Paul's epistle."

"I know what's to be done with it," Phoebe smilingly said. "And if Aquila won't do it, then I will. As for Castor's letter, I think it's time I took some action on that also."

From Priscilla's glance, Phoebe knew she, too, was being reappraised. Reopening the chest, she continued unpacking, turning the conversation to other subjects. They talked of the people Priscilla had known in Corinth, of business conditions, of the new fashions in Rome. The afternoon passed pleasantly but as the sun got lower in the western sky, Priscilla started becoming more and more apprehensive.

"It's not like Aquila to be gone so long," she volunteered.

"I'm afraid the news Rufus has for us must be serious indeed. If your Castor is involved, and from what you've said, I'm afraid he is, then it may fall to you to solve the problem he's brought."

When the sun dipped below the western hills, Priscilla excused herself and went downstairs to supervise the preparation of the family dinner. Phoebe followed her into the hall and then went to Debra's room. The girl was standing at her window watching the sunset when Phoebe entered. Turning around, she asked, "Do you need me, my lady?"

"Yes, dear," Phoebe answered. "Find Polax and have him come to my room." The girl hurried away, and the mistress of the Dolphin retraced her steps to her room at the head of the stairs. She was standing on her balcony watching the Tiber flow toward the sea when the Persian arrived. Her orders came out with an anger that surprised her.

"Polax, I want you to question the kitchen staff and learn where a Christian leader named Rufus lives. Go there and get Castor. If he's not there, find him and bring him to me. I don't want him harmed, but he owes me an explanation, and I intend to have it!"

The Persian grinned with delight and silently backed from the room.

CHAPTER XI

Likewise greet the church that is in their house.

ROMANS 16:5

❧✦❧

FOLLOWING the Roman custom, Priscilla planned dinner for late in the evening. When Aquila hadn't returned by sunset, she suggested that Phoebe relax and take a nap. "He'll want to talk way into the night. You'd better get some rest while you can."

Debra woke Phoebe two hours later to dress for dinner. While the maid was brushing her mistress' hair, she reported on Aquila's arrival.

"He came in right after you lay down. I offered to awaken you, but he wouldn't hear of it."

"Did Aquila seem agitated?" Phoebe asked.

"Oh, yes, my lady. Priscilla told him of your arrival with Marcus, and he immediately led her off to the small parlor and closed the door for privacy." Between brush strokes, Debra giggled and added, "But privacy in a houseful of servants is hard to maintain. Aquila ordered wine and later called for cheese, and still later, Priscilla wanted some fresh fruit."

"Go on," Phoebe urged.

"Well, I was making myself useful in the laundry room just off the kitchen," Debra continued. "And I heard the running report the staff was getting from the parlor."

Phoebe's eyes caught Debra's in the silver mirror. She smiled and said, "I'm surprised at you for listening. But perhaps you'd better tell me what they said."

Slowly drawing the brush through a strand of Phoebe's hair, she answered, "Aquila's very disturbed about your visit. It seems he'd met Captain Castor at the home of a man named Rufus, and there was a meeting of Christian leaders. Castor gave Rufus a letter from Tertius!"

"Did you get any idea what the letter contained?"

"Not all of it," Debra replied, "but enough to know that it warned everyone against Marcus. Aquila believes the centurion was sent to Corinth to learn about Paul's activities among the Gentiles. He fears the emperor is disturbed by the increasing number of Christian conversions in the provincial governments and the army." Debra stopped brushing and came around to Phoebe's side before saying, "He fears the letter we brought from Paul will spread the Gentile poison in Rome."

"Did Aquila call it Gentile poison?"

"That's what the wine steward said," Debra admitted.

This information, coupled with what she'd learned from Priscilla earlier, caused Phoebe great concern. *Could it be,* she wondered, *that Aquila and the other Christian leaders have turned their backs on Gentile conversions for fear of gaining Nero's displeasure?* Were they afraid that large scale Roman conversions would attract undue attention to themselves and thereby endanger the security they'd found in being considered Jewish? Or did they truly feel a man had to become a Jew before he could be accepted by Jesus? The term "Gentile poison" could have sprung from either situation, but Phoebe sensed it resulted more from fear than from religious conviction.

Looking around her at the comfort and elegance of the house, Phoebe could understand Aquila's and Priscilla's hesitance to risk everything for Jesus. She'd seen this attitude before—in Corinth. People had been reluctant to defend their faith in the face of pagan power and scorn. Paul was aware of this, and his demand that every Christian testify for Jesus usually resulted in the controversy that seemed to follow his ministry.

Phoebe wondered if this would always be the case. Was it possible that down through the years men would become so prideful in their own intellects and accomplishments that Jesus' great love would become an embarrassment? Would fear of possible persecution prevent them from testifying to their belief in God? Would they rather have security in their jobs and pagan acceptance than the salvation of their souls?

Debra had finished with her hair and was holding the soft yellow gown she was to wear to dinner. By the time she was dressed, Phoebe had made up her mind as to the course of action she should take. If it were fear of attracting Nero's attention that restrained Aquila and his friends, then she must confront them with Nero's plan to declare himself a god. Would they then be willing to forsake Jesus and worship a false god in order to save their security? She felt sure this would be unacceptable to them. Then an additional comment from the maid brought her up sharply.

"Aquila suspects that Nero is planning some kind of action against all Christians in Rome," Debra continued. "He thinks Marcus escorted us here with Paul's letter, hoping we'd use it to identify them for the emperor."

"Is there anything else I should know?" Phoebe asked.

"Just one thing," Debra replied. "Priscilla told him that you planned on giving him the letter. He's going to accept it and sit on it. That way, according to the steward, Paul's letter will do no harm."

Phoebe was fighting back frustration and anger when Priscilla stuck her head through the doorway and announced dinner. As Phoebe followed her hostess downstairs, she felt certain that if Paul's letter were to accomplish the results he desired, she'd have to deliver it. She was now sure that Aquila would never read it to Nero or anyone else if it meant risking the security and prosperity they'd gained on returning to Rome.

Coming downstairs, Phoebe overheard the remembered, almost musical voice of Aquila. The atrium was lighted from the glow of candles blazing in the dining room and by a single oil lamp hanging over the staircase. A delicate scent of jasmine blossoms filled the area, and stars twinkled brightly through the opening in the roof over the rain pool. Hearing them on the stairs, Aquila broke off his conversation with the children and rushed to the bottom step. His voice was warm with friendship.

"My dear Phoebe, we've thought of you so often, and you're constantly in our prayers." Extending his arms, he smiled his delight in seeing her.

His lack of pretense was honest, and Phoebe felt truly welcome to his home. Accepting his embrace and a kiss on the cheek, she wondered if the gossip Debra had repeated was accurate. With his hands on her shoulders, holding her at arms' length, he dispelled all doubts.

"Phoebe," he said, eyes serious, "you'd be our most honored guest under any other circumstances, but I've received very disturbing news regarding your visit."

Studying her host, she could tell that his concern was genuine. Aquila seemed much older than she remembered. His gray, wool toga hung loosely on his sparse frame. Deep lines creased his clean-shaven face. In the Roman fashion, he no longer wore a beard. His hair was turning gray, and Phoebe thought that might be the reason for his bare cheeks and chin. The arch of his great nose still reminded her of a swift falcon, and his dark brown eyes still contained the fire and sparkle that inspired men to accept his leadership.

Phoebe felt less tense. "If your news came from Castor, you can be assured that it was delivered with selfish bitterness." Hugging him to her once again, she added, "I bring you and Priscilla warm, personal greetings from Paul."

"And we feel the same about him," Aquila said, taking her arm and leading the way to the dining room.

During dinner, Phoebe brought them up to date on the happenings in Greece. She told them that Paul was on his way to Jerusalem with relief funds and that he planned to have the council confirm his ministry to the Gentiles. At this point Aquila's interest sharpened. He broke into her narrative.

"I'm afraid Paul is due for grave disappointment in that regard. A Gentile must remain a Gentile until he accepts circumcision and keeps the law of Moses. Jesus was a Jew, and His followers must also be Jews."

"Peter would dispute that with you," Phoebe countered. "He baptized Gentiles in Joppa without their first being circumcised."

"But Peter was called to account for that in Jerusalem, and the elders agreed that it was a one-time thing done by God and not by man." Aquila glanced at his wife for confirmation while adding, "If Gentiles are to become Christians, they must become Jews first. And this can happen only through circumcision."

Priscilla nodded in agreement with her husband, then Aquila asked, "Does the letter you bring from Paul deal with this subject?"

"Yes—and other matters as well," Phoebe answered.

"What are your plans for the letter?"

"Paul suggested that I bring it to you, hoping you'd present it to the people of Rome," Phoebe answered. "But Priscilla has told me that you might not accept it."

"Let me read it, and then I'll give you my answer," Aquila said. "If it contains more of an answer than I've heard from Paul before, perhaps I can accept it for delivery." His voice filled with grave concern as he added, "I'm familiar with Paul's letters, and if it contains what I suspect, then I must refuse his request. We love Paul as a brother, and he's done great things for the Lord, but his so-called ministry to the Gentiles isn't one of them."

Getting up from her couch at the table, Phoebe said, "I'll get the letter. I want you both to read it with the understanding that it must be presented to Nero." Turning to leave the dining room, Phoebe was stopped at the doorway by Aquila's incredulous tone of voice.

"Phoebe, you can't be serious! Does Paul expect the emperor to read it?"

Phoebe glanced back, smiling softly. "Yes, and so do I.

136

We've both received confirmation from our Lord that it's His intention also."

Going to her room, Phoebe got one of the copies from the bottom of her chest. Holding it in her hands, she paused a moment to pray that God would give Aquila an understanding and receptive mind. Her heart was beating faster when she came back down the stairs. Giving the letter to Aquila, she volunteered to put their children to bed so that he and Priscilla could give their full attention to its reading. Phoebe watched her host and hostess leave the dining room, cross the atrium and enter the library before she led the two youngsters upstairs. Debra joined her from the kitchen, and together they entertained the children with their adventures in the Strait of Messina until their young eyes became heavy with sleep.

Returning to her own room, Phoebe waited until well past midnight for Aquila and Priscilla to come upstairs. When they didn't appear, she finally decided it would be best to talk in the morning and retired. She was awake in bed with her candles extinguished when she heard the couple come upstairs, quietly pass her closed door and go on toward their own suite at the north end of the hall. The night and its silence closed in around her and she slept.

Aquila was taking his breakfast at a table in the peristyle garden when Phoebe came down the next morning. Ready for a day of business at his leather tannery, he was dressed in a coarse, brown chiton and heavy leather half-boots. Paul's letter was in front of him, rolled up, tightly closed.

Phoebe had put on a simple rose-colored tunic and open Greek sandals with woven hemp soles. Her dark hair was braided on both sides and looped to the crown of her head. She was feeling apprehensive as she walked toward him.

"Good morning, Phoebe. Did you sleep well?" Indicating a chair across from him, he rang a tiny bell beside his plate. A servant appeared before she was completely seated.

"Sleep was no problem for me," she replied. "But did you rest well after reading Paul's message?"

He waited for Phoebe to order her breakfast of juice, sliced

137

leg of mutton and scrambled eggs before he answered. "I read the letter, and so did Priscilla," he paused until the servant was out of sight, "and we've concluded that it's not in our best interests."

"Why not?" she asked.

"Until the council in Jerusalem confirms Paul's teaching on Gentile conversion and we're so informed, I can't be party to its distribution and reading before the Christian groups here in Rome." Aquila's face grew graver. "And your suggestion last night that Nero should read it is sheer madness." He leaned across the table in concern. "The letter will not only anger a majority of Jews, but the emperor will see it as a condemnation of his own life style."

"How does it condemn the emperor?"

Unrolling the scroll to a place just after Paul's opening salutation, Aquila started reading. "Professing themselves to be wise, they became fools, and changed the glory of the uncorruptible God into the image made like to corruptible man, and to birds, and four-footed beasts and creeping things. Wherefore God also gave them up to uncleanness through the lusts of their own hearts, to dishonor their own bodies between themselves: who changed the truth of God into a lie and worshiped and served the creature more than the Creator, who is blessed forever."

Looking up from the scroll, Aquila slowly shook his head and ruefully smiled. "That's a pretty accurate description of Nero and the pagan gods he worships," he said. "The emperor will recognize the image, and if he doesn't, Paul gets even more personal further on. Even though Paul used the plural, Nero will know it's meant for him." Looking back at the scroll, where his finger had kept his place, Aquila started reading again.

"For this cause God gave them up unto vile affections: for even their women did change the natural use into that which is against nature: And likewise also the men, leaving the natural use of women, burned in their lust one toward another; men with men working that which is unseemly, and receiving in themselves that recompense of their error which is meet." He shook his head gravely.

Aquila was silent while Phoebe's breakfast was served. When they were once again alone, he said, "That summary of moral corruption is a direct indictment of Nero and the moral tone he has set for Rome. Anyone reading such a statement to the emperor and the conclusion Paul has drawn, will suffer a death too horrible to describe." Rerolling the scroll, Aquila leaned back in his chair and added, "I'll accept delivery of this letter, Phoebe, but I must hold it until we hear from Jerusalem and until we've been here in Rome long enough to be certain of our continued welcome." Picking up the closed scroll, he placed it in his lap.

Watching the scroll disappear below the top of the table, Phoebe took a deep breath. "I'm afraid I can't accept that decision," she said. "The reason for Paul's letter still exists. Paul, Marcus and I have committed ourselves to seeing that the letter is presented and understood *now*." Her eyes never left his as she continued. "This life and home which you value so highly will be in total jeopardy in just 13 days. You'll be offered the choice of worshiping Caesar or worshiping God. If you choose the wrong one, your home may be secure, but your soul could be lost!"

The expression on Aquila's face changed from solemn assurance to amusement. Bowing his head slightly, he murmured, "Castor told us you'd present some such reason, but even Tertius didn't suggest such a far-fetched idea. Nero will never proclaim himself a god. Caligula made that mistake, and Nero's too smart to repeat it." Straightening his head and shoulders, Aquila declared, "I'm afraid you and Paul have been taken in by the centurion. If Paul's letter were read today, it would expose most of the Christian leaders in Rome to imperial persecution."

"What persecution are you expecting?" Phoebe asked.

"The persecution that would follow Paul's condemnation of Nero," he answered.

"How would the leaders be exposed?"

139

"Paul saluted almost all of us in the letter," Aquila replied.

Looking up into the brilliant morning sky, Phoebe quietly thanked the Lord for the inspiration which led Paul to send greetings to so many people. This was her key to gaining Aquila's support. "I think you should know," she said, "that an exact copy of this letter is already being read in the major cities south of Rome."

"It's what?" Aquila rose out of his chair in consternation.

Thinking back on their visit to Tarracina, Phoebe marveled at how the Holy Spirit had guided her to the Urbanus family and had inspired some unknown Christian to scratch the icthus that caught her eye on the mile marker. As Aquila bent to pick up the letter that had fallen to the patio floor, she leaned forward. "By now several copies of the letter are in circulation. I wouldn't be surprised if one wasn't on its way to Rome in an imperial dispatch bag."

Aquila's reaction surprised her. Collecting his composure, he sat back down at the table. "I'd already assumed that was the case when the centurion brought you here," he said evenly. "He surely must have kept a copy for the imperial files."

"If that's what you thought, then why oppose its presentation to the people?" Phoebe questioned.

"Having it reported privately to the emperor without it being received by the people is one thing. We could live with that. But having it read in several cities is quite another problem." Laying the letter on the table, he added, "If the centurion is such a good Christian, then he is the one to read it to the people of Rome!"

"No, Aquila," Phoebe flatly stated, "I intend to claim that honor." She smiled as amusement again entered his expression. Holding up her hand to stop his expected remark, she declared, "I presented the letter in Tarracina, and I'll do it here."

"Phoebe, why expose yourself to that? The Christians in Rome won't listen to you. They're Jews and you're a woman! Can't you see it? The centurion knew you'd be ineffective as a teacher; that's why he convinced Paul to send you. All you'll accomplish is the exposure of the brothers."

"Then you must do it."

"No, and that's final!" Aquila exclaimed.

"Can't you understand?" Phoebe pleaded. "The only hope you have of saving yourself and the others is with a large-scale conversion of Gentiles to the faith. Just the threat of it will stop Nero from proclaiming himself a god."

She told him how Marcus had been sent to Corinth to drive Paul to Rome. He shook his head in disbelief. Her explanation of how Poppaea was being influenced by the Sanhedrin created additional head shaking. He was impassive when Phoebe told of the danger Marcus was facing. His head shaking ceased as she told of how Castor had tried to kill Marcus. When she explained how Tertius had disbelieved Marcus' conversion, his reaction was strong. "Without circumcision, he's not a true believer! He hasn't made the irrevocable commitment. He can still turn away from Jesus."

"Can't you do the same thing?" Phoebe asked, emotion surging through her. "Can't you still deny Jesus as the majority of Jews have done? Is your circumcision a sign of Christian commitment? Are you still a Jew like those in the Sanhedrin? Aquila, think about it. Are you a Jew at all?"

Phoebe picked up the letter from the table. Tears glistened in her eyes. "I'll present Paul's letter to the people, Aquila, but I'm asking you to help set up the meetings. I'm going up to my room, and I'll expect your answer within the hour. If you still feel you can't help me, I'll leave your house so as not to cause you any further embarrassment."

Once inside her room, she broke down, then knelt and prayed. "Why, Lord, did I have to be so emotional in front of Aquila? That will just confirm his opinion that women are too weak to take any responsibility in matters of faith." She asked God to give Aquila a sign that would convince him that Paul's letter was within His will. She pleaded forgiveness for herself if she had overstepped the authority of the ministry she'd been given.

Phoebe was about to call for Debra to start packing when the girl breathlessly burst into the room. "There are soldiers in the courtyard!"

"How many?" Phoebe asked.

"Twelve . . . maybe 15," Debra answered. "And their commander is demanding to see you!"

Turning to the mirror, Phoebe quickly checked her hair and wished she were dressed in something finer than her tunic. "Is Julius with them?"

"No," the maid replied. "But someone important is with them; 12 slaves are carrying his chair!"

Rushing from the room, they were halfway down the stairs when they heard Aquila's voice at the front door.

"I'm the master of the house."

A commanding voice asked, "You're Aquila, the leather tanner?"

"Yes. May I be of service?"

"My lord, Seneca, wishes audience with the lady named Phoebe," the commanding voice replied. "Is she here?"

A softer, older voice entered the conversation. "Please excuse the centurion's tone. I'm Seneca, the father of Marcus, and I have urgent news for Phoebe. If she's here, it would greatly please me to meet the lady."

Descending the rest of the stairs, Phoebe stood in the rectangle of brilliant sunlight slanting down through the opening in the atrium roof. The polished yellow tiles of the floor felt warm through the soles of her sandals, and her gleaming black hair seemed edged in gold. She watched Aquila escort the nobleman inside.

Though of medium height, his toga hung on a broad frame. Except for his full head of unruly, graying hair, his face reminded her of Paul. He had the same prominent nose, craggy eyebrows, and his mustache and beard were neatly trimmed. Being Roman, she hadn't expected hair on his face, but then she remembered he was Spanish and supposed that made a difference. The lines on his forehead and at the corners of his dull, brown eyes reflected worry and dissipation. As a whole, his appearance was more that of a worldly scholar than a powerful statesman.

Phoebe acknowledged their introduction with a graceful curtsy and extended her right hand in welcome. Accepting it with his left hand, Seneca seemed to be appraising her. She read approval in his eyes which was confirmed by the gentle tone of his voice and the content of his speech.

"You're truly the beautiful woman Marcus described, and it grieves me to bring the news that I bear. Is there someplace where we can speak alone?"

Aquila suggested the peristyle and ordered refreshments served. When the servant brought wine and thin slices of cheese, Phoebe dismissed him and served Seneca herself. The nobleman watched her with kindly eyes, and when she joined him on a long marble bench in an alcove of lacy ferns, he finally spoke.

"My dear Phoebe, Marcus has told me of his love for you and your love for him." Smiling in a fatherly way, he added, "You know, of course, that he plans asking you to marry him once he's free of his current problems?"

"That, too, is my hope," Phoebe replied. "But you spoke of news?"

"Now that I've met you," he murmured, "I want you to know that I approve of his choice in a possible bride. You both have my support and affectior " He paused to sip his wine. "Marcus has been arrested, strippe of h rank and charged with treason."

Feeling faint, Phoebe shakily placed her wine goblet on the bench and steadied herself with both hands. A whisper was all she could manage.

"How could he be charged with treason for what he's done?"

"Nero terms his failure as treason," Seneca answered. "And that exaggerated charge, made in anger, may save him."

Phoebe took a deep breath. "Where is he now? Can I see him?" Closing her eyes, she waited for his answer.

"He's been turned over to the guard and is being held a prisoner in the Praetorian barracks at the Campus Martius." She felt Seneca's hand gently pat her shoulder. "As a last resort, we might be able to arrange Marcus' escape, but that entails great risk to the lives of the men guarding him. I'm not sure Marcus will accept their sacrifice."

Phoebe opened her eyes and saw deep concern on the man's face. Tears streamed down her cheeks, and he smiled, trying to reassure her.

"In answer to your second question," he added. "Under the charge of treason, it wouldn't be wise for you to see him. Nero is prone to consider a traitor's visitors as being part of the plot, and you could be arrested as well."

"Is there anything I can do?" she asked.

Seneca's eyebrows knitted together in question as he said, "You can do nothing for Marcus, but he did ask me to tell you this: if you've concluded your business in Rome, he wants you to wait for him at your ship in Puteoli."

"But I can't," she sobbed. "My job here isn't finished."

"What kind of job?" he asked. "Perhaps I can have it done for you."

Taking a firm grip on her emotions, Phoebe pulled herself together. His question told her that Marcus had made no mention of Paul's letter. Knowing there must be a reason for this omission, she didn't feel free to tell Seneca of it. Looking him directly in the eyes, she softly answered, "I may be able to complete my business in the next few days. How soon can we expect to know Marcus' fate?"

"The longer it takes, the better," Seneca replied. "If the heat of Nero's anger subsides before he's forced to consider the case, we may be able to save him."

"How can it be delayed with Poppaea taking such an interest in Paul's affairs?"

Seneca's eyes searched her face with fresh interest. "You know of Poppaea's activities?" he questioned with some surprise.

She nodded and sipped her wine.

"Then you understand the reason for Marcus' journey to Corinth?"

Again she nodded.

"Then you'll understand me when I say that Marcus has served the empire by what he's done." He observed her nodded reply and continued. "Burrus and I have failed to turn the lady away from her goal. The emperor is still planning his proclamation of divinity. This may overshadow Marcus' immediate danger, but his execution could become part of the ceremony."

Phoebe gasped at the matter-of-fact way Seneca spoke of his adopted son's possible death. She heard a subdued feminine reaction come from the library behind her. Either Debra or Priscilla was evesdropping, and she searched Seneca's face to see if he'd heard it too. There was no reaction, and the counselor continued talking.

"I will divert the emperor's attention away from Marcus with affairs of state. As I said, Nero was angry when he ordered the arrest. I'll do everything in my power to help Marcus, but it will take time." Seneca grimaced and added, "If all else fails, I'm certain the emperor's attention can be diverted by a requested performance of his poems."

"It all seems so childish," Phoebe remarked.

"Believe me, my dear, it isn't," Seneca observed as he finished his wine. "Nero isn't accustomed to disappointment at having his desires fulfilled. He wanted Paul either dead or brought to him in Rome. Marcus failed to do either. So far, Poppaea doesn't know what's happened, and I think this news can be kept from her. But the emperor still intends to become a god. Paul or anyone else teaching the contrary will be killed." He stood and poured more wine for himself. "When Marcus told Nero that Paul was still alive, the imperial rage was monumental. If the heat of it lasts, Marcus can't be saved."

"Perhaps I could plead for the emperor's mercy," Phoebe volunteered.

Almost spilling his wine, Seneca bitterly laughed. "Nothing would please Nero more. He loves having beautiful women beg for his mercy. He'd ravish you in front of Marcus and then give you to his slaves for their enjoyment. Marcus told me you were a Christian and had converted him. Nero would make an example of you both if you refused to worship him."

"Knowing this," Phoebe asked, "why did you let Marcus go before the emperor?"

Seneca's shoulders drooped as he answered, "It couldn't be helped. Nero was at my villa when Marcus arrived. My son was given a hero's welcome until he confessed his failure."

"When did Marcus tell you about us?"

"This morning," Seneca answered, "when I visited him in prison." He settled once more beside her on the bench. "Nero knows nothing of your connection with Marcus or that you're in Rome. Do nothing that will attract his attention. Finish your business here and go back to your ship. If Marcus can be saved, I'll send him to you. Otherwise, I'll send word of his death." Patting her hand, he concluded, "I wish it could be different. You'd be a lovely addition to the family, but I'm afraid the gods are against us."

He got up and said good-by, asking her not to come to the door with him. Watching him walk away, she knew he loved Marcus but was actually powerless to help him beyond a possible arranged escape. Phoebe quickly stepped to the library door, surprising Aquila and Priscilla who had been standing there. Both blushed at being caught listening to the conversation between her and Seneca. But Aquila's reaction made Phoebe glad they'd heard what was said.

"Rufus must be told at once that Castor's report is a lie!" he exclaimed. Stepping toward Phoebe, he took both her hands in his and added, "The letter Tertius wrote is wrong and that too must be made clear to everyone." As tears filled his eyes, Phoebe squeezed his hands in forgiveness.

"Has your opinion of Paul's letter also changed?" she asked.

"Yes, Phoebe," he confessed. "I still disagree with Paul on the conversion of the Gentiles, but in view of Nero's plans, I think the Christians in Rome should hear it." He looked down at his feet. "But I can't do it. You'll have to read it. I'll help arrange everything, but the rest is up to you. We'll send messengers out today, telling the people when to expect you, and I'll call my own church together for a meeting tonight."

Phoebe embraced him as Priscilla, wiping her eyes, said,

"Please forgive us, and let's pray for the safe return of Marcus. I'm ashamed of the attitude I displayed yesterday." As Phoebe hugged her friend, she marveled at the way God achieved His purposes.

CHAPTER XII

For there is no difference between the Jew and the Greek:
for the same Lord over all is rich unto all that call
upon Him.

ROMANS 10:12

SENECA'S visit accomplished several things, and Phoebe was
grateful that he'd come in person. She was now painfully aware
of what Marcus faced, and sitting alone in her room, she allowed her tears to flow unrestrained. It was conceivable, she
admitted to herself, that she'd never see him again. Having
come upstairs to prepare herself for the meeting of Aquila's
church, Phoebe couldn't push Marcus from her mind to con-
centrate on Paul's letter.

Aquila had been true to his word. Messengers were being
sent throughout the city announcing her arrival in Rome and
requesting invitations from each group for the reading of Paul's
message. He, himself, had gone to tell Rufus what Seneca
had said. Priscilla, extremely solicitous, was planning a special
dinner before the meeting so that Phoebe could meet the key
elders and gain their support for a teaching by a woman. Aquila
had suggested it, saying, "If they understand she's merely reading a letter from Paul, they may listen. Otherwise, they'll be
very rude and demand her silence."

The absence of Marcus concerned her for this reason too.
He had paved the way for her in Tarracina, but tonight she
would be on her own. This thought brought her out of her

melancholy. If she failed in her delivery, she'd be failing him as well as Paul and God. After an hour of studying Paul's phrasing, Phoebe was interrupted by an urgent knocking on her door. Then it opened and Debra burst into the room.

"Polax is in the kitchen with Castor!" she exclaimed.

Following the girl downstairs, Phoebe entered the kitchen with anger growing in her heart. The sea captain was standing in the center of the room before hostile eyes glaring from every direction. His clothes were torn; there was dirt and blood on his right cheek. Polax was right behind him with a large hand gripping his shoulder. Phoebe stopped just inside the door.

"I requested that he not be hurt."

Shifting from one foot to the other, Polax innocently observed, "He's not hurt; he's just been convinced that he should be here."

Phoebe's anger left her as she tried to hide a smile. Stepping forward, Phoebe stood grimly in front of her ex-captain.

"You have lied about Marcus and me. Your lies have caused great damage to the message I brought here from Paul. I suspect that it was you who got Tertius to write the letter that you carried. I want that letter."

Polax interrupted. "I'm sorry, my lady, but we lost Tertius' letter while we were discussing Castor's need to see you. It fell in the Tiber and floated away."

"That must have been some discussion," Phoebe dryly observed. She turned her attention back to Castor.

"You attempted to kill Marcus on the voyage to Syracuse. You're also a liar and a thief," Phoebe said. "You leave me no choice but to turn you over to the authorities."

"When did I lie?" he demanded. "And how can you call me a thief? I've stolen nothing from you." He glared at her, trying to regain some of his composure. "I told Rufus and the others that Marcus was a false Christian. In his letter, Tertius said the same thing. We warned them not to trust the centurion. We pointed out that he wore the emperor's medallion and was sent to Corinth to find Paul. I tried to warn both you and Paul of the danger he represented, but you wouldn't heed me. How could a centurion of Rome, favored by the emperor and the adopted son of the powerful Seneca, become a simple Christian?"

And now Castor's voice took on a plaintive tone. "How could you choose him over me when my loyalty was above question, and his was doubtful?" He turned and glared at Polax as he continued. "What right did you have in sending a thief after me to stop my witness against such a dangerous man?"

Castor's outburst gave Phoebe most of the answers she required. Just one question remained. "Did you convince Tertius he should write his letter?"

"Yes," he proudly declared. "In fact, I dictated it for him to sign."

Phoebe caught his eyes and held them. "You've betrayed the trust I placed in you as one of my captains. You've attempted to commit murder. You've been a false witness against a fellow Christian. You're a thief and a liar. Marcus is in prison under the charge of treason because he refused to kill Paul." Looking at Priscilla, she asked, "Can we hold Castor prisoner here until the meeting tonight? I want him to give his witness before I read Paul's letter. We'll turn him over to the Roman authorities in the morning on the charge of stealing a horse—which he did on his way to Rome."

Priscilla nodded her head. "Place him in the cellar. See that he has food and water."

Looking at Polax, Phoebe asked, "Will you guard him?"

"With pleasure," the Persian grinned.

As she went back upstairs with Priscilla beside her, her friend confessed: "Castor's attitude reflects a great deal of my own attitude when you first arrived, Phoebe." She stopped on the stairs and put her hand on Phoebe's arm. Her eyes were moist. "I was impressed with Marcus' position and the powerful prospects his favor with the emperor and his father seemed to represent. The fact that he might love God more than all these things never occurred to me. Is it possible that Aquila and I have allowed false values to cloud our faith in the Lord? Have we become possessed by the things we've acquired?"

Priscilla continued up the stairs. "Please forgive me, Phoebe, but when you arrived I couldn't believe that you and Marcus would risk your lives and the wealth you both represent for the sake of Paul's letter."

"Of course I forgive you," Phoebe replied. "You and Aquila have known great tribulation, and the peace you've achieved here has become important to you. Now, Priscilla, please pray that God will find a way for me to read Paul's letter to Nero."

"Phoebe, are you serious? Do you really intend reading that letter to Nero?"

Nodding her head, Phoebe turned and started to her room.

Priscilla quickly followed her. "Phoebe, but you can't! God can't expect a woman to carry such a burden."

"Nevertheless, He does," Phoebe replied. "And so does Paul. I think it's our only hope of stopping the emperor's proclamation of divinity. Somehow God's words may touch him. If he's not stopped, none of our lives or possessions will be safe. He'll demand that we worship him and deny Jesus or die. You heard what Seneca said." Turning, she gripped her friend's hand. "Pray with me, Priscilla, for the safe return of Marcus and the guidance of the Holy Spirit with Nero."

In addition to Phoebe there were four other guests that evening at dinner. She was placed on the couch to the right of Aquila with Andronicus and his wife, Junia, who were both greeted in Paul's letter. Andronicus was of extreme age. His head was totally bald and his eyebrows were snow white. Most of his teeth were gone, but the timbre of his voice was strong, as was his appetite. Junia was somewhat younger, but her hair, too, was white. She was silent in the tradition of Jewish women and spoke only when directly addressed. They both wore the traditional toga and stola of the older Roman generation.

Priscilla was reclining on the couch across the low table

151

from Phoebe. She was wearing a white silk gown, simply tailored to display her classic neck and shoulders. Her auburn hair was piled high and held in place by carved-bone combs. Beside her was Rufus, also mentioned in Paul's letter. He was younger than Aquila, and his wife, Marian, was a beautiful woman with long, shining blonde hair. Her gown was dark blue, cut in the style of an abbreviated stola. The aquamarine necklace she wore matched her eyes. Rufus' toga was white, and his handsome face carried a scar below his left eye. His almost black hair was in keeping with his Semitic birth and background.

Both men were elders in different Christian groups in Rome. They were Jewish and typical of Roman church leadership. Andronicus had been on the portico in Jerusalem on the day of Pentecost. He knew Peter, James, John, Andrew, Philip, Thomas, Bartholomew and Matthew. His ministry had been confirmed by the apostles. Rufus was the son of Simon, the man who carried Jesus' cross to Calvary. Both men had seen Jesus and called Him Lord. Their willingness to allow a woman to teach would silence all protest from the others. Phoebe knew that she had to make it clear to them that she didn't consider herself an elder or a deaconess or a presbyter of the church. She had to impress them with the fact that she was only a servant of God, sent to Rome by Paul with his inspired letter.

Phoebe had dressed simply in a gown of pale blue linen trimmed with white piping at the edges of the high collar. Her hair was parted at the crown of her head and combed long to her shoulders. The only jewelry she wore was the cross Gaius had given her.

The candlelight flickered softly as the dinner was consumed amid casual conversation. When the dessert of honeyed rhubarb pastry was served with brimming goblets of cherry wine, the conversation died and all eyes turned to Phoebe. She sipped the wine, took a bite of the pastry and put down her fork.

"As you all know," she started, feeling her heart pound and her throat tighten, "I've come to Rome with a letter from

Paul. Feeling that it is the inspired word of God, Paul has sent it to you with the hope and prayer that it will deter Nero from proclaiming himself a god."

They nodded their understanding.

Feeling a bit encouraged, she continued. "Paul asked me to bring the letter to Aquila for presentation to all the groups in Rome, but he feels he can't . . ."

Andronicus held up his hand and interrupted her. "We all understand Aquila's feeling regarding circumcision," he said in his heavy, rich voice. "I know of Paul's teachings and agree with them, but I'm only one man. The point we must decide now regards your status as a teacher. As a woman you have no authority over men. You're commanded to silence."

Phoebe felt stricken as he continued, his voice quivering with emotion: "The Lord, our God, has proclaimed that woman shall be submitted to man, and he shall rule over her. Eve led Adam to the tree of knowledge and enticed him to eat the forbidden fruit. She was in transgression, not he! His sin is on her and by his sin we are all sinners." He looked at Phoebe and asked, "How can you justify standing before men and speaking the word of God?"

The room was still. Phoebe took a deep prayerful breath. "God created man in His own image," she began. "He created man as both male and female. When God created Eve, He took the female out of man and in doing this, He made both male and female incomplete in the likeness of God. By God's own command, we can now only approach the completeness of God by cleaving one to the other as man and wife. We are equal in the eyes of God."

She stopped and looked at Andronicus. He nodded his acceptance of her argument at this point, and Phoebe pushed on.

"Eve's transgression caused the fall of man, and by Adam's sin we were all made sinners. Yet by the sacrifice and the righteousness of Jesus we've been forgiven of Adam's sin. Jesus treated women as they were originally intended to be—as sisters. We are His servants, the same as you. I don't claim to

153

be an elder or a presbyter." Observing their nods of approval, she continued. "During His earthly ministry, if Jesus had wanted women to be ministers over men, He would have called them to that purpose."

Again they nodded their approval.

"Jesus did, however, use women and give them ministries." Their eyebrows arched at this statement, but Phoebe went on. "He sent Mary Magdalene to the apostles with the message of His resurrection." The eyebrows came down. "He accepted the service of Martha and the anointing of Mary." Rufus nodded his head. "His disciples marveled that He talked to the woman of Samaria. Yet Jesus spoke to her of Himself so she could give witness of His coming. Jesus proclaimed the equality of us all when He said, 'For whosoever shall do the will of My Father which is in heaven, the same is My brother, and sister, and mother.'" She halted for a moment and looked at each of the men present. "Are you going to deny me that kinship with our Lord?"

The three men were silent as Phoebe gazed on each face at the table. Tears of love for her were streaming down Priscilla's cheeks. Marian's eyes were pleading with those of Rufus. Junia's face reflected joy and approval of what she'd said.

Andronicus broke the silence. His voice rumbled with emotion. "Tonight I have been taught by a woman. What she has said is true. From this day forward, when I worship, Junia will worship beside me."

Silently thanking God, Phoebe asked, "Then will you allow me to read Paul's letter?"

Being the oldest among them, Andronicus spoke for all. "Yes, Phoebe, and I will teach the people what you have taught us before you address them."

Prayer and discussion followed. Priscilla suggested and received Aquila's approval to gather together small groups of Christian women so they could begin receiving regular instruction in the principles of faith. "If women know the word of God, they will not be consumed with idle chatter in church," she observed. "They'll know when it's proper to speak and when they should remain silent."

Andronicus and Rufus agreed and proposed that this instruction be given by the elders. Sensing an additional victory, Phoebe added, "When you've heard Paul's letter, you will see how it can be used for such instruction. It outlines our faith and will assure everyone of receiving knowledge given by the Holy Spirit."

"Having read the letter," Aquila declared, "I can see the teaching value of such a document, but we must first accept all that Paul has written."

Chuckling to himself, Andronicus observed, "My dear brother, when you consider the limited success we've had in converting the Jews and compare it with Paul's success in converting Gentiles, can you still claim Paul is wrong?"

"That may be," Aquila countered, "but Jesus was a Jew."

Phoebe could have kissed Priscilla when she said, "But, darling, wasn't He first a man?"

Startled by her question, Aquila turned to his wife and answered, "But Mary, His mother, was Jewish. She's from the line of David."

"Aquila, by your own definition," Andronicus interceded, "Jesus didn't become a Jew until He was circumcised in the temple on His eighth day. Would He have been any less the Son of God had He not been circumcised?"

Excitement showed in Rufus' face as he held up his hand to gain their attention. "I recall something my father told me." He paused. "Let me remember his exact words. When they took Jesus to the temple that day, Mary and Joseph met a man named Simeon. This man was filled with the Holy Spirit and knew that he would not see death until he'd seen the Lord's Christ."

"Yes, go on," Andronicus said.

"Simeon took Jesus in his arms and said, 'Lord, now let Your servant depart in peace, according to Your word: for my eyes have seen Your salvation, which You have prepared before the face of all people; a light to lighten the Gentiles, and the glory of Your people Israel.' All this happened," Rufus excitedly added, "before the circumcision!"

Junia broke her silence. "We must sound like Pharisees, splitting hairs over a point of law. The words of Jesus, which Phoebe spoke just a few minutes ago, are all the answer any of us should need." Turning to Phoebe, she requested, "Say them again."

Making eye contact with each of them before she spoke, Phoebe repeated the Lord's words. " 'For whosoever shall do the will of My Father which is in heaven, the same is My brother, and sister, and mother.' "

"So be it!" Aquila declared. "I'm submitted to Jesus. His will is my will. I bow before the Lord. Let the will of God be done on earth as it is in heaven!"

Phoebe never dreamed her prayers would be answered so completely and so fast. Again she yearned for Marcus to be there as she followed Priscilla and the other ladies across the atrium and upstairs to refresh themselves before the full meeting started. Once inside the room, Marian threw herself on Phoebe's bed and giggled with glee. When her laughter subsided, she happily proclaimed, "Now I know how Joshua felt when the walls came tumbling down!"

The full meeting was held in the atrium, with benches arranged on both sides of the rain pool, facing a table set up in front of the archway to the peristyle. Coming downstairs with Paul's letter under her arm, Phoebe found the women all sitting to one side and the men on the other. The smile Andronicus flashed her indicated that this would change. It wasn't a large group; there were only about 30 people present. Standing at the foot of the stairs, Phoebe watched several men go up to Aquila at the head table and whisper in his ear. His expression darkened as each man made his report.

Calling the meeting to order with a general prayer, he introduced Andronicus for his teaching. While the older man was giving witness to what Phoebe had taught him, Aquila walked back to where she was standing.

"All the other groups, except for those of Andronicus and Rufus, have refused to listen to Paul's letter," he whispered, "But I think I have a solution. Tonight's dinner worked so well, I think we should invite all the other leaders here tomorrow night. Andronicus and Rufus will join us, and you can repeat your teaching."

This appealed to Phoebe. She had enough copies of the letter to provide each leader with one of his own. It would be the fastest way to cover them. Then only Nero would remain. She didn't have time to think about this because Andronicus was calling her forward while many of the men and women were changing sites in their seating. Asking Aquila to go and bring in Polax and Castor, she walked briskly to the front of the room. Smiling faces greeted her as she faced the crowd. Bowing her head, she prayed.

"Dear Father, may the lips of my mouth speak and read the words of the Holy Spirit for Your everlasting glory and the blessing of Your Son, my Lord Jesus. Amen."

Searching the crowd, Phoebe found two faces that she would speak to; by gauging their reactions she would temper her response accordingly. She selected a young girl sitting beside her father on the left. The second face was that of Andronicus, sitting on her right with Junia beside him.

"Our Lord Jesus is here tonight, walking among us with His gentle touch of love," she began. Pointing to a man sitting alone in the back, she softly proclaimed, "I see Him there in that man's face." Her moving gaze settled on a pregnant woman in the front row. "And He's here in this woman's eyes, nurturing her unborn child."

From the corner of her eyes, she caught sight of Aquila, Polax and Castor standing in the doorway on her right. The ex-captain was downcast and staring at the floor. Her heart suddenly overflowed with compassion for Castor.

Phoebe told the people how Marcus, wearing the emperor's medallion, had come to Corinth searching for Paul. She told them of his purpose and how God had changed the centurion. Explaining briefly how, in the interest of secrecy, Paul had

157

chosen her as his messenger, she related why the teacher had written his letter. When she described how the love between her and Marcus had grown, the women leaned forward with quickened interest. Castor's expression darkened with bitterness.

Her story of the voyage caught the imagination of everyone. When the attempted murder of the Roman brought gasps, Phoebe motioned Polax and Castor forward. Her voice contained no anger, no harshness and no judgement when she said, "And this is the captain I trusted with our safety." Polax pushed Castor to the front and stepped back. "I want you to hear his witness, keeping in mind that all things can serve our Lord."

Castor's testimony was reasonably accurate, though self-justifying. When he was finished, Phoebe extracted a promise from him that he would pay for the horse he had stolen. Then she forgave him for the damage he'd done to her and pointed over the gathering to the villa's front door, saying, "You're free. Go in peace. You say you're a follower of Jesus Christ. Be true to Him."

Surprise filled Castor's face, and he bowed to her, offering thanks as he sidled through the crowd toward the door. Polax groaned in disappointment but became silent under Phoebe's disapproving frown. The Greek stopped at the door after swinging it open. The darkness of the night framed him and the flickering candlelight added shadows to his face. Silently, he searched every face and then slipped into the gloom without saying another word. The lone man at the back quietly closed the door.

The girl sitting with her father was weeping. Andronicus solemnly approved what she'd done. Polax stiffly joined Aquila in the kitchen doorway. All eyes were on Phoebe. Taking the scroll from under her arm, she unrolled it and started reading.

"Paul, a servant of Jesus Christ, called to be an apostle, separated unto the gospel of God." Phoebe's voice was filled with the reverent love of the Holy Spirit. Glancing up from time to time, she saw understanding in the girl's face. Andronicus was attentive and occasionally nodded his approval.

"For I am not ashamed of the gospel of Christ," she read, "for it is the power of God unto salvation to every one that believes; to the Jew first, and also to the Greek."

Phoebe could feel the words come alive in her hands. She saw a smile form on the lips of the girl when she read, "But he is a Jew; and circumcision is that of the heart, in the spirit, and not in the letter of the law; whose praise is not of men, but of God."

Andronicus glanced at Aquila. His eyes reflected the love the old man had for his friend. Then they nodded in agreement as Phoebe read, "For the promise, that he should be the heir of the world, was not to Abraham, or to his seed, through the law, but through the righteousness of faith."

Faces lit up with joy as Phoebe voiced Paul's confirming words relating to the lifting of Adam's sin. "For as by one man's disobedience many were made sinners, so by the obedience of one shall many be made righteous."

That joy grew as she read, "For the wages of sin is death; but the gift of God is eternal life through Jesus Christ our Lord."

The living word of God filled the room, flowed into hearts, permeated the air and seemed to drip from the ceiling into their open ears.

Gladness entered her voice as she read, "I beseech you therefore, brethren, by the mercies of God that you present your bodies a living sacrifice, holy, acceptable unto God, which is your reasonable service. And be not conformed to this world; but be transformed by the renewing of your mind, that you may prove what is that good, and acceptable, and perfect, will of God."

The time it took Phoebe to complete the letter seemed to pass swiftly. When she was finished, the young girl's bright hazel eyes were glowing with new understanding. Andronicus got up and came to the head table with his arms outstretched in the love of God. Taking Phoebe's hand, he led her through the crowd and introduced her to each person while Aquila prepared for the breaking of bread. She was accepted as one of them, and the people clustered around her. Priscilla told them of Phoebe's fleet and how she managed the business her husband had left her. Rufus, Marian and Junia made room for her to sit with them beside Andronicus.

At the beginning of the sacramental service, Aquila gave special prayers of thanks to God for Paul's letter and then asked them all to pray for the release of Marcus. The joy Phoebe felt when it was all over was only dampened by Polax who came to her and quietly said, "It was a mistake to let Castor go. If he tells the Roman authorities of your connection with Marcus, you'll find yourself dancing to Nero's drum."

CHAPTER XIII

Professing themselves to be wise, they became fools . . .

ROMANS 1:22

STANDING high above the city at the peak of the Imperial Palace, Nero Lucius Domitius Ahenobarbus, Emperor of Rome, proudly looked down upon his domain. The low, morning sun edged Rome in contrasting blocks of deep, gray shadows and brilliant, reflective, stone planes. The sense of his magnificence became almost overwhelming. He not only ruled these people, he was a colossus of infinite power astride the lives of the stirring multitude below. Allowing his bulging, pale eyes to sweep the complete horizon, it gave him a sense of pleasure to think that every living soul in the empire breathed for his glory.

The palace beneath him was a source of irritation. He didn't feel it represented his true greatness. Lesser kings lived in grander surroundings. *Someday,* he thought to himself, *I'll build a golden palace worthy of me.* Looking down the northeastern slope of the Palatine, Nero's gaze raked across the ancient Forum. He noted the newer Forum, built by Julius Caesar, and the one beyond it, built by Augustus. As his eyes swept the columned halls of the Roman Senate, he laughed contemptuously. "Their seat of power is constructed over an old swamp. Mine rests at the crest of the city, nearer the abode of the gods."

Looking down at the temples below him, his thoughts ranged from the divine Julius to the deified Augustus. His mother, Agrippina, was the great-grandaughter of Augustus and sister of the Emperor Caligula. Nero smiled as he remembered the stories of how she had shared the incestuous bed of love with her brother. His smile broadened when he considered how Caligula had enjoyed the intimacies of both his mother and grandmother.

Stirred by a breeze, Nero's deep purple, silk toga caressed the naked flesh beneath it. The soft touch heightened the sensuous thoughts his active brain had conceived. He turned away from the view and slowly walked across the balcony. Pausing halfway to the guarded staircase, he waved aside the soldier's salute and sat down on a pink marble bench.

"I've been the emperor of Rome for two years," he mused bitterly, "and Agrippina still tries to dominate me. It was right for her to divorce my father and marry Uncle Claudius." He chuckled. "And how clever of her to poison old Claudius so that the Praetorian Guard could declare me emperor. But now she expects to rule it with me. Why am I plagued by possessive women? Agrippina had me marry Octavia who is a prude and a bore. Only the beautiful Poppaea understands my needs."

With the thought of Poppaea, Nero's full lips formed a slow smile as he recalled her husband's parting remark when he was ordered to extended duty in the provinces. "It grieves me to leave the fair Poppaea in Rome, Sire. Will you find a use for her?"

"That I have done," Nero murmured sensuously. "But why this consuming interest in Judaism? Why is she so obsessed with having this wandering scholar, Paul, killed? Until Poppaea, I had never thought of Paul and his Christians as any threat to the throne." Then he smiled thoughtfully. "Now she thinks I should follow the example of Caligula and declare myself a god. I think I'm going to like that." But slowly his smile faded. "All I've ever wanted to be is a poet and musician. It's the women in my life who seek other things. Seneca and Burrus can rule in my name, and if I declare myself a god, maybe I can rule the women around me. Britannicus is out of the way and now only the women remain to plague me. Once I'm a god, anything I desire will be considered divine." His eyes sparkled at the thought. "Agrippina can be a priestess and worship her son. Octavia too can worship me, and Poppaea, being older and wiser, can fill the requirements of my flesh and soul."

Running his pudgy fingers through his golden hair, Nero stood and walked back to the balcony rail. His eyes once again rested on the temples below him. In his mind's eye he could already see the temple he'd erect to himself. It would be greater than all the others. His fondness for older women, men and children would no longer have to be justified or explained. What he demanded of them would be considered divine service. Seneca and Burrus could charge people for the privilege of serving their god and emperor. *And best of all,* he thought, *I can devote myself to the arts as is befitting a genius of my talent.*

A concern darkened his dream of divinity. Would all the people accept him as their god? For this reason, he guessed he would have to subvert Paul and his Christians. The Jews would be easy to handle. Their priests could be appointed and they would obey. "I can buy their devotion," he mused. "And if not that, their silence. But the problem of Paul remains. The centurion failed me, and because of Poppaea's fury, he must be punished." *Poppaea is so clever. She says that if I can't get Paul to bow before me, perhaps someone authorized to speak for him could bend the knee in his place.*

His 19-year-old brain whirled with the possibilities of this line of thought. He turned to his bodyguard, standing stiffly at the head of the stairs. "Send a servant to Burrus and order the centurion, Marcus Paetius, brought to me." As the man turned to obey, Nero stopped him. "And have Seneca summoned for the questioning of his adopted son." He watched the soldier pass the order down the stairwell. *Marcus will know who can speak for Paul.*

For a while the view of Rome occupied Nero's attention,

but then his mind turned again to Paul who so infuriated Poppaea. What did he have that so enraged her and her Jewish friends? "It is Poppaea who demands his death if he refuses to acknowledge my divinity," he thought aloud. "Knowing what I crave from her, she uses her body to gain her way with me." Taking a deep breath, he sighed, "Will I always be cursed with such a driving need? Will I ever arrive at the day when her taunting smile and haughty hand will no longer excite me?"

To Nero's surprise, Seneca was waiting for him when he descended from his lofty viewing platform. The emperor was aware of his advisor's ability to forsee his desires, but it bothered him when this ability was demonstrated in matters of personal importance. The long years of close association had marked both men. Since Nero's childhood, Seneca had been at his side, first as a tutor and friend and now as the emperor's principal advisor. Agrippina had chosen him, and now it pleased Nero to see his mother's growing resentment of the influence Seneca carried in the reign of her son.

Nero's footsteps echoed along the marble corridor, matched by his armed escort. Seneca was standing alone, dressed in his scholar's toga before the great double doors on the chamber of state. He bowed low to the emperor and remained facing the floor until Nero spoke.

"Counselor, you seem to have anticipated me this morning."

"How so, your majesty?" Seneca inquired, straightening from his bow.

"I wanted you here during the questioning of your son." Walking on through the open doors, Nero accepted the guard's salute and added, "I'm determined to discover why a centurion of my personal guard would fail to carry out my direct orders and then dare to flaunt his failure to my face."

Moving fast enough to catch up with the emperor, Seneca's brain assessed Nero's remark and came up with the response Caesar expected. "But, Sire, Paul left Greece before Marcus could execute your command."

Nero stopped short and whirled on his advisor. "And why

didn't the centurion follow Paul? He didn't have orders to return to Rome."

"His first duty was to you, Your Majesty," Seneca reasoned. "Had he left Greece in search of Paul, you might have incorrectly assumed the Christian was dead. It wouldn't do for you to be wrong."

Pondering this argument, Nero walked on toward his throne. The muffled footsteps of his old tutor followed him. Stepping up on the dais, the emperor took his seat and asked, "Why couldn't he have sent a message?"

"Would a message of failure have pleased Caesar?"

Nero's eyes narrowed as he studied the empty hall. Seneca's question required no answer. The advisor had witnessed the arrival of too many messages of failure and already knew what the imperial reaction would have been. The marble busts of noble Romans silently stared back at Nero from their alcoves in every wall. They were judging him. His wisdom was on trial. The sightless eyes of the divine Julius were the most condemning. Seneca's reasoned voice, so familiar to Nero after years of tutoring, then advanced a different argument.

"Marcus Paetius is a simple soldier, loyal to you and his oath. There's no intrigue in what he did. A calculating man would have sent a message claiming success in finding Paul and announcing intentions of following him." Seneca leaned forward to emphasize his next statement. "Knowing that wherever Paul runs, he cannot escape the power of Caesar, because you have centurions all over the world, this centurion returned to confess his failure." Standing very erect, the counselor added, "You should have generals with such loyalty!"

Twisting sideways on his throne, Nero looked down over his shoulder at Seneca. That last statement seemed to echo through the polished marble chamber. In less than two hours the room would be full of selfish people seeking Caesar's favor or justice. Ambassadors would present claims from minor kings, and generals would request funds for the payment of troops. Senators would claim his attention, and without Seneca, Nero knew he couldn't face them all with the wisdom they required. Pulling at the rings on his fingers, the emperor conceded. "I'll consider this, but your adopted son still must be punished. I can't allow his failure to pass unnoticed." Turning and directly facing the advisor, he ordered, "Send word to Burrus delaying the centurion's arrival until I've had time to consider his case more fully."

Seneca motioned a guard forward and dispatched him with the emperor's order.

Watching this take place, Nero wondered what Seneca's next move would be. He knew his counselor would continue to maneuver for leniency on behalf of his son. *Perhaps,* he thought, *I should let Seneca face Poppaea's wrath and order him to find a substitute for Paul. Maybe there's someone already in Rome with sufficient Christian stature to satisfy my mistress' desire for their humiliation.* He watched as a page entered the hall with Seneca's carrying case of state papers. Seeing the counselor extract a sheet of parchment, the emperor decided to wait a little longer before pressing for Paul's replacement.

Nero's boredom was obvious as Seneca presented his agenda for the day. But when the last item was revealed he became alive.

"Your Majesty," Seneca summarized, "it's common gossip among the intelligentsia of the imperial court that you've composed a great musical poem telling the story of Antony's love for Cleopatra. It has been suggested that a reading of this poem, with accompaniment of the lute, would establish your creative genius beyond compare."

The emperor leaned forward with intense interest. He could hear the subdued murmur of the daily court gathering beyond the hall's closed doors. His mind brushed them aside and concentrated on what Seneca was saying.

"I've brought this to your attention, Sire, so you might consider a time and place for such a presentation. Musicians and actors can be gathered and rehearsed, under your direction, for this purpose."

This last remark brought Nero to his feet. "No," he cried,

"I'll do the music and the reading myself." Stepping down from the dais, he grabbed Seneca's white toga in his fist. "You're forgetting, counselor, that my talent exceeds that of common actors and musicians. It's my poem and my music, and I'll perform them!"

"But, Sire, you'll need time to prepare, and the affairs of state demand . . ."

Releasing his grip on the toga, Nero interrupted Seneca. "You can handle everything you've listed for today. My decisions would be based on your advice, and you have my authority to act." Stepping back, he smiled with satisfaction and added, "I'll order a banquet prepared for this evening and spend the day in my apartment rehearsing. You'll act the host tonight, and I'll present my poem."

Turning away before Seneca could remind him of his imperial duty, Nero strode toward the chamber's side entrance. The guard opened the door and snapped to attention, crossing his chest with a sharp salute. Pausing in the doorway, the emperor looked back.

"Counselor, command the entire court to be present with their ladies." He smiled and added, "This is a poem of love and inspired imagination. It will lead to an evening of uninhibited joy."

Watching his advisor bow to his wishes, Nero experienced an odd feeling of having been manipulated. He studied the older man for a moment and wished he'd paid more attention to the day's agenda. The vision of presenting his poem and the resulting public proclamation of his genius flashed before him, and he quickly shoved the other throught from his mind. He was several paces down the corridor when he heard the door close behind him.

Having escaped a tiring day at court, Caesar was pleased with himself. The Nones of April was still 12 days away and after that, he would no longer have to be concerned about the petty affairs of state. He would rule by divine decree and his immortality would be assured. His advisors would become priests and they alone would be allowed to approach him for his divine decisions. Poppaea would become his chief priestess, and she would stand between him and all the others.

Nero's ever-present bodyguard matched him stride for stride as he marched the length of the palace's north wing hallway. The emperor's apartment was at the very end and consisted of eight rooms which included a luxurious private bath and complete kitchen. Octavia's quarters, with only three rooms, were located in the south wing as far away from him as he could arrange. His thoughts formed around the empress.

She was a simple girl, a child really, even though he and she were the same age. Agrippina had arranged their marriage just a year before she poisoned Claudius. Knowing the history of Messalina, Nero secretly suspected that Claudius was not Octavia's father. *At least,* he mused to himself, *I'm certain of my father.* He was Ahenobarbus, a Roman of noble birth. Aloud he said, "But why must I be married to the ugly daughter of a royal slut? And why must she, like my mother, continually meddle in my affairs? I'm the emperor. Why can't they leave me alone and let me enjoy the fruits of my poetic genius? Only Poppaea understands me. When I'm a god, she alone will share my greatness."

Once inside his apartment, Nero summoned his personal staff and gave them his orders for the day. Hector, his chamberlain, was sent to the great palace kitchens to arrange the menu for the banquet. The slave was ordered to return immediately, once the arrangements were made, to help the emperor prepare for his poetic triumph. Nero planned to use Hector's sweet, effeminate nature in the role of Cleopatra during his presentation. He, himself, would don the uniform of the noble Antony while Hector would wear the royal gown of the Nile queen.

An hour later, both men were diligently rehearsing when a commotion broke out in the emperor's atrium. When Nero sent Hector to investigate, the slave didn't return. Instead, an angry Agrippina stood framed in the doorway of Nero's study.

"And you call yourself emperor," she loudly declared, "while that damned Spaniard school teacher sits on the throne of Rome!"

From the low position on his couch, Nero looked up at his mother. Her grey hair was firmly styled close to her head in tight curls that appeared painful. With hands on her hips and black eyes flashing, she strode into the room. Knowing her temper, Nero remained silent.

"You," she roared down at him, "are an insult to the blood that flows in your veins!" Her long pointed finger stabbed the air with a thrust of contempt as she added, "Seneca just received the ambassador from Gaul when I'd promised him an audience with you. How do you expect to rule the empire while reading poetry to a slave?"

Putting aside the scroll containing his composition, Nero slowly got to his feet and faced her. "You're forgetting yourself," he sternly said. "I didn't promise the ambassador anything! You made the promise without consulting me, and if you had, I'd have sent the bastard packing! All he wants is money and I don't intend for him to have it."

"Well Seneca gave it to him," she gloated. "Not all that he asked for but a large part of it nonetheless. Your school teacher now enjoys the gratitude of Gaul which rightly belongs to you!" Throwing her head back, Agrippina studied the ceiling as if searching for words. When her eyes returned to those of her son, she grimly said, "You and your poetry disgust me. I will not be at your banquet tonight. Nor will Octavia. We're leaving for Ostia within the hour."

Her long blue gown flared as she whirled toward the door. Nero's cold command stopped her.

"Mother, you and Octavia will grace my table tonight, and at the slightest indication of displeasure from either of you, I'll have you banished to Ostia for the rest of your lives!"

"You wouldn't dare," she snarled, turning slowly to face him.

"Try me," he challenged.

"Well, I won't sit at the same table with Otho's whore."

Nero knew he had won the argument and pressed his advantage. "Yes you will. Poppaea will sit on my right with you next to her."

"Where will Octavia be?"

"On my left, of course, next to Seneca."

Agrippina bowed her head. "I suppose the Spaniard's Saxon wench will also be present?"

Nodding his head, Nero laughed at his mother's defeat. *Someday I must have her killed. But today she learned who is the emperor of Rome.* His thoughts continued in this vein while he half listened to her continued protest. When she had finally vented her feelings, he allowed her to withdraw, knowing she and his wife would spend hours primping for the banquet.

Hector returned to the study, and the rehearsal was resumed, but Nero's heart wasn't in it. He couldn't shake the effect of Agrippina's visit. Seneca had taken the court before, and it hadn't raised her hackles. It wasn't the ambassador's visit either. Slowly, the true cause of her displeasure came to him. It was his poetry. His mother didn't want him to perform on the stage. She considered it beneath his dignity as emperor. Agrippina held his creative ability in low esteem. She didn't recognize the true value of his work and talent. Looking at Hector, Nero suddenly thought of a way to impress her and everyone else with the value he placed on his work. The simplicity of his inspiration both startled and pleased him.

"Hector," he quietly said, "I don't want you to play the part of Cleopatra tonight."

"Why, Sire?"

Nero didn't bother to answer because he knew the slave would soon understand. "I want you to select the most beautiful slave in the palace for the part." Hector allowed his disappointment to show, but Nero went on. "I want you to costume and rehearse her in the role, but tonight there'll be a difference in the climax."

"How, Sire?"

"When she reaches in the bag for the serpent, it won't be a toy! The entire court will understand the importance I place on my poetry when my Cleopatra dies just as Antony's did!"

Hector was a man of many talents, not the least of which was a great affinity for reptiles. Nero had encouraged him in this, and deep beneath the palace they maintained a den of death. Snakes of every description had been collected from the length and breadth of the empire. An asp would be selected from this collection for the climax of the evening's performance.

Brushing his long black hair away from his face, the slave smiled with understanding. Nero was fascinated by the fluid grace that seemed to enter the man's slim body whenever an encounter with his pets was anticipated. This sensuousness was part of Hector's charm and the primary source of Nero's pleasure in the slave. Nodding his dismissal, Caesar watched the man withdraw.

Turning back to his manuscript, Nero read aloud the lines he was to recite, pacing back and forth in the room as he did. Passing the scroll from one hand to the other, he practiced his gestures until he felt they were perfect. Then laying his script aside, he began again from memory. About halfway through, a servant's discreet cough from the doorway stopped him.

"What is it now?" Nero demanded.

"Sire," the servant replied, "a centurion of the guard is at the door with a Greek sea captain." The emperor was about to have them turned away when the servant added, "The Greek claims to have important information about the centurion, Marcus Paetius, and his dealings with a man named Paul."

Glancing out the window, Nero could tell from the sun's shadows that almost half the day was gone. He wanted to return to his poem. The rehearsal had to be completed, but the thought of Poppaea's reaction if she learned he'd turned the Greek away decided his course.

"Allow them to enter, but tell them to be brief," was his reluctant order.

A few moments later the soldier and his seafaring companion were standing stiffly before Caesar. Nero coldly appraised the pair and directed his question to the soldier.

"What possible news could you have that must intrude on my day?"

The soldier's eyes didn't waver from an imaginary spot on

the emperor's chest as he answered, "Sire, this man has news of a plot against you."

Nero's glance swept over Castor, taking in his rough, woolen toga, the toes of his scuffed seaboots and his swarthy, handsome face. Nero sensed an arrogance in the Greek's attitude and quickly resolved it.

"On your knees, Captain," he commanded. "Greek sailors speak to me only from a begging position." While Castor obeyed, the emperor directed a second question to the soldier. "How did this man come to us?"

"Sire, he stopped my patrol on the street this morning with a tale of being kidnapped and held prisoner by a group of Christians on the Aventinus. His story implicates the centurion, Marcus Paetius."

"The *ex*-centurion," Nero corrected. Turning his attention back to the kneeling Castor, Caesar questioned him regarding his identity. Once satisfied on that score, he sat down on the couch and listened to the Greek's story.

At first Castor seemed unsure of himself, but as his narrative progressed, he gained confidence and eloquence. He told of Marcus' voyage to Greece and the questions that were asked at every port. He explained how he had gained the confidence of Paul's secretary Tertius and learned of a letter the teacher had written to the Christians in Rome. With great relish, Castor told of the relationship between Marcus and Phoebe. Nero leaned forward with intense interest when the centurion's baptism was described. It was proof, beyond doubt, that Marcus had met and talked to Paul. The emperor questioned the kneeling Greek about the letter Paul had written.

"Do you know its contents?"

"No, Your Majesty. I escaped before it was read." Castor allowed his eyes to meet those of Nero for the first time as he added, "But I'm certain it condemns the gods of Rome."

"Who has the letter now?" Nero asked.

"The lady Phoebe, Sire," Castor replied. "The woman Marcus brought to Rome under the protection of the imperial medallion."

172

Suddenly Nero was on his feet, towering over Castor. His brain was seething with eagerness as he demanded, "Does this woman have the authority of Paul? Can she speak for him?"

"Yes, Sire," Castor answered. "She's a woman of great wealth and power." The Greek smiled for the first time and added, "It was she who converted your centurion. It was she who convinced Paul that he should send a letter, instead of coming himself. It's she who's preaching the contents of the letter here at the very heart of your empire!"

Checking his appearance of eagerness, Nero once again sat back on the couch and asked, "What else can you tell me about this Phoebe?"

Castor continued by telling Nero of Phoebe's beauty. He told how she controlled the lives of the men around her. Admitting that he, himself, had fallen under her spell, the Greek intimated that Phoebe was a sorceress who used Christianity to add to her power over men. When he told of the return voyage, he implicated Marcus by saying, "I tried to free the centurion from her power during a storm at sea, but he resisted and turned me over to her for punishment. She relieved me of my command and put me ashore at Syracuse. Having failed with the centurion, I came to Rome as fast as I could to warn Caesar."

An image of Phoebe was forming in Nero's mind, but one question still remained to be answered. "Tell me, Captain, when this woman preaches Paul's letter, do the Christians believe her?"

"Yes, Sire," was Castor's solemn answer.

Holding up his hand for silence, the emperor leaned back and considered what he'd heard. Questions began forming in his mind that he knew Castor couldn't answer. What kind of man would send a woman to represent him? What kind of men would follow a woman? This last question caused him some uneasiness. His mother controlled a faction of Roman power. His wife had her followers. The men who followed Agrippina and Octavia were dangerous men. That's the kind of men who follow women!

His eyes caught sight of his manuscript lying beside him, and he was reminded of another women. Cleopatra had commanded armies and navies. She, too, had controlled the minds and emotions of brave and honorable men. Was this Phoebe going to be his Cleopatra? Was she going to lead to his downfall? His mind briefly flashed on Poppaea. The whole problem of Paul and his Christians rested with her. *Somehow,* he thought, *I've got to gain control over these women. If I don't they're going to plague me to my tomb.*

Castor twisted uncomfortably in his kneeling position, and Nero waved him to his feet. "Captain, you've been of some service to me. How can I repay you?"

Grimly Castor replied, "Sire, I'm without funds and unemployed."

"Not any longer," Caesar observed. "You'll remain here at the palace as our guest until a ship of the Imperial Navy can be found for its new captain." Glancing at the soldier, still standing at attention, Nero ordered, "See to the captain's comfort and obtain the location of this woman Phoebe from him. I want a complete report before sunset." Getting up from the couch, he added, "Your report is for my eyes only. Is that understood?"

"Yes, Sire," the soldier answered while acknowledging the order with a salute.

The Greek thanked Caesar for his generosity and praised him for his greatness while pledging his undying devotion. Nero smiled at the two men as they backed from the room. *That Greek is not to be trusted,* he said to himself. *I must keep him here until this matter is resolved. After that, he'll be given a chance to prove himself by committing suicide.*

Picking up the scroll from the couch, the emperor walked across the room to the window overlooking the palace gardens. He tried to remember his place in the poem, but his mind refused to return to his composition. What Castor had told him of Phoebe forced itself into his thoughts.

How could a mere woman accomplish all the things Castor had claimed? Another question slipped into his thinking. Was she in fact a woman? She was from Greece and her name was Phoebe. Recalling the lessons he'd learned at Seneca's feet as a boy, Nero's brain seized on the tendril of a thought. Could it be the old gods, the ones he held in such contempt, were sending this woman against him? Was this their way of testing him for his coming divinity? Did Phoebe actually represent Paul, or was she an oracle from Olympus?

Nero's mind reeled under the impact of his thoughts. His body quivered with nervous energy. Unwittingly, he'd played into the hands of the gods by sending Marcus after Paul. Even Poppaea's role in the enterprise had been ordained by the ancient deities. They'd used Paul to lead his centurion to Phoebe. The emperor smiled at the cleverness of the gods. They'd even used his medallion to protect her during the journey.

Closing his eyes, he once again heard Seneca, as his tutor, instructing him about the Greek gods. "The goddess Phoebe is the wife of Zeus and the mother of Asteria and Leto. She presides over the oracle at Delphi as the successor of Apollo. Her name means 'the radiant one' because she's the goddess of the moon."

Blindly leaning against the window sill to steady himself, Nero hissed the words out loud. "Yes, she is my test!" Opening his eyes, his mind raced ahead. *If I can make her worship me, I'll truly be a god! And, because the Christians believe her, they too will accept my divinity. I must impress her with my greatness. Let her see that I rule an empire of learned and great men.*

Nero tried to still the wild beating of his heart. The way was clear for him. The goddess of the moon was in Rome for his benefit. She must not be allowed to pass him by. In his heart Nero knew this was to be his moment of greatness and glory. He rationalized the meaning of Phoebe's visit to Rome into an overriding obsession. It suddenly occurred to him that neither Julius, Augustus or Caligula had received such divine confirmation of their godly proclamations. Their declarations came from the lips of mortal men! They were not truly gods!

175

The emperor's eyes sparkled with inspiration as he planned Phoebe's reception. Speaking to himself, he laid it out.

"I'll have her escorted to the Hall of State tomorrow night under a guard of honor. I'll even go along with the gods and ask her to read Paul's letter to the men of Rome." Moving back to the divan, he had one final thought as he unrolled his poem. "Perhaps," he whispered, "I'll devise a test for Phoebe's divinity. It will let the gods know that I haven't been fooled." Chuckling softly, Nero resumed his rehearsal.

CHAPTER XIV

*Salute one another with a holy kiss. The churches of
Christ salute you.*

ROMANS 16:16

FOLLOWING the success of Phoebe's presentation the night
before, Aquila sent his messengers out a second time. At
Phoebe's suggestion, invitations to dinner were issued only
to those elders mentioned in Paul's letter. These included Ampliatus, head of the Aurelii family; Caleb, chief of the Narcissiani and a scribe of the Imperial Court; Eli, a wealthy former
slave and elder of the Aristobulus group; and Hermes, a wheat
merchant and leader of the Christians in the Suburra section
of Rome. Phoebe felt that after winning the support of these
four men, together with the backing she already had from
Andronicus, Rufus and Aquila, her mission would be 90 per-
cent completed. Reading the letter to Nero and obtaining Marcus' freedom remained her only major problems.

Priscilla spent the next morning briefing Phoebe on the size
and location of each group represented by the men invited.
They were sitting on the balcony outside Phoebe's room, and
the sounds of the river front, half a mile away, could dimly
be heard. Priscilla was still in her nightgown, but Phoebe was
dressed in a high-girdled chiton of light unbleached wool. The
Aurelii family was prominent, according to Priscilla, not only
among Christians, but also among the Roman nobility. Its

177

position in society was due to the land it controlled north of Rome. The Narcissiani group was made up of the remnants from the household of Tiberius Claudius Narcissus, an influential freedman advisor to the Emperor Claudius. The majority of them were employed in Caesar's service.

As Phoebe's hostess, Priscilla felt obligated to warn her about the Aristobulus leader. "Eli has gained a great deal of wealth from the sale of privileges. Being the former slave of Herod the Great's grandson, he's considered an authority on Jewish history and his influence has grown with the increasing Jewish popularity. It's possible he's associated with Poppaea."

"That's all the more reason he should hear Paul's letter," Phoebe observed. "It might make him realize the importance of keeping the faith."

"Be that as it may," Priscilla conceded "I'd be just as happy if Eli couldn't make it tonight."

"What about Hermes and his group in Suburra?" Phoebe asked.

"They're a group of hard-working Christians," her hostess replied. "You'll like Hermes. He's as common as an old sandal, and his sense of humor is delightful. I can't understand why he didn't welcome you to his group." She wrinkled her nose and chuckled before adding, "He probably thought it would infuriate Aquila. You should hear those two when Hermes is buying wheat bags from us."

Walking to the balcony rail, Phoebe stood silently and studied the view below. Her pensive mood carried to Priscilla as she asked, "Do you think there's any hope for Marcus?"

Priscilla's expression was noncommittal. "Seneca is a very powerful and clever man. If there's anything to be done for Marcus, he'll do it."

"My fear for his safety increased with every mile we traveled closer to Rome," Phoebe admitted. "As I began to understand the kind of man he had to face in Nero, I realized Marcus was at the mercy of a madman. He admitted as much the night we spent at a Roman encampment south of Tarracina." Dropping her arms to her sides, she admitted, "I love him too much to even think of returning to Greece without him."

Priscilla retired to finish dressing just as a sedan chair, carried by four slaves and accompanied by two armed men, pulled up at the villa gate. The Persian went to investigate, then sought out Phoebe.

"My lady, it's Marcus' mother. She wishes to see you."

As Phoebe arrived in the courtyard, the curtains enclosing the chair opened, revealing the reclining figure of a well-dressed, middle-aged woman. Her flaxen hair was set in small curls that framed her lovely face and provided a sharp contrast for brilliant blue eyes. Gold earrings caught the flash of the sun as she ducked her head and emerged from the silken cage.

Why is it, Phoebe mused, *that I'm always dressed like a drudge when someone from Marcus' family arrives?* Glancing down at her feet, she compared her ugly sandals to the beautifully embroidered slippers the woman was wearing. The lady was dressed in a gown of shimmering purple. Her robe was cut of the same material with wide lapels trimmed with a narrow border of gold thread. Stepping forward, she seemed to float toward Phoebe. Her voice was as delicate as Corinthian procelain.

"I've come to see you because my son loves you." Looking into Phoebe's eyes, she said, "I'm Ellsbeth, the woman you're replacing in my son's affections."

Phoebe curtsied and extended her hand in welcome, saying, "I'm Phoebe, the woman who loves your son."

"I had a moment alone with Marcus before they arrested him," she said. "And my lord, Seneca, has told me of his visit with you. Both of them are liars," she declared. "You're more beautiful than they said."

With a glance at Debra, Phoebe requested that refreshments be prepared and served in the peristyle. As the girl turned away, she added, "And ask Priscilla to join us." Offering her arm to her guest, she suggested, "Please come inside. We have much to talk about."

The early afternoon sun filled the columned garden with warmth and cheer. Noting that Ellsbeth didn't partake of either

179

the shelled nuts or wine, Phoebe feared she'd earned the woman's disapproval. This fear was quickly erased when her guest explained.

"I'm at that age when my diet is critical. Wine, sweets and nuts seem to enlarge my body and limbs way beyond the proportion I consume. My position and security depend entirely on my appearance. My lord, Seneca, claims he'll never abandon me, but when you take Marcus, I'll probably lose my hold over him."

Phoebe had never really considered the situation of Marcus' mother. It hadn't occurred to her that Ellsbeth might find herself in desperate need if Seneca could no longer enjoy the company and companionship of her son. She could offer one solution.

"You'll always be welcome with us."

"No, my dear," the woman replied. "I've become too much a Roman to leave Rome, but I thank you for the offer."

Ellsbeth rose from the marble bench as Priscilla came through the archway. Phoebe made the introductions and then watched the two women size each other up. Marcus' mother made the first observation.

"I had no idea that Christian women were so lovely."

"We model ourselves after the women of Rome," replied Priscilla.

The older woman laughed and returned to her seat. "The women of Rome are ugly. It's the non-Roman women who are desired here. Every soldier of the empire brings one back with him and the emperor so resents their freedom of selection that he claims their conquests for himself."

"I've heard as much," Priscilla said, helping herself to the nuts. "Did I interrupt something?"

"As a matter of fact you did," Ellsbeth answered. "I was about to explain the purpose of my visit. Please stay. I'm commanded to attend a banquet at the palace tonight, and I wanted Phoebe to know that I intend asking Agrippina, the emperor's mother, to order the release of Marcus. I'd ask the Empress Octavia, but she's more of a child than Nero and lives in deadly fear of her husband." She directly faced Phoebe and continued. "It may mean nothing, but I want you ready to leave Rome tonight."

Shaking her head, Phoebe watched surprise enter Ellsbeth's face. "I can't. My work here isn't finished."

"Then finish it this afternoon."

"Perhaps you can help me," Phoebe said. "How can I gain an audience with the emperor?"

"Why, in the names of all the gods, do you want to do *that?*" Ellsbeth demanded.

"I have a letter for him."

"Give it to me. I'll deliver it tonight, and you can start packing. By this time tomorrow, you and Marcus can be on your way toward a better life."

From this statement Phoebe knew that Ellsbeth wanted Marcus to do more with his life than serve Caesar. This was a mother trying to save her son from the corruption of a decadent society.

"I'm afraid," she responded, "that delivery of this letter requires its reading, and I can't allow you to do that."

"Phoebe," Priscilla interjected, "let Ellsbeth take Paul's letter to Nero. He can have any number of people read it to him."

"Seneca will do it gladly if I ask him," Ellsbeth said.

Phoebe considered this. She knew the word of God didn't need her voice to have meaning, but still, God had told her to do it. Seneca might wait until after the Nones before he acted on it. He might read it himself and then cast it aside as having no importance to Nero. Everything she, Marcus and Paul had done to this point was aimed at the emperor hearing the letter before his proclamation. Shaking her head, she thanked Ellsbeth for the offer, but declined.

"I'll be no party in making you available to Nero," Ellsbeth said. "With a body like yours, he wouldn't hear a word you said."

Priscilla agreed with Ellsbeth and the talk ended in a polite stalemate. As Marcus' mother rose to leave, she told Priscilla,

181

"If Phoebe changes her mind, get the letter to me at my villa on the Palatine before sundown." Standing, she turned to Phoebe and said, "Marcus has chosen a beautiful woman but a stubborn one. If you both survive this foolishness, I'll consider accepting this God of yours because you're going to need divine help." Suddenly bending forward, she took Phoebe's face in her hands and kissed her on the lips. When Ellsbeth straightened, she studied Phoebe for several moments and then whispered, "My heart goes with you, dear. Take Marcus back to Greece and let him be the father to your children in the way that I never allowed his father to be for him."

Getting to her feet, Phoebe embraced Ellsbeth. "Thank you for coming. If you can get Marcus released, do it. And remember, you will always have a place with us. I have ships in Puteoli every spring and summer; they'll be instructed to serve you."

Ellsbeth kept her grip on Phoebe's arm as they walked to the courtyard and her waiting attendants. After climbing into her sedan chair, she had one final statement.

"Marcus loves you, and I'm giving him up. Don't send him back to me as long as I'm in Rome. He achieved a peace and maturity that I can't describe while he was in Greece. If he ever comes back here, Seneca and this city will destroy him."

Phoebe watched her leave and praised God for giving Marcus such a loving mother. She knew that the woman's sins had been the cause of his father's banishment, but she felt a love for her that was warm and deep. *After all,* she thought, *we're all flawed and need the prayers of each other. We can't pray for someone else without loving them. And that's what God has commanded us to do.*

Returning to the house, Phoebe found Priscilla and Debra standing in the atrium. Closing the front door, she leaned back against its cool paneling and considered what Ellsbeth had said. If she did obtain Marcus' release, he might consider it expedient to leave the city. At least she could prepare for that even though she herself couldn't go. Aquila couldn't help because he was at the tannery.

Phoebe asked Debra to find Polax, then explained her intentions to Priscilla while leading the way back upstairs. "I'll send the Persian to buy horses and supplies. He can take them to the Emperor's Cloak. If we have to leave Rome suddenly, we'll leave everything else here, and you can send them to us on one of my ships later."

"Then you've come to your senses," Priscilla exclaimed. "You've given up that mad idea about reading Paul's letter to Nero!"

"No, that still must be done. But Marcus can at least get away."

"He'll not leave without you, and you know it," Priscilla declared.

"That may be," Phoebe admitted, "but even after I see Nero, we may need fast horses to leave Rome."

Feet slightly apart, hands on her hips, Priscilla faced her guest with flashing eyes. "If you somehow manage to get an audience with the emperor, you'll never leave the palace alive. Let Ellsbeth deliver Paul's letter. There's no earthly reason for you to risk everything this way."

"Not an earthly reason," Phoebe said, "but one from Heaven."

After providing Polax with the gold he'd need, she sent him on his way with instructions to find Julius and include him in their plans. "He may be at Seneca's villa or at Campus Martius. If he has access to Marcus, have him tell the centurion what we're doing. Let him know that his mother is appealing his arrest to Agrippina. Keep one of your horses for yourself and return here as soon as everything is ready. If Julius is with you, have him do the same." The Persian smiled and departed without saying a word.

Taking some action, any action at all, was a relief. Phoebe felt less helpless. Fear had been her enemy. She had taken her eyes off God. A short phrase from Paul's letter popped into her mind: "For you have not received the spirit of bondage to fear; but you have received the Spirit of adoption, whereby we cry, Abba, Father."

The rest of the day was spent preparing for the coming dinner and meeting. Aquila arrived home early and was told all that had happened. He agreed with Phoebe's actions, but learning that Ellsbeth had volunteered to deliver the letter to Nero, he, too, protested Phoebe's refusal.

As early evening came, their first guest arrived. It was Caleb, the chief of the Narcissiani.

Dressed in the same long-sleeved, high-necked gown she'd worn the evening before, Phoebe was introduced to the early arrival in the peristyle. Priscilla also wore her costume of the previous night, and Aquila was still in the off-white, single-girdled chiton he'd worn to work.

The imperial scribe was a tall, thin man. His long, narrow face was highlighted with blue eyes and heavy, shaggy eyebrows. He was wearing the scholar's toga of unbleached wool. Coming alone, he explained his early arrival.

"I thought it best to come before dark. The emperor's reading one of his poems at the palace tonight, and an orgy will probably follow the performance." Smiling indulgently at Aquila, he added, "You know what that will mean in the streets tonight. Every hellion in Rome will be out to join the fun. I hope to leave in the company of Hermes and his escort."

Phoebe recalled Seneca's remark about diverting Nero's attention from Marcus with a poem presentation. She wondered if tonight's palace activity was part of that plan.

Ampliatus of the Aurelii family was the next to arrive, accompanied by his wife and daughter. The women were dressed in matching stolas of pale blue silk. Both wore jeweled combs in their light brown hair, but the mother's attempt to resemble the daughter stopped there. The girl was thin and pale, her brown eyes were overly large and she seemed to carry an aura of sadness. The wife was plump with sharp, critical, dark eyes. Ampliatus was almost nondescript in his purple bordered white toga. He was of medium height with thin frame and large, rather sad eyes. Phoebe sensed he was a dominated man and seeing the girl cling to her father's arm, she felt the daughter shared the same fate. The mother spoke for them all.

"There's something going on at the palace tonight," she announced. "I've never seen so many chairs being carried in the streets. That heathen on the Palatine will probably gorge himself on our taxes and then lead his godless rabble through the streets to our discomfort." She flashed a swift smile at Phoebe in greeting and added, "Thank God, I insisted on an escort tonight."

Eli and Hermes arrived soon after. They were an unlikely pair. Eli was diminutive in every way. He had little hair, little shoulders and stood only five feet tall. Coal-black eyes sparkled in his small face revealing a lively interest in everything around him. Phoebe felt his silent eyes studying her while she was introduced to Hermes.

Hermes was a man equal to Polax in size and strength. It was obvious the wheat merchant handled his own merchandise. His arms were gigantic and rippled with power. A wide, open face, containing pale blue eyes, smiled in delighted greeting as he swept Phoebe up in a strong but gentle Christian embrace. Both men were wearing simple white togas and had come without their wives.

They commented on the traffic in the streets and helped themselves to the refreshments Priscilla had provided. Every time Phoebe glanced at the smaller man, he was appraising her. Hermes, on the other hand, had separated the daughter from Ampliatus and was pressing a full goblet of wine in her hands while regaling her with tales of high adventure in the wheat business.

Andronicus and Rufus arrived and apologized for the absence of Junia and Marian. They felt it best for the women to remain at their homes with so much activity going on at the palace. This opinion was quietly stated, out of earshot of the Aurelii women.

Aquila started the dinner with the ceremonial breaking of bread and sharing of the holy cup. He gave thanks to the

Lord on behalf of the group and asked His protection for their safe return to their respective homes.

Leading the discussion during dinner, Andronicus told the newcomers what Phoebe had taught him the night before. Rufus added his own evaluation of the teaching by saying, "If mankind is forgiven all sins through the sacrifice of Jesus, then surely the transgression of Eve is lifted from the shoulders of our women. They are partners with us in the service of the Lord."

The other men looked to Aquila for his opinion, and Phoebe's host agreed with an added observation. "We must teach our women the ways of the Lord. Let them be edified in the mysteries of our faith and worship beside us. They must still be submitted to their husbands, as we must be submitted to Jesus, but we must honor them with our love and cleave unto them as God commands."

Phoebe waited for silence and then added, "In his letter to us in Corinth, Paul explained what Aquila just said in a different way. He said: 'Let the husband render unto the wife due benevolence; and likewise also the wife unto the husband. The wife has not power of her own body, but the husband: and likewise also the husband has not power of his own body, but the wife.' "

"That's all well and good," Eli observed, "when you're talking about reproduction, but spiritual authority is another matter." He smiled thinly at Phoebe. "Jesus was a man, and His disciples were men. He didn't call a single woman to follow him."

Phoebe returned his smile and softly conceded. "He didn't have to; the women were already there. The ministry of women is not the same as the ministry of men; that I'll readily admit. We can't replace the figure of our Lord in the ceremonies of our faith, but we can minister to the needs of the church."

Eli warmed to the subject. "Coming from Corinth, you must be aware of the dangers involved in a feminine-based religion. The temples of Aphrodite are carnal houses of lust and greed. Christianity doesn't need the temptation of a goddess!" Pointing a finger at Phoebe, he charged, "Are you, with your beauty and charm, claiming to be a spiritual authority of the church in Greece?"

"No," she replied, "I'm a servant of our Lord—His adopted sister, and nothing more."

"Sister!" Eli roared. "You're nothing of the kind. You're not even Jewish! There's no blood from the line of David in your veins."

Without the presence of Christ to sustain her, Phoebe knew she would have been devastated by now. But a strange calm filled her and surprised them all when she quietly retorted, "My lineage goes beyond David. It stems from Abraham. And his from Adam. Abraham was a Gentile until God made him a Jew. A Jew is Jewish by faith alone. You can't be a Jew and call Jesus your Lord. When you claim Jesus as the Christ, you become a Christian. The same applies to the Gentile. A Gentile can't proclaim Jesus as Lord and remain a Gentile." She held Eli's gaze and added, "As for being a sister of my Lord, Jesus declared my sisterhood Himself."

"Where and when?" Eli demanded.

"She's got you there," Andronicus interceded with a grin. "No less an authority than the apostle Matthew reports Jesus as saying, 'For whosoever shall do the will of my Father which is in heaven, the same is my brother, and sister, and mother.' She's kin to Jesus just as you and I."

Hermes nodded agreement, as did Ampliatus. Caleb, who'd been silent to that point, sealed Phoebe's victory.

"Jesus also said, 'Full well you reject the commandment of God, that you may keep your own tradition.' It's time we drop the binding traditions of the Jews and more closely follow the example of Jesus. I declare that Phoebe is my sister in Christ. She is as much a vessel of His love as I, and I drink deeply of her cup and pray she'll share mine."

As the climax to a beautiful evening, Phoebe read them Paul's letter. She thanked them for their support and each guest carried a true copy back to his people.

CHAPTER XV

*. . . Tribulation and anguish, upon every soul of man
that doeth evil . . .*

ROMANS 2:9

ROLLING to his side and throwing back the silken covers
from his bed, Nero swung his legs over the edge and sat up.
A brief period of dizziness possessed him, but after sitting
stiffly for a moment, it passed. Running his left hand through
his hair, he pulled the bell cord to ring for his body slaves.
While waiting, he pleasantly recalled his triumph of the night
before.

Closing his eyes, he once again witnessed the naked expres-
sions of lust that filled so many faces at his banquet tables
when the young slave girl who played Cleopatra unbelievingly
held the live reptile that had bitten her. Then he relived the
exquisite thrill of watching her die. Her scream of terror was
an inspired climax to the reading of his poem. True, she was
only a slave, but what happened to her was just one indication
of how unlimited was his power.

Poppaea's response to the girl's death had proven the erotic
value of this kind of power. The unbridled desire he'd seen
in her gleaming, dark eyes had stimulated his responses to
her caresses and demanding lips. Otho's whore, he mused,
had been whorish beyond measure and in perfect contrast to
Octavia's prudish reaction.

Nero admitted to himself that his wife's humiliation by his open display of lust with Poppaea had been delicious. Octavia had been shocked by the girl's death, but the resulting orgy had shocked her even more. The destruction of innocent beauty, he decided, was a desirable impetus in the creation of carnal pleasure. In the future he would find more such victims to satisfy his imperial need. His poem had been worthy of a girl's life, and certainly his coming divinity would demand a sacrifice equally as great.

Walking to the open balcony doorway, Nero looked out on the wooded hilltop of the Palatine. His stomach rumbled, and he irritably rang again for his slaves. The midmorning sun was bright and warm on his naked flesh, but his mood was rapidly becoming black with imperial impatience.

Nero watched three slaves enter the bedchamber. One went through to his private bath. The other two, avoiding his dark glance, busied themselves with his preparation for the day. After being presented several combinations for his approval, he selected a rose-colored, silk toga and slippers of embroidered pink damask. Both men bowed before him and followed the emperor as he stepped through the side door to the steamy, perfumed atmosphere of the bath.

Relaxing under the tender attention of his slaves, Nero's mind moved ahead to the pleasure he expected this night with Phoebe's appearance at court. Through the written report he'd received following Castor's visit, he'd learned where Phoebe was staying. His imperial brain had reeled with possibilities of actions he might take, but the decision he came to was, in his opinion, a stroke of true genius.

He would have Marcus Paetius escort her to the court under a guard of honor. He'd impress the goddess of the moon with his own divine majesty and give her justification for worshiping him. *Tonight,* he mused, *will result in an intellectual orgy with the best brains in Rome standing as witnesses to my fitness for divinity.* Nero had been tempted to tell Poppaea of Phoebe's coming appearance, but now he congratulated himself on keeping his secret. She was expecting his proclamation to come

189

in 10 days, but he'd surprise them all by having Phoebe make the claim for him this very evening. As the goddess of the moon, her proclamation would have greater meaning than any he could command from the senate. He softly chuckled as a thought from the previous day jelled in his mind.

If the gods are going to test me through Phoebe, then I shall test her divinity for them. The court would be arranged for a formal hearing, he decided. Phoebe would be directed to a low couch placed in front of the dais below his throne. The intellectuals would be seated in rows to his right, with Seneca facing them. The members of the senate would be on his left, with Burrus' grim visage reminding them of his power. Marcus Paetius would escort the goddess forward from the door and remain at her side. *I'll have captain Castor sit at my feet on the steps of the dais to remind her that all men of the empire are subject to my will. Only Hector and I will know of the three vipers he'll place in Phoebe's couch. If she's truly from the gods of Olympus, the reptiles will not harm her, but if she's mortal, she'll die at my feet!*

After being bathed, massaged, perfumed, dressed and fed, Nero sent for his chamberlain. When Hector arrived, the emperor accepted the man's act of submission by allowing him to crawl across the dining room floor and kiss the imperial feet. It pleased Nero to have Hector remain on his knees while he heard the emperor's wishes.

"Do we have three African vipers in our collection?"

"Yes, Sire," the chamberlain responded.

Hector smiled with special knowledge as the emperor detailed how he wanted the three serpents placed inside an open-ended cushion on Phoebe's couch. The fatal bite of an African viper was almost painless. They would remain docile in the darkness of the cushion cover until disturbed. Vipers never gave warning before an attack, and their venom killed quickly. With three of them, the victim would die within minutes. He begged permission to be present for the event, and Nero finally agreed. "You'll wear the tunic of a scribe and keep a record of whatever is said."

Nero watched the man crawl from the room and then sent a slave for Burrus, prefect of the Praetorian Guard. When the old soldier arrived, orders were issued for Marcus' release and the restoration of his rank. Nero stated that he now considered the centurion guiltless in the matter of Paul's escape. "After all," he reasoned with Burrus, "how could a mere centurion do otherwise when the gods were preparing a divinity test for the soldier's emperor?" Nero laughed at the surprised confusion he saw in the prefect's face. "The gods even used Paul, Poppaea's enemy, and the letter he wrote, as an excuse for the goddess of the moon to come to Rome. It's only fitting that my centurion protect her during the journey."

Burrus made no comment regarding the emperor's reasoning. He acknowledged the imperial order pertaining to Marcus and started to withdraw. Nero stopped him with an additional order.

"Bring Marcus Paetius to me this afternoon, and I'll require your attendance at court tonight. Please notify the senate that I also expect every member to be present."

Nodding his understanding, Burrus turned to leave, but Nero stopped him again.

"Tell Seneca that he's expected together with all his intellectual friends."

"Sire, can you tell me the reason for such an august gathering?" Burrus finally asked.

"Yes, my dear prefect: tonight the goddess of the moon is going to proclaim my divinity, and I want the power of Rome to witness the event."

Burrus' face reflected none of his thinking, and Nero accepted the prefect's silence as agreement with his reasoning.

Nero considered Burrus to be loyal and devoted in a pragmatic way. As the officer withdrew to carry out his orders, the emperor realized that what he'd done in regard to Marcus would please Agrippina. The old woman had quietly requested the centurion's release last night. Now he could go to her and request a return favor.

Agrippina enjoyed great influence with the Vestal Virgins,

and Nero wanted sacrifices made on their altar for his approaching divinity. It would be her motherly duty to see that such was done. Preparing to go to his mother with his request, Nero stopped in the apartment entrance. A frown creased his young brow. Women were such gossips. *If I tell her what is about to happen, she'll tell the virgins. They'll tell the priests. By the middle of the afternoon all of Rome will know, and my surprise will be no surprise at all.* Giggling with delight at his cunning, he backed into the atrium of his apartment, called for his body slaves and led them into his dressing room.

They spent an hour selecting the wardrobe he'd wear that evening. He chose the hero's toga, or toga picta as it was called by the imperial tailors. Nero loved the feel of the heavy crimson silk on his body, and the embroidered border of gold would set him apart from all the others. A gold crown of laurel leaves was set aside for him to wear in the Hall of State. He selected sandals with thick, leather soles and straps faced with gold. This would set him off from the scholars whom he knew would be wearing the plain togas pura, while the members of the senate would be trying to out-dazzle each other in the purple bordered togas candida, impregnated with fuller's chalk. Burrus would be in the sparkling brilliance of his uniform, and Seneca would wear his traditional toga virilis, the color of natural wool.

Nero had moved to the balcony of his apartment when Hector returned to say that everything was ready. "The senate is in an uproar," he said. "Burrus appeared before them as they were about to adjourn for the day and commanded their attendance tonight. They demanded to know the reason for such a session and the prefect simply told them, 'Caesar commands it!' They're still protesting, but none of them left the senate chamber."

"What of the scholars?" Nero asked.

"The libraries of the city have been swept clean of fuzzyheads and the waters of the public baths are turning black from manuscript dust," the chamberlain said grinningly.

"And our little friends—will they stay safely in the lady's cushion until she rests on it?"

"Yes, Sire," the man whispered. "I have arranged it."

Languidly waving his hand in the air, Nero jokingly complained, "Such exciting prospects make me hungry. Have sweets and wine served to me on the balcony."

Sunset was still a few hours away when the emperor's chamberlain announced that Marcus was waiting in the atrium as ordered. "Burrus is with him, Sire, but the centurion may not please you. He is not in his uniform."

"What's he wearing?"

"A toga pura, Sire, and his hands are chained."

Nero pushed away the dish of fresh fruit and petulantly took a long drink of wine. This was an unexpected development and the question of it furrowed the emperor's brow. He'd ordered Marcus restored to his rank, and now the man was here in chains.

"Show them in," he ordered and assumed a position by the balcony rail, wine goblet in hand. He would receive them with the hills of Rome behind him and the sweet innocence of a kindly ruler on his face.

Marcus stepped onto the balcony alone and stiffly bowed to the emperor. The chain was loosely wrapped around his wrists and its small, gold links were not secured. His blond hair was beautifully waved and even the proper folds of his toga did not conceal his youth or the vigor of his trim body. When he straightened up from his bow, the brilliance of his blue eyes flashed like aquamarines in the deep tan of his handsome face. Nero viewed him for what he was: a chosen officer of the Praetorian Guard and a prime example of the manhood of Rome.

The emperor raised his goblet in greeting. "I salute you, Marcus Paetius, but I question the symbolism of your chain."

"It represents my failure, Your Majesty, and until I'm released from my oath to you, I must continue to wear it."

Nero chuckled and spoke with a smile. "You're a mistaken young man and brave beyond your years. I've restored your rank, and you defy me by wearing chains." Placing his goblet on the stone balcony rail, the emperor extended his hands and commanded, "Come here."

193

Stepping forward, Marcus raised his hands to meet Nero's, saying, "I wore your medallion on this chain, and now it wears me."

"Not any longer," Nero proclaimed as he unwound it from the centurion's wrists. "You served me and the gods by bringing the lady Phoebe to Rome. You were powerless to do anything other than what you did." Nero opened Marcus' hand and slowly coiled the chain in his palm. "Tonight I pray that I will pass my test as well as you have passed yours. How can I reward you for such service?"

Nero was amused by the confusion in the young man's eyes. Clapping his hands for service, the emperor spoke to his chamberlain as Hector stepped into the balcony doorway. "Bring parchment and pen and join us."

While they waited, Nero poured wine for Marcus and explained the divine revelation he'd received concerning the true identity of Phoebe. He told of how she, as a goddess, would test him for divinity and if he passed, proclaim him a god with the authority of Olympus. The emperor was unaware of Marcus' quickened excitement, and when Hector appeared with the writing material, he ordered the slave to sit on the balcony floor and write.

Dropping into a crosslegged position, Hector placed the parchment on his lap with the ink well on the floor beside him. Nero turned in deep thought and slowly began dictating as he looked out over Rome.

"I, Nero Lucius Domitius Ahenobarbus, Emperor of Rome, do hereby command that Marcus Paetius, my loyal servant, be rendered all courtesies due his rank of tribune within my empire. I further confer upon him all the privileges of my imperial medallion and release him from further service to my person and throne." Turning around, he faced Marcus and added, "By these presents, I declare Marcus Paetius a knight of Rome."

Looking down at Hector, both Nero and Marcus watched him date the document and hand it up for the emperor's signature. Taking it to the smooth stone rail, Nero signed it with a flourish and then read it back aloud. Before handing it to Marcus, the emperor reserved one last command.

"Tonight, you will escort the lady Phoebe into my court and remain with her afterward until she dismisses you. Your life is hers until she is safely back at Olympus." He handed the royal commission to Marcus and smiled, saying, "You see, Tribune, you're my gift to the goddess of the moon, but I still possess the power and the pen to reverse my proclamation should you displease her!"

Nero was momentarily puzzled by the expression of absolute delight that filled Marcus' face, but the tribune's words dispelled his puzzlement.

"Your Majesty, this commission," Marcus indicated the parchment in his hand with a nod of his head, "is the answer to my prayers and the order that goes with it will be obeyed. I will serve Phoebe and the God she represents with all my heart, body and mind." Snapping to attention, Marcus saluted Caesar and waited for dismissal.

The lowering sun was emblazoned on the hills behind Nero when he nodded his permission for withdrawal. As Marcus backed away, the emperor said, "I shall miss you, Marcus Paetius, but the sacred duty you've assumed will be a continuing service to Rome." He stopped Marcus at the doorway. "As part of my last command, I ask that you now lead the guard of honor to the house of Aquila and bring Phoebe before the men of Rome."

With a final salute the tribune backed from the balcony, while Nero stared after him, a sly, twisted grin on his face.

CHAPTER XVI

Render therefore to all their dues: tribute to whom trib-
ute is due; custom to whom custom; fear to whom fear;
honor to whom honor.

ROMANS 13:7

LATE afternoon sunlight was filtering through the grillwork
of the windows in Phoebe's room. She was alone with her
thoughts. All day, her mind had been pressured by the demanding need to see Nero. She felt as though God were trying to
speak to her, but her agitated mind wouldn't remain calm
long enough for His voice to come through. In desperation,
she decided to take action on her own. She would simply go
to the gates of the palace and demand an audience. If the
rumors she'd heard of Nero were true, he'd see her. She would
dress in her finest gown and look her most beautiful. God
gave her this beauty, and she'd use it to gain the emperor's
eyes and ears.

Polax and Julius were both at the villa. They would be
her escorts. Paul's letter had been delivered to the Christians
in Rome. Even Eli had accepted it. Nero was her only remaining objective and while she was there, she would beg for Marcus' release. Tears threatened as she thought of him languishing
in prison, cut off from her and subject to the insane punishment
Nero would conceive. Wiping her eyes, she sat up on the edge
of her bed and called for Debra. With great care, she and
the maid began her preparations.

Debra arranged Phoebe's gleaming hair with tiny seed-pearls forming a halo at the crest of her upswept dark curls. They seemed to radiate a lustrous glow of their own that added to the sparkle of her flashing eyes. For the first time, she allowed Debra to add color to her lips and a trace of tint to the trailing corners of her eyes. Looking at her reflection in the mirror, she saw a Phoebe she'd never seen before. Closing her eyes, she remembered how her mother had looked when she played the lute for her father.

The Grecian peplos gown she'd chosen for her palace visit was composed of a form-fitting, light, gray silk with a diaphanous cloak of white, silk gauze. The creamy glow of her slender arms and bare, delicate shoulders blended perfectly with the petite fullness of her breasts. Her confidence began to grow as the delicacy of the physical impression she was creating materialized from the combination of her lovely gown and natural beauty. Slipping into matching, gray silk slippers, she stood before her mirror for complete self-appraisal. Pearl earrings and necklace were added. The necklace clasp was being closed at the back of her neck when Julius burst unannounced into the room.

"Marcus is here!" he exclaimed. "He's downstairs with two full squads of mounted guardsmen and a golden sedan chair!"

Wearing the uniform of his new rank, Marcus interrupted from the doorway. "No, Julius, I'm right here with my heart in my hands."

Phoebe's eyes darted to the tribune's happy face, and her heart exploded with joy as he rushed across the room and took her in his arms. A weeping Debra quietly pulled Julius from the room.

Reluctantly breaking their embrace, Phoebe suggested they needed to thank God for his deliverance. As they knelt together, she could feel God's love engulf them, and her tears flowed. Then Marcus' deep voice joined hers in praising God the Father, God the Son and God the Holy Spirit. A small, tender voice formed in Phoebe's head.

"I'm pleased with you."

Phoebe's damp eyes sparkled their way to Marcus'. This shared moment together, in total harmony with God, was a treasure beyond price, confirmation for Phoebe that man, united as one with woman, was closer to the Father. Together, they reflected the complete image of God.

Marcus arose, helped Phoebe to her feet and told her of his meeting with Nero. Taking his commission from inside his breastplate, he let her read it. Phoebe shook her head with amazement.

"What could be his motive for giving you such a commission?"

Smiling with delight, Marcus told her of Nero's last command and how it related to her. He explained how the emperor had rationalized all they'd done in Greece as being the actions commanded by the gods of Olympus.

"Nero thinks Paul sent you to Rome with his letter, rather than come himself, because you're the goddess of the moon, and you've been sent to test him for divinity."

"But this is insane," she murmured.

Nodding his head, Marcus continued, "And Nero is gathering the best minds in Rome to witness the test and hear you proclaim him a god. The emperor sent me, with a guard of honor, to escort you to the palace for this purpose."

Silently, Phoebe tried to sort out all the implications of what Marcus had said. She'd prayed for a means of reaching Nero with Paul's letter, but nothing in her wildest dreams could have conceived such a means as this. Waves of fear engulfed her when she visualized herself standing before Caesar, at the center of Roman power, with only Paul's letter in her hands. Marcus sensed her feelings.

"Has the letter been delivered to the Christians?" he asked. When she nodded, he looked relieved. "Good. Then we'll take a copy to Seneca for delivery to Nero and leave Rome tonight."

Phoebe's reaction startled him. "No, Marcus! We can't run! God didn't bring us here for that." Her self-assurance returned with a burst of confidence. "God will protect His Word," she declared. "Jesus said, 'For I will give you a mouth and wisdom, which all your adversaries shall not be able to gainsay nor resist.' We'll go before Nero and trust in the Lord."

"But he's a madman," Marcus protested. "He can just as easily have you killed as listen to you!"

"He thinks I'm a goddess," Phoebe replied. "And he's expecting some kind of test. We'll let Paul's letter test him. After all," she smiled and added, "I have a message from God for him, and he shall hear it."

Shaking his head, Marcus began pacing the floor. Gradually, the deep, inner conviction swept over him that Phoebe was right. They had a mission to perform together. God was working it out, and they were to be His instruments for something that was much bigger than their own personal needs and desires. Together they would present Jesus to Caesar and accept the consequences.

Calling Debra and Julius back into the room, Marcus told them what was planned while Phoebe nodded in approval. Then she ordered everything packed for their return to Greece and sent Julius downstairs for Aquila. When Aquila appeared, Marcus explained again what must be done and asked that he pray for their safety.

When Aquila strongly advised against their going to the palace, Phoebe and Marcus shook their heads. Standing at the window, watching the setting sun, the tribune seemed deep in thought. Aquila was about to leave the room when Marcus turned and spoke.

"Aquila, as an elder of the church in Rome, can you perform a marriage ceremony for Phoebe and me?"

"Yes," was his brief answer.

Marcus glanced at Phoebe for confirmation, and when she nodded her head, he continued. "It is our wish that we be married tonight before going to the palace."

A broad smile filled Aquila's face. "It shall be done. Rufus is downstairs. He and Priscilla will stand with you. But are you sure that now is the right time?"

"Only God knows what lies ahead for us," Marcus replied. "With Nero being the kind of man he is, we may not have another chance." Crossing the room, he placed both hands on Aquila's shoulders and softly added, "United in marriage, we'll be stronger in the Lord."

"As you wish," Aquila agreed. "Come downstairs when you're ready, and we'll share the sacraments in the garden."

An hour later Phoebe stood beside Marcus, and with all the company of the house in witness, she accepted his pledge and gave him hers. Aquila asked for God's blessing on the union, and they prayed in Jesus' name, pledging their lives to Him and to each other. When they embraced for the holy kiss of matrimony, they could hear God's words:

"You are one in Me. Let no man put asunder what I have joined together. Now, go without fear, for I am with you."

Having made all possible preparations for the journey together back to Greece, Phoebe picked up Paul's letter in its canvas bag and together with Marcus started for the courtyard and the waiting honor guard. Polax, dressed in the robes of a Persian warrior, barred their passage at the outside door. His gleaming scimitar reflected the candlelight of the atrium, and his firm, deep voice announced his intentions.

"Julius and I are going with you." He held up his hand to stop any protest. "We'll have horses outside the palace and should you need us to cut a path to freedom, we'll be waiting outside the Hall of State for your command."

Marcus embraced the Persian and the decurion, accepting their volunteered service. The tribune admitted to himself they might not have the honor guard for their return. Polax threw open the doors, and he and Julius followed Marcus and Phoebe into the night.

Using the sedan chair, Phoebe was carried between two columns of mounted guardsmen through the streets of Rome to the heights of the Palatine. Flaming torches lighted their way, and the people they passed bowed in respect to her entourage. Alone, behind the curtains of the swaying chair, Phoebe prayed. From time to time, her resolution wavered, but each time fears began to overwhelm her, the Lord restored her courage. She heard the challenge at the palace gate. Peeking through the curtains, she watched Marcus accept and return the guard's salute. The chair moved forward toward the seat of imperial power. Clutching her breast and closing her eyes, she tried to slow the curious beating of her heart by praying in the Spirit. Then as the chair was lowered to the pavement, her heart slowed its wild beating. When she opened her eyes, Marcus had pulled back the curtains and was leaning forward to assist her. His confident smile was now all she needed to face Caesar.

Marcus walked beside her down the polished marble corridor toward the great bronze doors of the Hall of State. The echo of his heavy boots and those of Julius and Polax announced their arrival to the guards at the doors. An officer stepped forward as they approached. He saluted the tribune and bowed to Phoebe. Julius and Polax were told to position themselves outside the hall. Two soldiers then swung the great doors outward and Phoebe caught her breath at the sight they revealed. Paul's letter suddenly seemed heavy in her hands. Marcus stepped forward and stood in the doorway. His commanding voice stopped the subdued hum of conversation within the hall. Every eye turned toward the door as the emperor stood to receive her.

"Hail, Caesar," Marcus announced. "Hail, noblemen of Rome," he continued. "I bring you my lady, Phoebe, from Cenchrea with the word of God for your ears!" Extending his right arm toward Nero, standing before his throne, Marcus stepped aside and proclaimed, "My lady, may I present the emperor and the men of Rome."

Advancing to the doorway, Phoebe bowed to Nero and then to each side of the hall. Standing still for a moment, she surveyed the gathering. Marcus offered his arm and she laid her small hand on the cuff of his gauntlet. Other than the whisper of her slippers and the click of his boots the room was silent. Phoebe recognized Seneca standing to the emperor's right and guessed the soldier to his left was Burrus. The old man smiled at her just as she caught sight of her former captain, sitting with a smug expression on the dais steps. The heavy thump of the closing doors stopped her and as the sound echoed in the chamber, a tiny voice in her mind whispered, "Don't sit in front of Caesar."

Feeling the strength of the Holy Spirit inside her, Phoebe felt totally secure. Her breathing was slow and regular. She nodded toward Caesar and the emperor spoke.

"We are honored, my lady. Please come forward and sit on the divan we've arranged for your comfort."

Keeping her eyes on Nero, Phoebe moved to the front of the couch. The stiffness of Marcus' arm indicated that he hadn't expected to find Castor at the foot of the throne. He waited for her to withdraw her hand before he lowered his arm. Taking a deep breath and looking full into the face of Caesar, she opened her mouth without knowing what she was to say.

"Nero, emperor of Rome, you sent for me, and I have come. What is it you desire?" It was her voice, but it contained a power she didn't possess.

Her question appeared to surprise him, but he smiled as he replied. "Phoebe of Cenchrea, your appearance here with a halo of moonbeams in your hair and the shimmering silver glow of your gown is proof that you're more than you seem to be. I will answer your question with a question. Why are you in Rome?"

"I'm a servant of God, and I've brought His word, as revealed to the Apostle Paul, for your people."

Indicating the divan behind her with a wave of his hand, Nero invited, "Please be seated and let us hear this word."

"Sire, I prefer to stand."

Nero leaned forward. "Why?"

"God has told me not to sit before Caesar."

"But surely you'd be more comfortable on the soft cushions we've provided," Nero pressed.

Phoebe turned and glanced at the divan. Her eyes caught a slight movement in the center cushion. "You ask that I disobey God by tempting me with the soft caress of death," she said softly. "For surely if I disobey God, I will die, but if I live in Him, I will live forever."

The impact of her words on Nero surprised Phoebe. His expression was one of total satisfaction. Without knowing it, she had passed his test. To him, she was indeed the goddess of the moon.

When Nero's eyes swept over the entire chamber, Phoebe followed his glance. She was the only woman in the hall. Men of all ages were seated in ranks behind her on both sides of the center aisle. Countless torches flamed brightly in their gold sconces on walls and columns. An old senator tittered as her eyes passed him. The sound was quickly hushed by a cold stare from the throne. The torchlight wavered from polished marble in every direction.

Nero leaned back in his throne. "Very well, then, you may stand and tell us the inspired words you bring from Olympus."

Phoebe was amazed at her own bravery. "From Olympus?" she laughingly asked. "Marcus told you I'm from Cenchrea."

The emperor had a retort on his lips but apparently thought better of it and remained silent. Phoebe watched his expression change from one of certainty to one of doubt. Untying the canvas bag in her hand, she withdrew Paul's letter. Looking around for a place for the bag, she carelessly tossed it on the divan. she unrolled the scroll and held it before her. She didn't see the emperor's quickened interest. Looking up, she thought he was waiting for her to start and she began reading.

Marcus' eyes were on Phoebe. He didn't see the three triangular heads emerge from the cushion's cover. But nearly everyone else in the room seemed hypnotized by the slow, deliberate, slithering movement of the serpents. With her back to the couch, Phoebe couldn't see them, and her clear, sweet voice continued with the reading.

". . . Wherefore God also gave them up to uncleanness through the lusts of their own hearts, to dishonor their own bodies between themselves: who changed the truth of God into a lie and worshiped and served the creature more than the Creator . . ."

She was standing only a few feet from the divan and when the plop of the first coiled body sounded on the marble floor, the snake was already between her feet.

As Phoebe felt something coil around her ankle, she looked up from the scroll at Marcus. His eyes cautioned her to stand perfectly still. The second plop sounded like thunder in Phoebe's ear. As if sensing for direction, the reptile's tongue darted in the air. Phoebe forced her eyes back to the scroll and continued reading.

"God gave them over to a reprobate mind, to do those things which are not convenient; being filled with all unrighteousness, fornication, wickedness, covetousness, maliciousness; full of envy, murder, debate, deceit, malignity; whisperers, backbiters, haters of God, despiteful, proud, boasters, inventors of evil things, disobedient to parents, without understanding, covenant-breakers, without natural affection, implacable, unmerciful; who knowing the judgment of God, that they which commit such things are worthy of death."

Marcus slowly turned on the third serpent as the second slithered across the floor toward the dais. Frozen with fear, Castor couldn't move. He crouched as if stricken and watched it slither over his extended legs and continue climbing toward the throne. A deep sigh marked his fainting.

By now Nero had pulled his legs up into the seat of his throne. He was watching the snake's slow progress. Phoebe felt the reptile at her ankle uncoil itself. As she stopped reading, she glanced down to see it crawl across the floor toward Marcus. The swish of his sword blade passing through the air seemed loud in the forced silence of the room. Its sharp cutting edge neatly separated the poisonous head from the writhing body. The third serpent was likewise dispatched in one sure swift stroke. Answering Nero's scream, Marcus charged up the dais steps, past the unconscious Castor, and pinned the last remaining reptile under the flat of his blade. Phoebe's voice filled the hall.

"You offered me a nest of vipers to test my faith." Pointing directly at Nero, she turned and spoke to the men behind her. "Is that the man you want for a god? Shall I test his divinity by having Marcus lift his blade? Do you want proof that he's mortal?" Whirling back on Nero, she asked, "Do you believe you're a god?"

Nero's terror-stricken eyes gave her the answer, but again she loudly demanded, "Are you a god?"

"No," he screamed, "I'm not a god and never shall be!"

Marcus turned his blade from the flat to the edge and severed the life from the twisting viper. A silence settled over the chamber which Phoebe broke with firm resolution.

"I've done God's will!" She threw Paul's letter on the couch beside its bag. "And I'm leaving His Word here for you all to read! If you abide in what it says, you shall be saved. But woe unto you who now have it, if you continue to disobey!"

Turning away from the dais, Phoebe started for the great doors. Marcus sheathed his sword and saluted Caesar. "I go now to obey your last command. We will leave Rome at once and I humbly beg that you consider what Phoebe has left for you."

Then he followed behind her as the great doors swung open.

As Marcus and Phoebe walked toward the great doors, the hall was silent. Many of those present were not sure what had happened. Astonishment transfixed the assembly now frozen in the light of the torches. Three vipers had been killed. The emperor had been strangely cowed. And now he sat on his throne dazed.

Phoebe wondered too about Nero's silence as she and Marcus headed for the open doors. She wanted to run, but knew this would break the spell. She wanted to scream but resisted this too. Everything depended on the confident attitude they assumed before the assembled gathering. God had protected them. *Please Lord,* she prayed, *get us out of here!*

The open doorway was very close now. Once through it, they would have support: Polax and Julius. Then there was a good chance of escape. If only . . .

Then came the cry, strangled at first, then shrill: "Guards, stop him! Touch not the woman, but arrest Marcus, the tribune!"

Soldiers suddenly blocked the door. Marcus stopped and

205

turned to Phoebe, anguish flooding his face. They had come so close. But the baseness of Nero's shame had robbed the emperor of even a shread of dignity.

Phoebe fought off tears. She had a wild urge to call for Polax and Julius but bit her tongue. That would only bring disaster to two faithful friends. She looked into Marcus' face and knew she must give him hope and reassurance. *But how, Lord?* And then she remembered. *Of course.* Paul had given them words for just such a time. They came to her now so that she could say them softly to Marcus in that long moment frozen in time:

". . . neither death, nor life, nor angels, nor principalities, nor powers, nor things present, nor things to come, nor height, nor depth, nor any other creature, shall be able to separate us from the love of God, which is in Christ Jesus our Lord."

EPILOGUE

Dearly beloved, avenge not yourselves, but rather give place unto wrath: for it is written, vengeance is mine; I will repay, saith the Lord.

ROMANS 12:19

HISTORY tells us that Nero never publicly proclaimed himself a god, nor was this action taken by the Roman Senate. Approximately eight months after Phoebe delivered Paul's letter, Nero ordered the murder of his mother, Agrippina. Seneca and Burrus had to support the emperor in this or lose their positions of power and throw the empire into Poppaea's hands.

In A.D. 62, Burrus died, and Seneca lost favor. He was forced into private life. Still unable to become empress because of Octavia, Poppaea drove Nero to the brink of sexual madness until he ordered Octavia's execution on false charges of treason. Poppaea then became empress.

About this time, Paul was nearing the end of his two years of house arrest in Rome. He had been arrested in Jerusalem and brought to Rome as a citizen for trial before Caesar. After a two-year wait, Paul was not tried before Nero. He was finally given a preliminary hearing and released.

The apostle may have gone on to Spain as he'd planned and worked among the Gentiles until Luke brought him word of Peter's death in Rome. This was during the persecution of the Christians which followed the great fire in A.D. 64. Paul returned to Rome early in A.D. 65 to find that Seneca had committed suicide on Nero's orders. Paul was arrested at the height of the persecutions and beheaded outside the city on the road to Ostia.

Nero gave himself over to shocking displays of drama and poetry, turning his back on the function of emperor. Late in A.D. 66, he traveled to Greece and took part in the musical and drama competitions where he, as emperor, won all the prizes. He'd hardly returned to Rome in A.D. 68 when revolt broke out in Gaul and Spain. The revolt in Spain was suppressed by a Roman General named Galba.

Learning that Galba was coming to Rome to overthrow him, Nero fled the city. He lacked the will to commit suicide and was killed, on his own order, by a faithful freedman.

There's no record of what happened to Phoebe, other than she did return to Greece. Think of Phoebe when you read the second epistle of John and perhaps the Holy Spirit will let you join me in thinking that she and Marcus were reunited, raised Christian children and served our Lord.

ACKNOWLEDGMENTS

Many kind and loving people encouraged and counseled me during the writing of *Deadline in Rome.* Among those to whom I owe a great debt are: the Rev. Wesley "Ted" Nelson, the Rev. Richard "Dick" Copeland, the Rev. John Urban, Clare Weakley, John Sherrill, Richard "Dick" Schneider, Jean Reith, Louise Boggess, Lee Ann Nelson, Andrea Copeland, Ruth Urban, Barkley Rice, Daymon Schulgen, Susan Daniel, Dorothy Everts, Maggie Cowart, Jill Garrett, my daughters Karen Twombly and Kirsten Call and the best editor in the world—my wife Murney. Some of the physical and mental attributes of my characters were borrowed from the people I pray with at the Episcopal Church of the Resurrection in Dallas, Texas. Lucy Lee Lane and Billie Branum sustained my strength.

Invaluable assistance was provided by the Bridwell Library of Southern Methodist University. The life and times of Phoebe couldn't have been assembled without the priceless volumes from their extensive shelves. The staff and resources of the Nicholson Memorial Library of Garland, Texas, must also be praised.

Specific counsel was also provided by the Rev. Michael Harper, the Rev. Patric Hutton, the Rev. John McDonald, the Rev. Francis McNutt, the Rev. Everett Fullam, the Rev. Sudduth Cummings and the incomparable Rita Bennett. Sister Jean Hill inspired the use of singing in the Spirit. The Rev. Claud Behn was a constant sounding board. On-the-scene research in Rome was provided by Ginny and Michael Marrinan. By prowling the streets of the "Eternal City," they gave me a semblance of ancient Rome.

BIBLIOGRAPHY

Brunner, Emil. *The Letter to the Romans: A Commentary.* Rev. ed. Philadelphia: Westminster Press, 1959.

Cartocci, Sergio and Gluco. *Yesterday's Rome.* Plurigraf.

Dodd, C. H. *The Authority of the Bible.* London: Nisbet & Co., 1952. New York: Harper & Bros., 1962.

———. *The Epistle of Paul to the Romans.* London: Hodder & Stoughton, 1934.

Earl, Donald. *The Age of Augustus.* New York: Crown Publishers, 1968.

Enslin, Morton Scott. *The Ethics of Paul.* Nashville: Abingdon Press.

Everyday Life in Bible Times. Washington, DC: National Geographic Society.

The Excavations of Corinth. Athens, Greece: American School of Classical Studies, 1927.

Geer, Russel M. *Classical Civilization: Rome.* Englewood, NJ: Prentice-Hall, 1950.

Grant, Michael. *Cities of Vesuvius.* New York: Macmillan Publishing Co., 1972.

———. *Saint Paul.* New York: Charles Scribner's Sons, 1976.

Hadas, Moses. *Imperial Rome.* Alexandria, VA: Time-Life Books, 1965.

Haenchen, Ernst. *The Acts of the Apostles: A Commentary.* Philadelphia: Westminster Press, 1971.

The Holy Bible, Authorized King James Version. "Open Bible Edition." New York: Thomas Nelson.

Phillips, J. B. *Letters to Young Churches.* New York: Macmillan Publishing Co.

Rome. Arti Grafiche Bellomi.

Rome of the Caesars. Translated by Michael Hollingworth. Bonechi-Edizioni.

Steele, David N., and Thomas, Curtis C. *Interpretive Outline of Romans.* Phillipsburg, NJ: The Presbyterian and Reformed Publishing Co., 1963.

Wight, Fred H. *Manners and Customs of Bible Lands.* Chicago: Moody Press, 1953.